Bitter Kind Of Love

Nicole Snow

Content copyright © Nicole Snow. All rights reserved.
Published in the United States of America.
First published in October, 2014.

Disclaimer: The following ebook is a work of fiction. Any resemblance characters in this story may have to real people is only coincidental.

Description

BITTER LOVE: DEFIANT, SEETHING, AND UNSTOPPABLE...

Alice James tried like hell to forget soul killing tragedy. Running from her gun runner father's murder and dark days with the Prairie Devils MC was pure survival. But escaping nightmares is never easy. Neither is erasing *him* from her memory.

Lucas "Stinger" Spears can't forget the walking mystery with the killer body who shared his clubhouse for a few glorious weeks. Too bad Alice rebuffed his wild charms like no woman has, and nobody – nobody! – says no to the VP of the Devils Montana crew. Now, his own dark memories and raw passions are perfect fuel for a midnight ride to find his woman and stake a claim.

She can't remember what love's supposed to be. He can't live another second without her on his bike and between his sheets, screaming his name and wearing his brand. And neither of them knows a dead man's secrets are about to drive a terrifying wedge between their hearts, threatening their fragile love and the entire club...

Will Alice and Stinger's bitter love turn sweet – or will it become pure poison?

The Prairie Devils MC books are stand alone romance novels featuring unique lovers and happy endings. No cliffhangers allowed! This is Stinger and Alice's story.

I: Shades of Betrayal (Alice)

When I felt the knife against my throat, I knew I'd fucked up bad.

Stinger wasn't coming to pull me feet from the fire either. Not this time, not when I'd run away from him and his club like the terrified girl I was.

He'd offered me the world, and I'd forsaken him. Now, I was going to pay the price.

"I'll ask you again, little bitch. *Where. Is. It?*" My interrogator's eyes were pitch black.

God, how many times had I seen eyes like that before? They were as black and dead as the last few months of this new life, lost to the world, abandoned in the deep cold darkness.

"I…I can't remember. I already told you that. I'm not lying!" I spat at the floor and looked up, trying not to shake.

My eyes passed over the patches on his cut: NERO, PRESIDENT, 1%, WRECKING CREW, SLINGERS MC. Skulls wearing cowboy hats and smoking pistols menaced their way out of the leather. Above it all, his black eyes devoured me, darkness set in a bald head and cheeks pocked with scars.

Sick irony twisted my stomach. I'd fled to Idaho to get away from biker gangs intruding on my life, only to have a truly feral MC threatening to make sure I never had to worry about intrusions ever again. And all because I couldn't give him something I didn't know I had, that fucking map my father hid before they murdered him.

"Bullshit!" Nero lowered the knife and gave me a good shove against the wall.

Behind him, another man laughed, giggling like a hyena while he scratched his arm. Nero's head whipped back and he gave the psycho an evil eye.

"Shut the fuck up, Hatter." He drew in a heavy breath before turning back to me, bathing me in those inverted spotlights he had for eyes. "Your amnesia act's not pulling the fucking wool over my eyes, girl. Maybe it worked before, getting every fool from here to Missoula to swallow your shit, but I'm not biting. I know the Rams kept you for days in that shitty clubhouse after we killed your old man and ripped through his fucking truck. Don't tell me the Feds took it. I won't believe that shit for a second."

I looked up at him, hatred swirling in my veins. My fiercest look didn't faze him. All it got me was the knife at my throat again, cold and threatening as ever.

"Who the fuck took it, slut? Did you bring it out here when you decided to move West and shake your pussy on stage? Should I rip apart this whole fucking house looking for it?" Nero looked up at his men and snapped his fingers.

His crew moved behind us, stomping into my tiny kitchen. Crashes blasted my ears as they turned over the table and started to open every drawer and cabinet they could find, hurling out the contents, killing the grim silence with a ferocious clatter.

Shit. He knew damned well I wasn't hiding anything in plates and cups, didn't he?

Maybe it was a new, sick form of torture. I didn't give a damn that they were destroying what little I had. It was the noise that got to me, the thunderous explosion of dishes, silverware, glass, and food hitting every surface within striking distance.

The one called Hatter added his high, insane laugh to the chaos too, a soulless cackle that drummed into my bones.

"Okay! You fucking win! I'll tell you everything I know. Just please…make them *stop,*" I screamed, jumping in his arms, wishing I could get his gross hands away.

I nicked my neck on the knife while I was thrashing around. Nero tucked it away, satisfied with my surrender, but not before I felt a warm trickle of angry blood pooling in my cleavage. He blinked, his eyes wide, allowing me to hold one hand to the wound while he clapped his hands and yelled at his men.

"All right, boys! Keep your peckers down and stop ripping shit to kingdom come. Our little raven's gonna sing…"

He smiled, reaching up to run the back of his hand through my black hair. I twisted away, stopping just short of slapping his stupid hand. Jesus, it was tempting, but I knew I'd get pure hell if I laid a finger on him.

The crashing stopped, replaced with wintry silence. Hatter's sick laughter faded into their heavy, excited breaths. They came tromping back to their boss, surrounding us in a cruel circle that would've made the biggest badass in the world sweat bullets.

My memory gathered itself while I stared into Nero's cold eyes, collating all the terrible things I'd forgotten for months. Everything I'd tried to escape forever.

I was an idiot to think I could run from it. Evil things always caught up with me, no different than this pack of vicious murderers.

"I watched Dad die in their clubhouse. The Rams kept me prisoner," I said, remembering the worst days of my life. "I couldn't have been there more than a few days..."

"You gotta do better than that, little lamb. That shit's the first thing I learned through the Grizzlies grape vine, and it's fucking useless!" His last word exploded in my face like a bomb. "I want those fucking routes. I need your old man's map. Don't give a shit hearing about the Rams' escapades while you were chained down like a bitch."

Don't shake. Don't cry. Don't give him anything except stark, bitter truth.

"The Prairie Devils picked me up. I was with them for...damn, it must've been several weeks. They held onto me while their drama with the Rams dragged on. This man, Stinger –"

It hurt to say his name.

Stinger repulsed me, fascinated me, and stirred more conflicting emotions than any man I'd ever met in my life. I couldn't handle him. I ran, as fast and as far as a bus ticket and a little cash could get me, hoping I'd never have to say his name again.

Nero held up a hand, hissing through his teeth. "I already told you, bitch, I don't need to hear all these little details. I don't give a fuck about hearing how many times they used your tight ass. If you don't spit out something useful in the next two minutes, Hatter and Wasp here are gonna use your holes instead. And I can guarantee they'll give you a pounding a whole lot harder than anything those Prairie Pussies gave you…" He turned the blade in his hands, bored beneath his rage.

I shouldn't have said his name. I'm not worthy to even think it.

My heart sank, thinking about the only man who gave a single crap about me since these demons killed Dad.

Stinger was a total angel, a guardian, handsome as he was strong, determined to keep the brutal world off my back. He protected me, the total opposite of what these idiots thought about the Devils, and I repaid him by fucking off without even saying goodbye.

"It doesn't matter," I whispered, the worst lie I'd told all night. "I didn't see much. The Devils had their own crap going on – one of their brothers almost went to prison. They barely told me anything about their business. Just asked me a bunch of questions until the Rams hit them that night."

"Yeah, yeah. Poison," Nero grunted. "I know all about what those sloppy motherfuckers did. Didn't off a single Prairie Pussy, did they?"

I shook my head, remembering my last night with the club, nearly all the men laid up and suffering. The tainted whiskey did a number on their stomachs.

But it wasn't the club that mattered. It was *him,* and I was right by his side, holding his hand while he writhed in pain, then laying next to him – repaying the same favor he'd done me the first night I left hell.

Then there was the kiss the next morning, when he was still delirious…

I closed my eyes. It was too damned much.

I was an idiot, and the world didn't offer second chances.

"You're right. None of them died," I said, reluctantly forcing my eyes open.

"Fucking amateurs," Nero growled. "So, what, then? The Pussies cut a deal with the Feds, I know that much. How did the Rams die? That fucking thing had to be at their clubhouse. I know they fucked us over. And I know the Feds didn't tear them a new asshole. Their dicks are too limp these days for massacres and media spectacles. Who killed them?"

I swallowed the painful lump in my throat. Nero stepped closer again, catching the glint in my eye that told him I was holding back.

"You coming clean, or what? Fucking tell me, bitch! You got one chance, and you're losing it by the second." He grabbed my shoulders and pressed me to the wall, hot breath spilling onto my face, carrying the faint and sickly stink of whiskey. "We're not gonna do this same old song and dance all night, girlie."

My feet dangled off the floor as he lifted me higher, hanging my face just a few inches over his repulsive mug. No matter how hard I tried, I couldn't look away, knowing if he wrung out the next bit, it would seriously fuck over the people who'd saved me.

And Stinger too – especially Stinger!

I'd already stabbed him in the back by running. I couldn't twist the knife by fucking over his club – could I?

"I get it." His voice went cold, the anger doused to smoky rage. "Cutting up that pretty skin or having a dick inside you doesn't rustle your panties too much. Hell, you're probably already fucking guys in your off hours at the strip joint, yeah? You got a body worth a few dimes, bitch, and having us steal what you're selling doesn't get you in a fucking twist."

I refused to answer. I had to keep my lips sealed, had to stay quiet. No, my memory wasn't perfect, but I'd be damned if I let it go.

"Let me tell you something." He let my shoes drop to the floor with a shove. "You've never fucked the way we do. You see my bro, Hatter, over there?"

He grabbed my face and twisted it in the right direction. I was forced to look at the skinny, nasty freak behind him, the man who couldn't stop twitching and giggling like a lunatic.

"Show her your goods, brother!" Nero ordered.

Hatter laughed louder as he rolled his leather cut down his arms and pulled up his shirt. I gasped.

Crazy emblems lined his body like every biker, but they weren't tattoos. They were deep red scars, gouges in his skin. Several long lines of flame were deep red, nearly bleeding. The smoking gun on his chest was lined with thousands of little cuts designed to look like thorns.

The other two men laughed. I felt the blood draining from my face.

"This is what he does for fun," Nero said. "Likes to carve shit up like it's Thanksgiving dinner three hundred and sixty five fuckin' days a year. Not just his own skin neither. Fuck, you oughta take a good look at his dick…this man's the only bastard I've known in all my years who takes razors to his pisser."

The demon grinned and reached for his jeans, squeezing his crotch. Then he reached into the holsters near his waist and pulled out two matching daggers, holding them across the lump in his pants, giving me a smile straight from the darkest corner of hell.

Nero knew what he was doing. The bastard *knew* I'd take damage to keep my secrets, but not *this*. I couldn't fight the monster leering at me with his knives and manic evil, drool slipping down his chin.

No, no, Jesus Christ, no.

I couldn't let this sick animal have his way with me. I wouldn't survive.

Right then and there, I broke. My cowardly mind spun, ready to cough up anything to get me out of this. Anything to take away the pure fucking evil circling me in this room.

Hatter reached up, began to unzip his fly. I couldn't even stand to see it. Terror hit me like lightning, and I flinched in Nero's hands.

"Stop it. Stop. Call him off," I whimpered. "I know where the stupid map is."

"Okay," he said softly. "I'm gonna give you one more chance, bitch, and only one. *Who* killed the Rams? Who the fuck was there before the Feds rolled in? Who took it?"

"The Devils. The whole club combed the place over good before they gave it up to the cops. If anyone's got my Dad's stuff, it's them. The map's at their clubhouse, stuffed up in some office. Now, please...let me go."

Nero never smiled. He just nodded and did as I asked, letting me fall to the floor. He coughed once, watching me collapse in a sobbing heap on the ground.

Cold. Satisfied. Happy, maybe.

And why shouldn't he be? The bastard just watched me sell my soul.

"Come on, Shark," he said to the larger man in the corner. "Bitch finally gave us a gold nugget we can use. We'll call it in to the rest of the club and figure out the best plan of attack."

The man with the VP tag and the silver teeth nodded, and began to follow him out. I looked up, staring through my tears, wishing I could see through the walls, straight to the dense gray winter sky.

I'm sorry, Stinger. I'm sorry.
God, I'm so fucking sorry!

I saw it in my mind already. These assholes weren't going to waste much time. They'd show up not long after Christmas if they had to, a sneak attack. Nero and his men would burst in with guns blazing, brandishing their blades. They'll kill, torture, and burn anyone they had to for that damned map.

The Missoula boys would never see it coming. Blaze, Tank, Moose…Stinger.

They'd all fight like mad until their last breath. But it wouldn't be enough. They'd be flattened on the ground with holes in their chests.

I'd watched the club nearly get slaughtered in one ambush while I was there, and the Slingers promised hot lead instead of half-assed poison.

I thought about Stinger's strong face, lifeless and pale, a neat dark hole through his head.

Fuck. This couldn't be happening!

I couldn't let him or any of his guys die because of my screw up.

My hands stretched across my face and just kept going, pulling on my skin. I wanted it to hurt. My surrender was going to get a lot of good men killed, and probably their old ladies too. I might as well have put a gun to Stinger's temple and pulled the trigger myself.

I stopped stretching my face to total hell and looked up. The other two demons, Hatter and Wasp, lingered. I wanted them gone like yesterday. I wasn't sure there would ever be a way to bleach their evil presence out of my rental.

After this, I had to leave. I had to get out and go far, far away.

Maybe I could leave the Devils an anonymous tip, a letter or a call to tell them what was coming…but first, I needed these killers *gone.*

Shit, why weren't they moving, following their nasty leader out the door?

"Hey!" I screamed, my life returning. Nero stopped with his VP at my front door and turned. "We're done here, aren't we? Take your guys and go. I gave you what I promised."

At last, I saw his smile, evil and crooked as the rest of him. "There's a special place in hell for traitors and cunts who can't keep their lips sealed. Don't worry, baby, your friends from the Prairie Pussies will be joining you down there soon. Daddy's waiting too. Old Mickey's paying for some seriously fucked up sins on Satan's bench right now, I'd wager…"

My eyes bulged. My lungs felt like they'd been filled with cement. I couldn't even shake my head or ask him what the hell he was talking about. It was all there in his savage face.

"I'm gonna give you boys an hour with this bitch. Have your fun and then clean up the mess. We'll dump her body off on the way to Montana."

Nero was out the door, his VP behind him. I took one look at the two smiling assholes closing in on me fast, trying not to let my knees turn into mud.

Run. Get away. Fight.

I hurled myself downstairs, heading for the basement, listening to their heavy boots clomping behind me. The last thing I thought before my screams pierced the darkness was Stinger.

I hurled my frenzied wishes, my prayers, my everything high into the cold, indifferent winter sky. I would've given anything for a miracle, anything for him to hear it and come for me.

Yes, I prayed, even when I saw what a total, undeserving bitch I'd become, the last girl in the world who deserved a rescue by the man who haunted her dreams.

But I wasn't stupid. The universe never, ever worked like that. I didn't believe in coincidence or miracles, and I definitely didn't deserve one after what I'd done.

Shit! It was so fucking dark down here, and I didn't dare turn on the lights and give them an easier time. I ran into the washing machine, its cold metal slapping my hands. When I looked up, the bikers' dark shadows blocked the hall, boxing me in.

When Hatter lunged, pulling at my hair, I lost it.

The screams, the prayers, and everything else went numb. He whirled me around, slapping me against the wall before I lost my balance and began to fall. Nothing broke it. Nothing caught me. Nothing except brutal regret as I hit the floor and they started tearing at my clothes.

That thing they say about your whole damned life flashing before your eyes right before you die? I thought it was crap – until it happened.

I remember everything, past and present flashing like strobe lights, colliding jigsaws in my head. Every piece of Stinger, I tried to cling onto, but I couldn't. It was all coming in a blizzard, churning too fast, the few good pieces always out of reach.

I'd lived on a merciless ledge, and I was an idiot to think there'd be anything different at my life's sudden dead end.

One second, I caught a fragment. Just one.

I remembered Stinger's warmth, his strength, his powerful arms wrapped around me, so real my heart stopped shaking to tatters in my ribs. And then it was gone in a wink, replaced with the savage wolves behind me, grabbing me by the ankles and ripping at my clothes.

II: It Always Catches Up (Alice)

Months Earlier...

It was a run like any other. Or that was the way it started, anyway.

I was perched in the big truck's passenger seat next to my Dad, quietly humming to himself as classic rock blasted over the radio. On the lonely highway cutting West through Bozeman, we looked like any other truck hauling freight, and that was his goal.

Nobody would've guessed Mickey James was anything more than an ordinary trucker unless they'd done business with him. If they could've seen the way he lived, they quickly would've realized the lie...

I never knew how much my Dad made running guns and contraband over the years, but it must've been millions. Too bad the long stays we had in Vegas and Reno always managed to take his latest fortune. The odds never cared how big a man's fortune was. The hungry casinos devoured it just the same.

I'd been on the road with him since I was seventeen and he took me out of school for the very last time. Whoever my mother was – some junkie whore, he said – I doubt she'd have approved of the way we lived, if she was a decent soul.

And there was some serious doubt about that.

I was almost asleep when we pulled into the rest stop. Dad's humming stopped and he held his stomach, popping the door and quickly running to the bathroom. I straightened up, staring into the night, hoping it'd be morning soon so I could enjoy the familiar mountains heading into Missoula.

The stress was killing him. After years of wheeling, dealing, and killing when he had to, his lucky star was fading. I'd overheard him bitching to contacts about business being down ever since the Grizzlies and Prairie Devils, two warring motorcycle clubs, cut some kinda truce. In the blink of an eye, two of his biggest clients no longer needed to stockpile weapons to point at each other's heads. Worse, the Devils were running their own supply lines through Grizzlies territory into Canada, and Dad was just one of many suppliers vying for his tiny cut.

He came back wiping his mouth, shirt reeking like he'd just spat up his stomach. His eyes were bloodshot. I breathed the sickly smell deep, making sure he hadn't taken to drinking on the road. I didn't think he'd completely lost his mind yet, but I had to be sure…

No, he was dry. The foul scent was too gross to be whiskey. Thank God.

"You okay?" I whispered, reaching over for his hand.

He jerked it away. "One day, I'm gonna teach you to drive one of these rigs, Alice. I'm fine. Just a little older for wear and a bad hotdog back in Bismarck or something. Fuckin' gas stations…"

"This wouldn't have anything to do with the deal that's about to go down, right?" My eyes narrowed.

So did my father's. For a minute, I thought he'd chew into me for sticking my nose where it didn't belong. Instead, he started up the truck and chuckled as we got onto the road.

"Nah. Nothing like that. The boys we're going to see won't refuse the shit we've got in the back. We can do business with the Grizzlies. They're our ticket to making some bucks without having Throttle's little stamp of approval on fucking everything." He growled the name of the Devils' national President. "You're turning into a curious little cat, ain't you?"

I looked away. His tone sounded half-impressed and half-mocking. I could never be sure which feeling won out in my Dad's weird mind.

"That's okay, hon. If I can get a few things stitched together right, then maybe we can figure out some college or something for you after you get your GED."

"Yeah." My lips twisted sourly. How many times had I heard that? "Maybe if it doesn't all get pissed away at the casinos this time."

Dad's friendly expression melted. The sickly, grayness on his face returned. I turned away from him, staring out the passenger window and into the deep, dark Montana night. If I didn't know any better, I almost thought he was ashamed.

I couldn't blame him for wasting his money on games. Learning something practical sure as hell didn't interest me, and sending me to an art school I'd probably flunk was barely better than losing thousands at the tables. My fingers pinched the bag with my sketch book, all I had for company on these long, miserable trips, not counting the man next to me.

Dad kept his maps in there too. He left me in charge, knowing I never misplaced anything.

I closed my eyes and tried to sleep. Growing up was nothing but disappointment and feeble promises that never materialized into anything better. Time had done nothing but grind us down more, and I doubted it would change now that I was old enough to drink.

It was hard to imagine how it could be any worse. A shame, really, because if I'd seen the blackness coming, maybe I would've been prepared for the tragedy that came next.

"Alice? Honey, wake up." Dad pressed a cold bottle to my cheek.

I opened my eyes and sat up. A knot in my neck burned, always the same spot. Too many years spent sleeping in screwed up positions on the road with him left little quirks youth couldn't heal.

Like always, I snatched the cold orange juice out of his hand and popped the cap. We'd just left another gas station and the sun was high overhead. The mountains made me smile as I sipped on pure acid.

The cheap OJ was fake as hell, but at least it was familiar, the same as the rolling peaks closing in fast as the truck rumbled down the road.

"How much longer?" I asked.

"Just another hour or two. The Rams' place is up near the Idaho border, wedged between a couple little towns. Keep an eye out for toothless fucks with banjos and shotguns in them hills. From what I understand, these boys keep their clubhouse *way* back." He winked.

I managed a weak smile at his lame ass joke. Good thing a life of dealing with criminal buyers meant neither of us was truly likely to be rattled by some backwooded mouth breathers.

An hour later, the wisecrack took on a grim reality. Dad had to shift gears several times to force our heavy load up the narrow unpaved road, cut up the side of a mountain flanked with trees.

The place looked even dingier than I imagined. It was early afternoon when we rolled in, and nobody came out to greet us. Dad and I were in their clubhouse, taking seats at the bar, before anybody stirred.

A muscular man with gray hair and a beer belly came out of a room down the hall twenty minutes later, rubbing his eyes.

"Hello, Block," Dad greeted him. "You ready to talk business?"

The Rams' President eyed us warily. He looked gross, shirtless except for the cut draped on him, potbelly sticking through the opening.

"I'll be ready soon, but the other guys aren't. Hold your horses. I need the whole club in on this so we can vote. You know how this shit works. Nice and democratic." He picked up an open bottle of whiskey on the counter and chugged it down. "Make yourselves at home, you two. Must be a bitch and a half barreling all the way here from Michigan on such short notice."

"Desperate times," Dad said darkly. "Gotta do whatever it takes to drum up business. You got contacts who are interested in buying bulk at a good price. Can't do that with the Devils blocking the old routes going East to West."

"Fucking Devils," Block snarled, clanking the nearly drained bottle on the counter. "Those pussy bitches are supposed to show up here next week. Bastards want us patched over quick as a support club since this state's their territory now – otherwise they'll disband us."

Dad's face tightened up. I waited for an explosion, but I should've known I'd be waiting an eternity. He rarely let his real emotions out. *Very* rarely.

"Don't worry," Block said, settling an uneasy hand on Dad's shoulder. "I'm not gonna double-cross you. Those fuckers won't be keeping too close an eye on us out here as soon as things are settled. I got plenty of ways to hook you up with the right guys."

"That's what we're here for. Both of us."

I nodded, giving Dad my quiet support.

"Gotcha, dude." Block looked at me and slowly grinned. Not a smile I wanted to return. Thankfully, the dickhead seemed too drunk to care when I looked away from him.

Dad cracked a beer while the creepy Pagan Rams President made the rounds, trying to rouse his men from their rooms in the back. He looked high and low for something I could drink behind the bar, but came up with his hands dusty and empty. He shrugged.

"Looks like these fuckers are all out of Coke and water. Last beer too." He held up his bottle and shook it.

"How about a shot of something to take the edge off?" I said, looking over at the fresh bottle stacked up behind the bar.

"No," Dad said quietly, taking his seat next to me again. "Need us both to stay focused. This little club's new to me, but their big brothers aren't. Grizzlies are serious enough fuckers to keep us both on our toes, Alice. Remember that."

A chill crept up my spine. Living like we did, it was easy to forget that every one of these deals could easily go badly and end with both of us dead. I trusted Dad knew what he was doing.

He'd been screwed over a few times before, once when I was with him. He was selling weapons to some thugs in

Portland. They weren't waiting out on the street where he'd agreed to meet them. I knew something was wrong when he warned me to duck, pushing my head down beneath the widow.

Instinct told him they were waiting behind a rusted warehouse garage door, waiting for us to pull close to ambush. Dad never got that far. He picked up the automatic between us and shot through my open window, riddling the door with bullets, sending the men behind them to their quick and dirty deaths.

I trusted him after that. There was no reason to think he wouldn't be able to handle these sloppy, drugged out bikers past their prime if things got dicey.

The four Rams didn't shuffle out until another hour passed. Then they sat at the dirty tables away from us, bullshitting amongst themselves. The way these crude, coarse men always talked about the women they fucked and threw away made my stomach churn.

I looked at my father warily. Did he say the same things when I was out of earshot? Or did he have more respect for girls because he had a daughter? Obviously, he'd been wild in his younger days, only tightening the leash because I'd been dropped in his lap to raise.

I shook my head. No wonder I was still a damned virgin at twenty-one. How could I want *anything* to do with men when I'd grown up hearing old bikers and leering thugs talking about which hole they were going to fuck next?

Dating? Not in this life.

Good guys worth having relationships with were reserved for the normal, law abiding, civilian world. And that world was just as distant and strange as the idea of loving a man instead of just fucking him. Or, rather, being fucked by him, fucked and thrown away like an empty bottle.

Dad's ears perked up when we heard the rumble of motorcycles. He pushed away the empty beer he'd been nursing for over an hour and stood, giving me a serious look that said *look alive, hon. Here we go.*

He was halfway to the door the Rams were all gathering around when several guys pushed their way in. Dad took one look at their patches and his smile melted.

"Slingers? What the fuck? You're another support club." He turned to Block. "You told me full patch Grizzlies MC brothers were coming to cut this deal. Come on, Alice."

He waved to me. "We're getting the fuck outta here. I'm not wasting my good fucking time dealing with more middle men."

I'd never seen him so pissed. Well, not since he'd lost six figures one night in Vegas several years ago.

"Whoa, whoa, fuckin' whoa!" The tall bald man with the scarred face and the brightest SLINGERS MC patch threw out his hands and nearly hit my Dad in the chest. "What's the hurry, buddy? We just got here to party."

The other Slingers and the Rams moved to block the door, smiling the whole time. Dad was a big guy, and he bowed up right away, unused to taking shit from anyone like this.

But he wasn't a fool. We were so stupidly outnumbered it wasn't even funny.

My heart leaped into my throat. These men from the other club weren't slow moving old stags like the Rams. They looked lean, mean, and seriously hellbent on getting their point across – whatever it was.

If things went bad…then I wasn't sure the luck we'd always had in these deals would hold.

It'll be okay, I told myself. *You've seen him talk his way out of standoffs with gorillas bigger and more pissed off than these guys. Just keep it together.*

I backed up, taking the furthest seat from the bar I could. The man with the bright red colors looked past Dad and smiled at me. If the devil himself decided to crawl out of hell and take human form, I would've guessed he'd smile a lot like this guy. It was a strange smile too, evil because his teeth sat so *damned perfect* in his scarred face.

"Relax. Bring your slut over to the table, friend. No secrets here. We're all gonna sit down like gentleman and hash this out." He forced his hand on my Dad's and gave it a powerful shake. "Name's Nero. I'm the President of the Slingers MC, and I'm here to do business, just like Block told you. The Grizzlies are too busy with the cartels in SoCal to send their own boys out here. They need every man for the Mexicans. So, I came out with my main crew here: Shark, Wasp, and Hatter."

He pointed to several big, bearded, and brutal looking men next to him. The last guy was leaner, twitchy like he'd had too much caffeine. He also had a crazy glint in his eye I didn't like one bit.

"You got my advance?" Dad asked, grinding his teeth.

I swallowed hard. He still wasn't backing down.

Nero smiled and nodded. "Yeah, man, of course I do. It's in my saddle bag. Two hundred big, just like Block said. It's yours – long as we cut ourselves a deal here today."

Slowly, my father turned to me. I could see the rage boiling in his red face, tempered only by the possibility that things might not go straight to hell. If we played along and heard them out, maybe we'd walk out alive.

"Come on, Alice," he said. "Let's sit down and talk."

"Good choice, Mickey. You're smarter than you look," Nero said, walking over to the big table the Rams had formed with several smaller ones pushed together.

"Go get the drinks, Reaper. We've got special beer for a special occasion," Block ordered, tapping the man with the VP patch next to him.

We all sat down in silence, Dad and I taking our places across from the vicious looking Slingers. The Rams all sat on the ends, sans Reaper, who came back several minutes later pulling two huge kegs and a tray of heavy mugs. I watched him fill each glass from the tap, shifting to the second keg when he got to ours.

The beer landed in front of me. I started to drink it when I saw Dad doing the same. I guessed the earlier warning about staying focused had taken a back seat to mimicking these jackals across from us, all of whom were gulping down their brew in loud slurps.

Nero drained his mug and slammed it on the table. Dangerously close to Dad's hand. He wiped his mouth and smiled.

"Well, what's in the truck?" Nero lit a cigarette and looked at us.

Dad pulled a list from his pocket and began rattling off a long list of names. I'd heard the words lots of times, but I still had very little idea what these weapons were: AK-something-or-others and Kevlar vests, stun grenades and RPGs, guns and bombs with big numbers attached, only matched by the number of people they'd killed.

Nero's cigarette was half burned by the time he finished. He waited for Dad to stop, then exhaled a long snort of smoke, before replying.

"Fucking impressive," he said. Dad's fingers tensed on the list in excitement, rustling the paper a little. "But I got a different deal in mind."

We both blinked simultaneously. I looked at Dad nervously and saw the light go out in his eyes.

"Yeah? What kinda deal we talking?"

"The kind that lets me poach any weapons I want for free. You're the one guy in this biz who's got his supply routes tracked from Maine to California like nobody else. You know exactly what's coming and going, whether it's yours or not. I'm fucking impressed. I know you've got some way to keep track of everything. If you wanna hand over that pretty little map, we'll call it good and be on our merry way."

Dad laughed once and slammed his fist on the table. "You gotta be shitting me! Did you know about this, Block? What's in it for your ass?"

He turned to the Rams' President. The heavy man shrugged, then nodded. "Deal's a deal. Everything you need to know's right in front of you. I've kept up my end to get you here talking to Nero."

Dad's temple was throbbing. If he could've grabbed me by the hand and walked right out the door, he would've. But there was no easy way to stop all eight huge bikers from descending on us before we got a single step closer to our truck.

The nine millimeter I knew he had packed in a holster near his hip wouldn't do much good either. Not against so many bastards like this.

"Yeah? What the fuck are you offering?" Dad said quietly. "You're talking about buying out my whole fucking business and getting a price on my head if anybody ever finds out what I gave you. You'd better offer four – five times! – what I fucking talked about with Block."

"Yeah, about that..." Nero's voice deepened. He stubbed out his cigarette on the bare table. "We'll give you the two hundred big I brought with and something that's worth a whole lot more than ten mill – immunity from Slingers' raids. You get to keep on selling shit to the same assholes you've served for the last thirty years, and we won't stop you. Trust me, buddy, they're gonna need your business once we start draining their fucking inventory and turning it to gold ourselves."

Dad looked defeated. Tired. The anger causing his leg to tremble against mine faded inexplicably. Actually, I was starting to feel pretty damned exhausted myself. Foggy, even, the same kinda sensation I had when I got my wisdom teeth out a couple years ago.

I tried to stay focused. Dad rolled his shoulders, as if he was trying not to fall asleep right there.

"Then what? You think I'm some kinda god damned dummy? There's no fucking future in that...not when you're fucking up the entire trade...Christ, you assholes are *worse* than the Prairie Devils. I'm sorry I ever came." His hand was spread out on the table, shaking to hold up his body.

Jesus, I was feeling sick, like something had tapped my veins and drained every ounce of energy I had.

What did they *do* to us?

"Whatever, dude. Had a feeling you'd turn us down." Nero grinned, bearing his evil, perfect teeth. "It wasn't a serious offer. Don't worry, you won't be alive long enough to bitch about shit."

"Fuck!" Dad roared just as the realization hit me in my heavy, heavy brain.

My chin slumped on my chest and I looked at my empty beer glass. Sneaky, sneaky bastards! They'd put something in there, something in the beer they served from the other keg. Dad jerked up, reaching for his gun, teetering like a big tree about to collapse.

"You mudderfuckhers!" He slurred. "Poiswon. Alish – run!"

The last word was perfectly clear. I jerked to my feet and got three steps out before the whole world went black. I hit the floor and rolled on my side, trying to scream for help, fighting to call out helplessly to my Dad one last time.

Whatever the hell they'd given us, it paralyzed my body, but left my eyes open just long enough to watch his luck flicker out forever.

Dad was still on his feet, rocking in a tight circle, but his fingers were too screwed up to pull his gun. Nero stood slowly, heavy mug in his hand. He looked at me and winked while he raised it high in the air, then brought it down hard on the back of my Dad's head.

Thwack! The sick sound was like a rotten watermelon splitting apart. Dad went down.

I was still screaming bloody murder in my head when my vision blurred to pitch black, and all my senses numbed. The thick dark trail of blood spreading from the back of his head found its way to my cheek, too numb to feel anything except its warmth.

Then the darkness caught up to me, and I lost my mind forever.

Days passed in that dingy little room. I couldn't remember I'd been poisoned, couldn't remember where I was, couldn't even remember who the dead man underneath the sheet was on the bed across from me.

He was pale. Rotting. All I had was a name – Alice – the name of someone who'd been condemned to be forgotten like a ghost.

The corpse scared me. So did the gruff voices outside my room. Men were arguing about tearing a truck apart, searching for something. There were only bits and pieces, loud rasps and growls my screwed up brain tried to understand and failed to every time.

"Not here? How the fuck could it be anywhere else? That dead sonofabitch lived on the road! I ought to unload everything in that fucking truck on this shithole clubhouse and leave you assholes torched for the Prairie Pussies to find."

"We did what you asked, Nero. Got him here. We delivered. Go ahead and kill us. The Devils will find out and come for your asses before you can shake your tails outta this state, if Fang and his Grizzles don't go after you first." The voice was tense, artificially clam, like the man was hiding something.

"You know what? Fuck it. We're out. This whole fucking thing is a bust and I'm gonna have my guys comb his fucking house for the map. Come on, boys. We're done wasting our time here."

"What about the girl?"

"Block…you dumbass. You really think we give two shits? You can have her ass. Payment for keeping your mouths shut. You're worth a cheap cunt, but I'm sure as fuck not paying you fifty big for holding out on us."

"You're goddamned lucky I don't have time to shove my knife up your sorry ass. Remember, asshole, we were never here."

A door slammed so hard it shook the entire building. Then silence. The deadly still lasted at least an hour.

I tensed up when I heard footsteps approaching my door. The muffled voices got clearer right before they came through.

"Gotta feed the bitch something. 'specially if she's gonna start riding all our dicks and give old Ruby a break. Junkie slut deserves it for telling us how to mix that shit in the beer. Fuck, it's been a long time since we had a nice young cunt to get our dicks wet…"

"Easy, Reaper. Better to take her gentle tonight. You fuck her too rough on an empty stomach, after what she's been through, and she'll be like a dead fish." Block stepped into the middle of the room and grunted. "Where the fuck is she?"

The overwhelming grog and brain fog swarming through my veins earlier was gone. Now, I was full of so much adrenaline I couldn't feel the sharp pangs twisting my stomach. I didn't know who these men were, but I understood what they wanted, and I was dead set on defending myself like the wild animal I'd become.

A shadow pushed the closet door open. My eyes burned when the bright light in his hand tore through the darkness concealing me.

"Bitch is in the closet, Prez. I'm gonna get her out…"

The last little island of sanity I was holding onto sank to oblivion as soon as he laid his hands on me. Kicking, screaming, biting, scratching.

The sheer ferocity must've surprised him because it took several seconds for the big man to get his footing. His bulk dropped on top of me, crushing me to the floor, but my arms and legs wouldn't stop thrashing.

Jesus, he was tugging at my jeans! Snarling, I rolled, jabbing my fingernails at any bare inch of skin I could find.

The scratches cut deep, allowing me to feel the faint outline of a neck, a face, an ear. Reaper screamed bloody murder and ripped off my jeans, tumbling away as I kneed him hard above the groin.

The kick missed its target by a couple inches. Damn it.

"Fucking cunt!" He swung low, a full force fist aimed at my face.

I was too quick for the old bastard. Whatever I'd given up in memory must've been made up in speed because I rolled and crashed against the wall like a stunt woman. Reaper's fist dragged him through the air and cracked hard against the wall.

"Fuck! Fuck, fuck, fucking bitch…almost broke my damned hand." His voice weakened.

The punch caused real pain. Dark satisfaction welled up inside me, but I wasn't letting my guard down. I hunched in the corner, ready to leap and go for his eyes next if he came any closer.

Whoever these men were, I'd rather *die* than have their wretched hands on me.

"Reaper. That's enough." The older beefy man grabbed his comrade by the shoulder.

"What're you talking about, Prez? You lost your fucking mind? We ought to put a bullet through this bitch's head and lay her on top of daddy over there…"

His breathing came hard, rough. Pure rage possessed him like a demon. He stared at my dark corner with hateful promises in his eyes. *I will kill you,* they said.

"Don't. We don't got the time or energy for dealing with another body. Fuck it, Nero screwed us over. Again." Block sounded tired. "Just leave the bitch alone. Those Prairie Pussies'll be here in a few days and we can dump her off with them."

Reaper spun, staring at his leader. "You goddamned serious? What if she talks? Those guys are assholes, but they won't hesitate to gut us. You heard what they did to the Grizzlies before the bears fled the state!"

"I'd rather have 'em fixated on this feral slut and her dead daddy. We can feed them anything we want about this bitch and her old man. But if it looks like things are too quiet and they go sniffing around Mickey's cargo we buried out back…they could find out the Slingers were here. Then you might as well kiss your hard ass goodbye. Bruises'll heal, brother."

Block grabbed for Reaper's hand. Frustrated, the man with the VP patch tore himself away, standing up. He gazed into the darkness one more time. It looked like it was taking all the energy in the world to hold back and listen to his boss.

"Whatever. Fuck this," Reaper growled, clasping his wounded hand tight. "I'm not coming in here with that crazy fucking pussy again, however hot she is."

"No need to," Block said. "We'll have Ruby slide her some fucking oatmeal or something. It's only for a couple days. If the girl wants to act like an animal, then we're gonna treat her like one."

I couldn't breathe properly again until I heard them leave the room and slam the door behind me. I stayed in the corner a long time, well after the darkness in my closet spread across the room. The lone window lost its light fast as the sun set behind the trees. The dead man's stench was getting stronger every hour.

Alone. Alone in the dark with nothing for company except the corpse stretched out on the bed about ten feet away.

When I couldn't hear anyone stirring in the clubhouse, I crawled into the room. If I could get outside, then maybe I could find the main door to this place, make a run for it.

Didn't have a clue where I'd go, or how. But *anywhere* was better than here.

My meager hope melted as soon as I grabbed the doorknob and gave it a good pull. Locked. Feeling above it with my palm, I found a newly installed lock, something like a deadbolt controlled from the other side.

Shit! Exhaustion settled in, long overdue, making me slump against the door and rest my forehead on the cold wood.

Fighting, kicking, screaming, and scratching only would've brought unwanted attention. I had no choice but to slink by the dead man again, wondering why the hell they called him daddy.

Surely, he wasn't mine? Was he?

The darkness and the thin sheet over him prevented me from seeing his face. Deep inside my head, a voice warned against trying to take a good look. If I recognized him, then I knew I'd truly be done.

Was it only three days? It felt like three weeks.

I slept with one eye open, staying in the darkness, treating the pale light spilling into my room like it would burn me to ashes. My heartbeat woke me with a jolt every time the door creaked open. I was ready to fight the men, kill them or kill myself if I had to, but it was only some skinny figure who stopped at my closet door.

The woman was afraid. At least I had something in common with someone here.

"Here," she whispered, the only word she ever said, sliding a ceramic bowl with a spoon in it across the floor.

It was always the same: oatmeal or instant soup. Total crap, just as bad as everything in this rotten room. The stuff stopped the hunger pangs just long enough to tangle my intestines. There was no bathroom, and no fucking way was I going to ask the brutes keeping me prisoner for potty breaks.

I used an old cardboard box I found on the closet shelf, a humiliating necessity I couldn't ignore when the urge struck. I didn't understand why, but that made me cry like nothing else.

Pissing in cardboard box made me so sick the tears came. Not the dead man moldering mere feet away. Not even the constant fear Reaper or Block would come back and finish what they'd started. No, living literally like an animal was one bridge too far, one horror I couldn't process in my screwed up head.

The next days were quiet and miserable. I wondered if I'd die in here and join the body on the bed after all. I couldn't bother wondering who I was or what I'd done to deserve this.

All I cared about was survival, freedom, some way out of this hell. There *had* to be a way, if I just waited it out and didn't totally snap.

I never expected a man to be my ticket out. Much less a stranger from the same kinda ruthless thugs who'd already turned my life upside down.

Voices. New voices. Loud voices – far louder than the men I feared.

Block, Reaper, and the others sounded like children next to the men roaring at them. I pressed my ear to the wall and listened. The Rams' leader kept mumbling apologies, offering his full cooperation, something about earning a patch or support from these other guys.

When I heard the footsteps coming, I tensed up. Curled my arms and legs in a ball, hoping somehow I could hide. Not that I actually expected it to work.

"Fuck me," a gruff voice said, now right next to the locked door. "If these idiots have got a rotting corpse holed up in there, I swear I'm gonna –"

The doorknob jiggled once. Impatient, the stranger growled, and smashed something heavy against the door. Probably a boot. The deadbolt broke and the door swung back, smacking the wall. Heavy footsteps followed as three tall, massive, and deadly serious men entered.

It was daylight. The closet was dark – pitch black in the corner where I huddled – but I could tell from the second they entered the room that they were determined to scope out everything.

The trio were all big guys, but one of them was a total giant. The big man stopped, towering at the closet's opening, blocking out all the light. He lifted his arms, holding something.

No, aiming.

"Get your ass out here now! You've got five seconds to show yourself, and the countdown's already started."

One way or another, I was dead if these guys wanted me to be. The killer instinct that helped me against Reaper a few days ago was gone, faded, beaten into submission by shitty food and constant fear.

The giant's hands twitched. A second as long as half a lifetime ticked by. Without thinking, I stood up, my mind totally numb as I walked toward the raging hulk.

I just wanted this to be over. If this was the beginning of the end, then so be it. I'd rather die out in the open. It was better than being shot in the dark like a worthless rat.

The world was getting smaller and smaller as I took one trembling step at a time toward his huge shadow, and then past him, into the light. The giant kept his gun trained on me for several long seconds as I walked by him, and then lowered it with a confused look.

Christ, how long had I been holed up in there? The light was…overwhelming.

"Holy fucking shit," a man said, right as my legs gave out.

I started to fall. The whole world went spinning, breaking apart, blurring into a sickly haze.

My vision was fucked. But I never hit the floor. Two strong arms grabbed me just in time, yanking my body tight to his powerful chest.

I took a deep breath, relieved that he'd broken my fall. Musk, motor oil, and a faint spicy cologne teased my nostrils. I'd forgotten what it was to smell something good and fresh. I inhaled again, slow and steady, relishing his scent.

He smelled *wonderful*. Powerful. Safe. Maybe even pure.

"What's wrong? Are you hurt?" The stranger's voice was deep, demanding. "Talk to me, girl!"

I wanted to. But the nervous breakdown wouldn't let me. I bowed my head against his chest, burying my face on a simple gray shirt peeking out between his leather vest.

Of course I'm hurt, I thought. *I'm hurting like hell. But as long as I keep breathing you, I might be okay. Maybe.*

"Christ." The taller, angrier voice behind the man holding me exploded. "Bad enough we've got a body back here to deal with. Now here's little miss Dracula too. Soon as I find out who the fuck died here, I'm gonna slaughter those Rams…"

The arms holding me tightened. Amazing how they could be so reassuring without words, so gentle even though they felt like they could crush the life out of anyone who got in his way. He leaned down and breathed deep. His strong chest rolled, a steady wall of muscle beneath my cheek.

Exactly what I needed, though I hadn't known it until that very second. Time slowed each time he moved or flexed, as if to say I'd be protected for as long as I damn well needed.

After the last few days in this hellhole, his embrace was an oasis, and I never wanted to let go.

"Get her out of here," the giant said. "Don't know how Blaze wants to handle this shit, but there's no sense in letting her stew a second longer in this cesspool."

"Thanks, brother." His hands moved and he began to walk, nudging me forward with one strong arm cradled over my neck, ready to catch me if I stumbled. He slapped the big man on the shoulder as we passed through the broken door.

"It's okay, baby," he whispered, a storm building beneath those three words. "Whatever the fuck they've done to you, we're gonna make it all right. That's a fucking promise…"

What have they done to me? I wondered. I shook my head, questioning my feeble memory, pushing dirty strands of hair against his smooth skin.

Jesus, I needed a shower. Shame hit hard. I was surprised the stranger didn't shove me back in the closet when he figured out how gross I was.

He was right about one thing: I hated the assholes who'd held me under lock and key. For all I knew, my nightmare was entering another chapter walking with this strange man.

Whatever. I didn't have to trust him. I just had to wrap myself up in the powerful shield he offered, the rock hard body that bowed up when we passed by the Rams and went outside. His movements vowed if anyone wanted to get to me, they'd have to go through him first.

Good enough. I didn't know him, didn't know if he was truly as good as he seemed. But he was the first person in a long time hellbent on protecting me instead of offering more torture.

For now, that was enough. All I needed to leave this place. If I survived this, then maybe there'd be time to sort out the rest.

He helped me outside and sat me down on a big motorcycle, making sure I was fixed in safely. Jesus, I wasn't sure I was in any condition to ride. I'd never been on one of these things before. Something about sitting on the huge, sexy chrome rocket gave me new energy. Feeling the wild wind in my hair sounded lovely after I'd been cooped up for too long.

He gently pressed a blue helmet onto my head and then walked behind me. Flipping open a compartment, he began searching for something.

The man's hand brushed my bare leg as he bent down. I jerked, ready to bite and scratch.

"Shit, baby, calm down. I was just trying to see if I had something for you to eat in my saddlebag. When's the last time those assholes fed you a decent meal?"

For the first time, I gazed into his eyes, drilling down deep to see if I could find anything sinister. Thank God. There was nothing there but shock, surprise, and – was I seeing it right? – concern.

I shrugged, calming as I allowed him to reach by me. I eyed the patches on his cut. One tag said VP – just like Reaper. STINGER was stitched next to it.

"Fuck me. It's empty." He zipped up the bag and slammed the compartment shut. "Fucking forgot I gave my last jerky to Moose before the ride in…"

"That's okay," I said, ignoring the hunger rumbling in my stomach. "I've survived worse."

"I see that," he said, looking me up and down. "Shit, you're gonna need something to cover those legs for the ride. Can't get on the road with you like that. Hold on."

My ears perked up. He almost sounded reluctant when he talked about covering me up. He walked to the truck parked nearby, rummaged around in the backseat, and then returned a couple minutes later with an oversized pair of jeans.

"Put these on. They might be a little big, but they'll do. Had a feeling my brother, Moose, had something in there his daughter left behind…"

I rolled them up, trying not to blush. Something about dressing right in front of him activated my modesty more than him holding me in nothing but this crappy shirt and my panties. Having pants around my waist again made me feel more human too.

"Thanks," I said, giving them one more pull around my waist.

"No problem. And, baby, anytime you're ready to talk about what those assholes did to you in there, you come to me. I'll bring Blaze in on it. The Prez is looking for a damned good reason to tear into these pricks. If they hurt a single fucking hair on your pretty head, just say the word. We'll come back and make sure these cocks never fuck with anybody again."

His stare was so intense. For a second, I lost myself in his dark brown eyes, and then I began to notice the rest of his face for the first time.

The man – Stinger? Was that really his name? – was pretty handsome. Rough masculine beauty shined through, like bright stars breaking through my fog.

Medium, slightly shaggy brown hair hung down his forehead, flecked with sweat after the intense standoff inside the clubhouse. The imposing stare melted the longer I looked, and his strong jaw tightened in a smile, forming dimples on his cheeks.

He was older than me by a good ten years – maybe more – and what I could see of his body peeking through his tight clothes said he'd lived a very different life. His bare arms were hard, sculpted, ready for anything. Maybe some things I didn't want to know about.

He'd earned his wild strength somehow. I suspected it had a lot to do with the way he'd also gotten the fearsome looking ink crawling up his arms.

Several symbols on his skin jumped out at me before he moved: pitchforks, skulls, phrases written in small, crabbed writing I couldn't quite read.

The crap the Rams wore on their clothes and their skin had looked pretty ferocious too. That made it all the more surprising that the man next to me was acting like a perfect gentleman. Nothing like his devilish tattoos suggested.

"I get it. You don't need to say shit right now. Not to me, Blaze, or anybody else. Just rest, baby. You've been through the fucking grinder." He slowly slid his hand on my shoulder and urged me to lean back. "Hey, you got a name?"

Then he sat down on the bike in front of me, reaching for my hands, gently lifting them around his waist.

"Alice," I said.

I wondered why it was so easy to remember my name but nothing else. My mind was all twisted in knots, like I'd just gotten off a rollercoaster. Everything was like quicksand, shaken to pieces and slowly sinking.

God, could I even be sure the brutes with the Rams patches had tried to force themselves on me a couple days ago?

"No shit? You mean like the girl in the fantasy book?"

"Sure. Just as long as you take me home to wonderland on this thing."

He laughed. It was a marvelous sound, smooth and masculine as he looked.

"I'm Stinger," he said, tapping the patches on his breast with the name tag and VP lettering. "You remember that. That's the name you're gonna speak if you need anything, baby. Anything at all. Long as you yell, I'll come runnin', morning, noon, or night. Stick with me, and you'll be fine. Cross my fucking heart."

He slashed a sign across his shoulders like he really meant it. For all I knew, this whole damned thing was an act. If it was, then he deserved an award for the most charming, convincing liar I'd ever met. Or at least the best one I could remember meeting.

"I won't forget," I said. "Doesn't seem like the kinda name anybody forgets."

"Fuck no." A serious edge crept into his voice. "I always leave my mark on people one way or another. Friend, foe, brother…when I see somebody or something worth fighting for, I'm there, and it'll take a whole fucking army to keep me away. I'm not used to taking a damned thing lightly."

Is he serious? I started to wonder if my screwed up state was making me hear more drama, more promise, in his voice than what was really there.

"Lay back and hold on tight, Alice. I'll get you somewhere safe in no time. This ride's pretty damned comfortable once we get going, believe it or not."

I listened, settling back in my seat and folding my hands around him. It was a little awkward touching a man so close, so intimately, when I barely knew him.

Stinger wasn't fazed. He probably gave girls rides like this all the time, and I felt silly taking so long to realize it.

When he didn't feel enough pressure in my hands, he reached down, and shoved them together tight, pressing them around his waist.

"You keep them together just like that. Lean into me if you have to. I'm your support."

And he was. Seriously. I shifted up a little and took his advice, resting my head on his shoulder. His warmth and unforgettable scent instantly made things better. I didn't even flinch as the Harley rumbled to life and pulled up near the other empty bikes waiting for their riders.

I looked down. PRAIRIE DEVILS MC, MONTANA was written in a ribbon flowing across his back, surrounding a grinning devil's face flanked by pitchforks. A small red diamond patch off to the side contained the 1% symbol, outlined in blood red.

Didn't have a clue what it meant, except the Rams had it too, a pale white 1% patch stitched on their cuts.

A few minutes later, the same burly guys I'd seen before wearing Stinger's colors came walking out, heading for their bikes and the lone truck parked behind us. All the vehicles fired up and joined us. We rode out in the middle of the three bikes, with the truck in the rear.

Stinger was right about one thing: I was completely in his hands now, for better or worse. And all I could do was survive in the present while the past and future swirled like thick fog.

I pressed my hands tight to Stinger's waist, tracing his hard abs as the bikes hit the highway. Each time I shifted my hands, his belly jerked a little beneath me.

Mumbling apologies, I locked my fingers together and held them in a spot just above his waist. There was something oddly comforting about this close, human contact after I'd been away from the living and sane for so long. His warmth, his strength, the sturdy control he kept over his ride made me feel more secure than anything I could remember.

Exhaustion caught up to me and I relaxed my face on his shoulder. The strange half-dreamy state I slipped into was a hundred times more soothing than all the hours I'd slept in that rotten closet.

Just before I lost consciousness, I could've sworn I felt his hand on mine near the belt, strong and reassuring, making the same promise in his squeeze that I'd felt in his arms and seen in his face.

Stinger's the only word you need to know from now on, his fingers said. *Doesn't matter if you can't remember where the hell you came from or your last hot meal.*

As long as you remember me, you've got a fighting chance, and I'm gonna fight for you, baby. Cross my heart and hope to fucking die.

III: Herding Cats (Stinger)

Thank fuck Blaze and Tank were right by my side when I saw her. If it hadn't been for my brothers, I might've turned to stone gawking like a fucking idiot as she stumbled outta that ratty storage space, but only after my dick beat me to it first.

The girl was beautiful. Yeah, it was a strange kinda beauty with her messed up hair and dark smudge marks all over her hands and legs. But a red blooded man knows a girl who'd be a knockout with a hot shower when he sees one.

Christ, what the fuck was she doing in nothing but a striped shirt and panties? What the fuck did the Rams *do* to her?

I was on her before the Prez or the big guy could move another muscle. When she collapsed on my chest, I wrapped my arms tight and pulled her in.

It was like lightning, thunder, rain. A crazy typhoon surged up inside me, blasting every inch of my brain, trying to keep my muscles from twitching.

Lust died down a few degrees. Now, cradling her like this, I was fucking pissed. The MCs who treated their girls like shit always landed themselves a spot on my personal shit list. Maybe that had something to do with Beth, or maybe I just didn't like seeing dudes in my world acting like fucking worms.

Regardless, I had to hold on. I had to help her.

And I *really* had to make the filthy spot in my head that controlled my dick settle down and take a breather before I lost my fucking mind. I knew it wouldn't be easy just seeing her, but feeling her? Having her pressed up against me like this, shaking those pretty pert tits on my cut every time she trembled?

Fuck.

I was glad the Prez let me move fast to get her outta there. Blaze was just as pissed off as ever, and he wanted me out so he could lay into the Rams without her in the way. Not to mention get Mickey's body somewhere it'd never trouble anyone again.

When I got some pants on her and put her on my bike, I'd tamed the horny demon in my skull as much as I could.

I was really concerned. More than just wondering how I'd get my dick wet. No joke.

Everything about the girl said she'd been through some serious shit. We'd have to do something about that as soon as I got her back to the clubhouse. I wasn't used to playing nurse, no, but I'd damned sure do whatever I could to make her comfortable while we waited for the nod from Blaze to tear the Rams' dicks off for what they'd done.

We made small talk on my Harley, and then she finally laid against me to rest for the long drive to Missoula. Took real energy to keep my eyes on the road during the drive.

My brain was too busy feeling her curves against me, aching to feel her laid out in the other direction, right on my lap. Alice – that's what she said her name was – felt good. Fucking right.

When we stopped to refuel, she was still snoozing. I settled her back and let my goddamned eyes roam all over places they shouldn't have, across her plush tits, up her snowy neck, devouring her raven black hair. Then they shot down, crawling over her wide hips, burning every curve of her nice long legs into my memory.

My dick started straining again like the relentless fucker he was. I squeezed the pump in my hands hard, crushing the metal handle 'til my hand went numb.

By the time we got to the clubhouse, my pulse was going mad, beating like a hammer in my pants. Normally, I would've made a straight line for the club whores. I ached so bad I would've taken Marianne and Sangria both, hauling them into bed and fucking them blind, imagining they were both half as hot as the black haired beauty riding bitch on my bike.

Too bad there was shit to do, and nobody else seemed too concerned about making sure she was settled in.

It was all up to me. My job to make sure Alice was safe, settled, fed, and warm. Reb and big bearded Moose crawled out of the truck behind me, both of them shooting me curious nods as I stepped off the bike, knelt down, and shook her.

She didn't want to budge, moaning like it hurt to come outta the deep coma she was in. Girl must've needed a lotta beauty sleep with a bod like that.

Fuck it. No way was I leaving her out in the open. Scooping her up, I carried her straight to my club room, the same spartan little hole in the wall I called home. Soon I'd be looking for a proper place in town like some of the other brothers.

Wished like hell I'd gotten an apartment sooner for this, but my little room would have to do. Right now, a door between the rest of the club and a warm bed was all she needed, and I had that much to share.

"Wake up, girl," I whispered, laying her down on my mattress. "You need to eat."

She brushed her hands against me and whimpered. Struggled like a sleepy kitten. Sure, she needed her shut eye – God knows the last time she'd been able to sleep easy in the Rams' clutches – but she needed food and water too.

I told her I'd be back and went to the bar. I rustled up a leftover burger from the fridge and some water. After the shit that just went down with the Rams, it wouldn't be long before Blaze called church. Least I could do was get her fed before then.

Back in the room, she was snoring. I pulled her up, careful to make sure she didn't try to scratch me when I nudged her. She still struggled every time her eyes were closed, but just seeing me seemed to calm her, make her settle down and take the food and drink, if reluctantly.

I sat down as she came up, gnawing on the sandwich in quick little bites.

"Stinger, I'm full," she said, the burger half-eaten. "I need more sleep. So tired…"

I folded my arms. "We're on the same page. You can rest your eyes again after you finish your water. *All* of it."

She'd only taken a few sips outta the tall glass I gave her. Damn it, I had to get some fluids in her. I wasn't a nurse like our on call medic, Emma, but I had enough sense to know the girl had been through the wringer and was way too dry, halfway dehydrated.

"Come on, baby. Drink. Can't let you get sick on me."

I grabbed the glass and pushed it to her lips. Frustration flashed in her pretty eyes as she looked at me, then slowly parted them.

I tipped the cup 'til she took it herself, gulping down everything I gave her. Good.

Later, I'd make sure she got cleaned up too. I was sure I could scrounge up some fresh clothes from one of the whores or somebody's old lady, maybe Blaze's girl, Saffron. Alice was shorter than her, but about the same build. Looked like she'd have perfect, full curves if only she wasn't so damned starved.

"There," she grumbled, clanking the cup on the nightstand. "Empty. Do I get to sleep now, or are you going to watch me do that too?"

"No. There's a meeting I need to go to actually," I said. "I'll check up on you in a few."

"Whatever," she said, collapsing on her side. "Just turn out the light."

My eyebrow quirked as I made my way out. Anybody deserved to have some attitude after being imprisoned in a fucking closet, but I was surprised the change was so sudden. Where had that scared, whimpering little thing I pulled into my arms gone?

Whatever was right. I had plenty of time to figure this shit out later. I closed the door behind me and walked down the hall to meet Blaze. Didn't doubt the Prez was already fuming and waiting for all our asses in the meeting room.

Church lasted fucking forever. I shoved it along as best as I could, listening to Blaze vent all the ways he was gonna fuck up the Rams if the excuses they'd made for him didn't check out. Tank's mind was somewhere else.

Our huge Sargent-at-Arms had only recently pulled his ass outta the funk he'd been in for months. The drama between him and Em had been going on fucking forever, but it finally seemed to be going his way.

The other brothers sat with us too, Moose and Reb. Everybody except Roller and the two prospects, who'd followed one of our Dakota boys from mother charter out West on a special shipping run.

"You really believe them, Prez?" Moose asked, stroking his thick beard.

"Not for a goddamned second. That said, we couldn't turn up anything to prove Block was lying through his teeth," he growled, twisting his gavel in one hand.

He wasn't the only one who had thunder rolling through his system. I didn't give a shit whether the Rams were proven liars or not.

So what if the marks on Mickey's body corroborated their bullshit story? They were bullshitting us about the girl one way or another. What kinda sick fucks lock a young girl up with a dead body for days?

Too many unanswered questions. Too many roads leading back to the same damned place: any thought of seriously patching the Pagan Rams over as a support club was ludicrous. They deserved to be disbanded for the shit they'd done, preferably starting with their shriveled little dicks.

"How about that crap the guys pulled out of their backroom after burying Mickey? Anything good? I'll look it over myself if it hasn't been checked yet." I volunteered to take on the files, knowing how much Blaze and the other guys hated paperwork.

"Don't bother, VP." Moose shook his head at me. "Nothing too useful. Just a big fat folder full of old inventories. Looks like some routes too. Just a big ass map of the whole damned country with lines going through it. Had himself a sketch book too."

"Sketch book?" Blaze snorted. "What the fuck was he drawing? Directions for the numbskulls in that fucking clubhouse about how to fire the shit he was selling? Guess it's been twenty years since those mustangs fired a weapon. Don't now why Mickey was looking to do business with them at all."

Pissed as I was, Blaze's sarcasm made me smile. The Rams were fucking dumbasses, no two ways about it. Made it even harder to believe they'd managed to take out Mickey in a sour bar brawl and tortured the poor girl sleeping in my room.

"No, Prez. It's like…fantasy shit." Reb smacked his lips, chewing his tobacco. "Elves, castles, fairies…I dunno. See for yourself."

He reached into the pile of papers in the middle and grabbed the tall booklet. I intercepted it before it got to Blaze, quickly fanning my fingers through the pages.

One look at the drawings told me this shit wasn't drawn by a salty old smuggler like Mickey James. No way, no how. It had to belong to Alice.

"He's right," I said. "I don't think this is Mickey's either. The writing's real girly. Don't see blood or guns or naked ladies…"

The sketches were really pretty good. No, maybe not ready for Hollywood story boards or book covers. Still, it looked like they'd been done by somebody who'd have a shot at it one day if they just kept going.

I was flipping through the back pages when Blaze's gavel came down. I blinked, looked up, and flashed my trademark smile at his angry ass.

"What the fuck, Sting?" Blaze growled. "This isn't an art gallery. Put that shit away and let's chew on the facts that are useful."

"You sure we got any, Prez?" That really sent blood into his face. I straightened up. "We're not gonna know shit 'til I talk to Alice. She's the only one who lived with them and might've seen what went down with Mickey. Just give her a chance to rest, clean up, and I'll talk to her tomorrow."

"Sounds like a plan to me," Tank said, leaning in his chair, looking at Blaze. "The VP's right, boss. We don't know much. Even if we did, we've got two choices: make these assholes shape up, patch them in, and hope to hell they never bothered us again. Or else we send them packing with a sweep of Satan's Scythe and destroy every last Pagan Rams emblem we can find."

Blaze looked like he was ready to turn the table over. He was used to getting shit from me – what else was a VP in an MC like this one good for? – but taking it from Tank and the other brothers sealed the deal.

"All right, all right," he said, shaking his head. "We'll wait and see. Stinger, I'm counting on *you* to give us something we can use. Don't think I need a vote to know everybody in this room would rather chase the Pagan Rams off our turf and into Grizzlies' territory rather than deal with their nasty asses again. Or just kill the motherfuckers cold. Whatever we do, I need *something* to make sure we're not making a mistake. I'm not risking this club's blood again without a damned good reason."

"I'll have Em check her too," Tank said, his face lightning up when he said the nurse's name.

I studied his expression. Had a feeling the fucking guy was finally getting his dick wet after breaking the glacier between them. He sure as hell wasn't sulking around and drinking himself into a stupor like he'd been during all the months when Em gave him the cold shoulder.

"How 'bout tomorrow?" I asked. "Alice really needs her rest. She's tired as all hell."

"No," Blaze said, tapping his gavel a couple times when I gave him an angry look. "Em's already here waiting for us to finish up. The sooner we move on this shit, the quicker it's over. And I want *all* threats to this club wrapped up before winter. Then we've just got our shipments from the Dakota boys to deal with."

"That and your wedding, Prez." Moose smiled.

Blaze cocked his head and let his anger taper. The senior brother's words were the goddamned truth, and it only caused my rage to ratchet up a couple notches.

Blaze and his old lady were due to get married in Reno early next year. Wasn't hard to see those bells were ringing loud in his mind since he'd claimed her and proposed, but all I heard was bullshit if it caused him to make Alice suffer more.

"Come on, man." Reb said, sensing the invisible smoke rolling off me. "It's just a little check up. Em's fast and efficient, and you know it. She'll finish the girl in no time and send her back to you."

"Whatever. Let me get her up." I was rising from my chair before Blaze banged the gavel, bringing the session to a close.

Blaze shot me a warning look. The Prez took a lot of lip when it mattered, but he and I both knew I was damned close to shitting on his authority. I waited by the door 'til the other brothers began to rise.

Fuck it. I was out the door before he could get in my face, heading straight for the girl, the only one in this clubhouse who gave a damn beyond pumping her for info.

The checkup went fast. I was in the room with Blaze while Em did her thing. Tank wandered in a few minutes after us, and I instantly sensed some tension between him and Nurse Blondie.

God. Damn. It. Apparently, fucking hadn't resolved shit between them in any lasting way.

Not my business. Not my problem, I thought, turning my full attention to Alice.

I watched Em's gold locks bobbing as she checked her over. Helluva contrast against my girl's jet black hair, and I knew damned well what I preferred.

She's not your girl, I had to remind myself. *Not yet, anyway.*

Fuck, what was I thinking? Probably not ever. I wasn't sure what the hell was happening to my brain since I got her little hands around me on my bike, but it was freaking me the fuck out.

So did the bombshell that dropped next. Alice insisted she couldn't remember shit except her name, and it didn't look like she was fucking around. My jaw was left hanging, along with everybody else's.

Em broke out a bright light and beamed it into her pretty eyes. I tightened my jaw, wondering when she'd finally be through with this bullshit.

"Pupils are normal. No sign of brain damage." Emma paused, glancing at Blaze. "What is it you want to know?"

"What the fuck really happened the night she showed up at the Rams' clubhouse. She says she doesn't remember shit," Blaze said, pacing the room. "Is it possible she's fucked up her head, nurse? Or is she fucking us instead?"

Shit! My blood went from lukewarm to molten lava in a nano-second. My fists twitched at my sides.

I wasn't gonna clock my hotheaded Prez in the jaw for the same crap he gave everybody else, but it sure was tempting.

What the fuck was he thinking? The girl didn't have a single reason to yank our dicks around in the wrong direction.

The evilest warning look I ever summoned went his way while I wondered why Blaze's doubt against her felt the same as if he'd just spat on me, a fellow brother and his own VP. I shouldn't be taking this shit so personally, and I knew it. The reptile part of my brain refused to get the message.

I listened intently as Em explained that amnesia wasn't unheard of after suffering something really tragic. When she said it was probably a mental block instead of brain damage, the boil in my veins popped. Every muscle I had flexed, ready to march out to my bike and roar out to the Rams' place myself, not coming home 'til I cleaned their asses up good.

Blaze and the nurse ran through who Alice could be, wondering if she was Mickey's old lady or his slut. Maybe he liked them young.

Fuck! Thinking about her wrapped around that dead asshole's body – hell, any asshole, alive or dead – threatened to melt me from the inside out.

I stepped up when Em moved aside, throwing an arm around Alice's neck and helping her off the table. Knew damned well it was possessive too, but I didn't fucking care.

"Don't think she's that kinda girl, Prez," I said, trying as hard as I could to hide my rage. "She's not a club slut. I can spot those bitches from a mile away, and this isn't one."

"Yeah, yeah, you're right about that…" Blaze looked amused and frustrated as hell. "Whatever, bro. Just get her the fuck outta here and find the girl a room."

Done, asshole, I thought. Didn't bother saying goodbye as I took her by the hand and led her away, back to my room, the only place here where she belonged.

"You sure you got enough to eat earlier?" I asked, focusing my eyes on hers when we were alone behind the door.

"Yeah. Can I finally sleep, or are there are going to be more interruptions?"

"Hell no," I growled. "Lay down and rest as long as you fucking want. I'll wait here. Anybody who knocks at this door in the next hour's gonna get a fist to his face."

I was dead serious. She needed to get her head straight, dammit, and I intended to keep my secret threat, even if Blaze came sniffing around for more information. I'd had it up to hear with his shit. I'd rather risk a beat down from all my brothers than deal with him twisting Alice's arm again like a total asshole.

Fortunately, it never came to that. The other brothers had plenty other business to take care of. I should've been outside tuning up my bike with winter creeping closer, but I couldn't do shit with this angel laid out in front of me, shaking a little as she nodded off.

"Sweet dreams, baby." I pulled a blanket over her, wishing I had something nicer than this tattered old thing.

I must've stood there at her bedside for another ten minutes, just watching, studying her. My cock kept his cool for once while I waited for her to stop shaking. The boys hadn't fired up the furnace yet in the clubhouse, and it was too damned cold for her bones. Winter was right around the corner.

The blanket wasn't doing shit. With a heavy sigh, I rolled my cut off my shoulders and climbed in next to her, throwing one arm around her shoulder and pulling her close.

Christ, she felt amazing when I spooned myself over her, covering every curve with my body, hellbent on keeping her free and clear of a world that wanted to keep piling its shit on her.

Having Alice up against me was better than anything I could think of to keep warm in this clubhouse. Better than a few shots of Jack. Better than fucking Marianne and Sangria or any new whores at the same time.

Better than anything and everything except for one wicked, insane desire I couldn't ignore.

Just one thing would've beat this: tearing off the blanket, stripping down her pants, and sinking into the soft warm perfection between her legs…

Shit, just thinking about it turned my blood to steam, heavy magma heading south real fucking fast. It hit my dick over and over and over in heavy waves. It ached because I wanted to fuck her, and then hurt like hell because I couldn't.

Aching for women wasn't something I was used to – not for long, anyway, because I always took what I wanted in the past. Pussy comes easy when you're big, fit, tattooed, and brought up to take the world by its fucked up horns.

But for her, I waited. I waited and suffered. My pulse beat my dick stupid, the price of being a perfect gentleman curled up next to this shattered dove, a wolf in gentleman's dapper clothing, an animal who wanted this girl so bad his brain turned to hot mush.

All I knew was I wouldn't wait forever. One day, when she was well, I'd make the gentleman stuff it, showing her how there was nothing gentle or tame about how this man fucked. 'Til then, she didn't know shit about what I was hiding.

She didn't need to neither.

If she did, she would've thrown me off the bed and run for the hills. Only sane response to my inner freak who was all tongue, all cock, all lust. And just barely held in check by the tight fucking choke chain I had around his neck, fighting to keep control, for her good and mine…but just barely.

Barely.

Barely was fine for today, but it wouldn't be forever. Not by the longest fucking shot in the universe.

Damned good thing I kept control. I'd be a fucking monster as bad as the Rams if I took her like this, more vulnerable than ever, however much my devil cock wanted me to.

I made sure to keep the soft blanket between us so she couldn't feel my psycho hard-on if she woke. I had to keep that chain tight, hide my beast for just a little while longer.

No, dammit. Never thought I'd think it, but some things were more important than sex. When I eyed her in the darkness, she looked so small. Whether she knew it or not, she needed somebody to protect her from the fucked up world outside, and I was game.

I had to be. That promise I made all those years ago, after I fucked up with Beth…

No. I closed my eyes. The last few days had already been beyond intense. Bitter, angry shit. I sure as hell didn't need to add another bad memory to the fire.

Alice turned gently in my arms, pushing back into my warmth. I relaxed, even with brimstone lighting up my veins, aching need thundering at a primal level I couldn't completely switch off. Sooner or later, the Sandman would find my ass and knock me out.

Long as Alice was safe and comfy, that was all that mattered.

I slept late. Alice was still buried in her dreams when I eased myself up, tucking the blanket around her tight to hold the warmth I'd added over night.

Blaze was at the bar, cellphone in hand. Only took a second to realize something had gone straight to hell with the dark note in his voice about to go off the rails. Tensing up, I walked closer, just as he finished and slammed his cheap burner on the counter.

Saffron wasn't in yet. She'd been managing the bar ever since she became his old lady. Still, I seriously doubted she'd been on the line. This looked like a helluva lot more than a bad fight with his woman.

"What's going on, Prez?" He didn't answer me. "What the fuck happened?"

He slammed his fists down hard on the counter, narrowly missing the shitty phone. Blaze looked up, his eyes burning like nothing else.

"Tank's in prison. Killed some asshole cousin of Em's at her place last night. Beat him to death. The badges found him with that bastard's blood all over his fists."

"Fuck." My heart sank, and my whole fucking mouth went dry like I'd just swallowed cotton.

I thought dealing with Alice would be the hardest thing on the agenda for today. Now, the entire club had a real problem on its hands.

The next couple days were agonizing as fuck. I made sure Alice cleaned up, fed, and slept as much as she wanted.

Blaze was working on getting our brother out ASAP. Turned out the dead asshole who caused all of this was a rogue ATF agent trying to pump the club for info through Em. I saw the nurse walk outta Blaze's office after he grilled her, making absolutely fucking sure she hadn't ratted on us.

Somehow, the Prez managed to cut a deal. He'd offered the bastards Mickey's body, but of course they wanted more. The arms trafficker was no good to them dead. Turning over his bones was enough to get Tank out temporarily. The Feds were giving us our giant to help search for something useful, but he'd be going behind bars again in a week if we didn't give them some shiny new shit for their resumes.

If my plate wasn't already overflowing, I had another problem with my fucking plumbing. The morning after we picked up Alice at the Rams' place, my nuts started burning, and not in any way I enjoyed.

I thought back to the last time I fucked our whores on a drunken bender, a few days before we visited the Rams and their stinking clubhouse. Fuck, if one of those bitches gave me clap or something, I swore I'd stick to my hand for the next month.

Yeah right, a voice laughed in my head. *You're not gonna keep a damned thing in your pants with her here.*

Not that I could imagine fucking anybody except Alice. The sluts and groupies who came to our parties were like half-baked imitations to the pure, sweet slice of homemade pie the mystery girl offered.

A quick stop in Em's infirmary helped. She checked my sac and had me piss in a bottle – fucking humiliating, as always – but I needed to find out what I was dealing with. The nurse was as upbeat as she could be under the circumstances.

I tried to be too. She didn't need any more frowns over Tank. Besides, if there was a ghost of a chance at getting in Alice's pants when all this shit blew over, I was gonna make damned sure my equipment was all in working order.

I walked back to my room to check on Alice, ignoring the unpleasant burn in my balls. She'd played mute for the last couple days, sleeping off her injuries. That was fine with the club focused on Tank's situation, but damn, she couldn't keep quiet forever.

Blaze was starting to hold my feet to the fire with this deal looming. Sooner or later, he'd be on Alice's ass for info if Emma didn't get to her first. Anything she remembered that might help us get our brother out permanently and wrap up the bullshit with the Pagan Rams was top prize.

I had to try getting it outta her the easy way, before things got harder. The other brothers were treating her like she was fucking cursed, and I knew their kid gloves were coming off as soon as the big guy was released from jail on Friday.

Opening the door, I found her sitting on the bed, glumly flipping through an old motorcycle magazine I had on my dresser. She looked up at me, wrinkled her nose, and tossed it on the floor.

"Don't you knock?" Alice whined.

I kicked the door shut and folded my arms. One thing she hadn't slept off was the fucking attitude that started burbling up after we got her away from the Rams.

How the fuck did a girl so hot ooze pure ice?

"It's my room," I said, coming closer.

I pulled up the lone chair and sat down, throwing my legs over the backside. Having some extra space in my lap helped ease the pain in my balls. No fucking way was I letting that shit interfere with our chat when she already acted like she had my nuts in a vise.

"Why're you here? It's not dinner time yet, is it?"

I looked her up and down. Dammit, I didn't care how soft and sexy and helpless she was…I wasn't gonna put up with this shit forever. I had to get something I could use for everybody's good: hers, the club's, and Tank's.

"I'm gonna be straight with you, baby. Blaze and my crew are getting real anxious for shit we can use against the Rams now that we got a brother facing serious jail time. The Feds want to know what the fuck Mickey's body was doing there as bad as we do." I grabbed for her hand, closing my fingers around hers tight when she tried to pull away. "Come on, Alice. Give me something I can throw my club. You want somebody to knock? Fine. Everybody'll be knocking a lot harder on your door next week when the clock starts ticking to keep Tank free."

"I already told you," she said sourly, struggling out of my grip. "I don't remember anything!"

"And I don't totally believe that," I growled. "I'm not a pro like Em and I don't know how shit works inside your head. But I've seen plenty of guys in the past who took a beating and lost their brains for a while. Couldn't remember much more than their names – just like you. But it always came back after a few days…"

"You're calling me a liar? Great." She sniffed and turned her head, long black hair flapping on her shoulders.

Shit. A different burn circled around and around my dick. The damned thing was sick but it wasn't dead. She looked better than ever after being cleaned up and rested for a few days. Sure didn't act like she felt it, though.

"I'm saying you're gonna remember something sooner or later, baby. And I'm hoping like hell it'll be today, when you can get off easy telling me. I'm the good cop here. This is as low pressure as it's gonna get. Come on, girl. *Think.*"

She paused, beaming those icy brown eyes at mine. "You can't keep me here forever. I don't have to tell you or anybody else *anything*. How's what happened to me any of your club's fucking business?"

"Because your business turned into club business the minute we found you holed up with Mickey James' dead body."

Alice blinked, and then looked down, her wildcat anger softening. His name. Something about it struck a bell. I saw my chance and pushed the chair closer to her, reaching for her shoulder and giving it a squeeze. This time, she didn't move away.

"I'm trying to help you and help my club, Alice. Yeah, you're right to be pissed off. I wouldn't like being made to hang out here if I couldn't remember much beyond my own damned name. We're not in the habit of bringing in strays just for fun. You're here for your own damned safety and because you're the only one who rode in with Mickey, the *only* person who can tell us what the fuck happened there."

"I...I don't know...I'll try..."

Without thinking, I let my fingers wind down her arm, slow, almost sensual. Had to get off her before I went too far.

Fuck, the girl was like a magnet. Even when my dick was broke and she looked at me like I was the last asshole in the world she ever wanted to see, I couldn't stay away.

Wasn't just about fucking her either. After Beth, I had to protect her, and the best way to do that was making sure the bastards who'd fucked her over were six feet under.

"Stinger?" Alice was looking at me, both her small hands circling mine.

I blinked. Shit, something about her was bringing back bad fucking memories I'd been able to keep boxed up for years. This wasn't like Beth. No fucking way was this gonna be a bad re-run…

"I'm listening," I said.

"It's all mush in my brain. I remember him…the dead man, I mean. I don't know who he was or why I was with him. Just got these little flashes of being around him, but it's not clear why. I don't know if they're dreams or memories or just my own imagination." Her turn to squeeze my hand. "Give me another day. I'll try to come up with something."

Fucking finally. I laced my fingers with hers and gave her the biggest damned smile I could manage. No guarantees she wouldn't go cold. At least it was a start, and that meant there was a chance Tank's ass was saved too.

"Take the evening. Whatever happens tomorrow, I'll be there with you. Won't leave you alone to face anybody. I know how Blaze can be…" I clenched my jaw. Pissed me off just thinking about our Prez getting wound up and snarling in her face.

Not gonna happen, I vowed.

"I'll tell you whatever I can in the morning, and then I'm leaving." She looked up, the chill returning to her eyes, reluctant determination in her grip.

"What're you talking about?" I shook my head, wondering if I heard her right. "You've got no place to go. Can't let you loose if you give us something useful and the Rams are still out there. Hell, Alice, they've already been jerking Blaze around behind the scenes to get you back. Fuckers claim they never agreed to turn you over for good. Having you here's gonna start a war even if we don't decide to put a bullet through their fucking heads and save us all some trouble."

"I'll deal with all that on my own. I'm a big girl and I can figure it out, even if I'm trying to sort out all this crap in my head. I know I can survive. Look, I appreciate the way you've helped me, Sting. I know I've been nothing but a bitch until now…"

I shook my head, denying the bitterness. Yeah, some truth was starting to spill outta her, but not anything I wanted to hear. Definitely didn't want to hear about how eager she was to get up and go neither.

"You'll go when it's safe." I looked her right in the eye, feeling my arms flex. "Not my call. It's Blaze's. He'll let you out as soon as he's satisfied with what you have to say, and we can guarantee you're gonna go wherever in one piece."

That was only half-true.

As Prez, Blaze needed to approve her taking flight after he had her information. But the only man here who really cared about seeing her off safe was *me.* Shit, the other brothers would probably be glad to see her go, especially when she was just one more thing to deal with in an avalanche of shit this club had to clean up over the last few months.

"Whatever," she said, jerking away from me and turning her head. "I don't belong here and you know it. Whenever you decide I'm not fit to be your prisoner anymore, call me a cab and send me on my way. I'll pay back every dime it takes to get out of here."

What the fuck? Was it *really* so bad here with me and the brothers? Despite trying to keep a lid on it, now I was starting to feel my blood warm.

"You're not leaving with nothing except the clothes on your back. You wanna do a few chores around here for some money, we'll figure it out. This fucking place always has shit to do that the prospects never get around to."

That was an understatement. With all the endless drama and battling other clubs, our two prospects, Smokey and Stone, rarely got a second to ease into the club life cleaning the place and keeping our beers cold like most initiates did.

"Wow," she said with a sarcastic laugh. "Thanks, dad. Never knew losing my memory meant I'd get treated like a dumbass kid. Or is that the way all you bikers treat grown women around here?"

Fuck this shit. I jumped to my feet and let the chair fall. Had to blow this room before I went ballistic. Alice jumped when my seat hit the floor, and I was almost out the door before she called to me.

"Stinger! Wait!"

I stopped, one hand on the doorknob, looking back. Couldn't fucking tell if she was done bullshitting, or just winding up something else.

"I never asked for any of this. I just want some distance…I don't need you to watch me like I'm going to fall and wreck what's left of my mind. Don't need you bringing me food or tucking me in. I can handle basic day-to-day crap, and I can handle this too."

Fuck. I wasn't sure she was aware of me laying next to her that night, pulling her close. She sure hadn't acted like it was a chore then.

"You helped me and I'm grateful, Stinger. I really am. But I don't need you –"

"Just fucking stop, baby," I growled. "I'll see you here tomorrow when Blaze is ready to talk. You can use me as your damned punching bag all you want, I don't give a fuck. But you better try to swallow some of that shit when you're dealing with Tank and Em tomorrow. They won't be as forgiving or as patient as me."

I was gone without another word, heading for the bar. Doctor Jack would do me some good, and Saffron served it up real nice. I tried not to wince as I climbed on the bar stool.

God damn. I regretted not asking for several shots from the get-go. Tonight, Jack was all I had to blow off steam with my nuts acting up. If it wasn't for that, I would've been heading straight to the whores' room, taking one rough fuck for every needle the little ice queen in my room just jammed in my fucking heart.

I hounded Blaze all morning, trying to convince him to stay outta Alice's interrogation and leave it to Em and me. At last, he relented. The Prez was plenty distracted dealing with the Feds and Tank's homecoming tomorrow, and he seemed glad to have one less thing to deal with.

As 'glad' as fire breathing Blaze could ever be, anyway.

A little later, I pounded on the door to her room. Alice came out without saying a word. She wouldn't look at me as I led her to his office, where Em and the Prez were waiting.

"Need you to try to get something useful out of her, Em," Blaze said, barely holding in the storm welling up inside. "The Rams are riding our asses. They can smell the shit that's about to come down with Tank and the Feds. The assholes spotted our prospects when I sent them out to move Mickey's corpse to a safer place. The fucks have been laying off the meth and booze long enough to do more spying than I gave 'em credit for. Bigger balls too since they're giving us shit about the girl."

"Fuck the Rams." I stared the Prez down first, then gave the same evil look to Em and Alice. "If those bastards want her brought back to their ratty little clubhouse, they'll have to come here and take her."

There was a second of silence. Then Blaze broke, hissing through his teeth and shaking his head. "Christ, Sting. Get some fucking pussy that's used to taking dick and stop worrying. Like I said in church, she's not going anywhere. She's too valuable."

Alice looked at me nervously. The bitch gaze she'd had yesterday was missing – dormant, maybe. I held her gaze as Blaze told Emma to get something juicy one more time before he left to do other shit.

Em started out asking the usual crap, circling around the chair where Alice was sitting like a shark, asking her every little detail she could remember about that night. I warned her to go easy.

Tank's situation had the nurse pretty shaken up. He'd been hauled into jail right after they patched things up, thrown in the slammer because he was helping to keep her safe from the piece of shit cousin blackmailing her ass. Now, the soft, shy nurse we all knew was melting away with her man's freedom on the line.

Em cracked a little more by the second, letting out her inner bitch. She asked my girl about the dead man.

"I don't remember anyone named Mickey," Alice insisted.

My heart sank. If she'd truly given remembering all her focus last night, it hadn't turned up shit. Still, she looked so disappointed, so sad, so fragile I couldn't get pissed. Emma, on the other hand...

Didn't like the way she was looking at Alice one bit.

"Don't understand what the fuck Blaze expects you to do. Alice doesn't know shit," I growled. "Whatever the hell happened with the Rams, it was bad enough to make her forget, just like you said."

Em kept her eyes fixed on Alice the whole time, even when she was speaking to me. "No. She can't give us the big picture, but she might remember some details. There's got to be somebody home in there."

That did it. Alice looked up, frost shining in her eyes, sharp and angry as ever.

"Stop talking about me like that. I didn't ask to be here. I don't understand why you and these bikers are keeping me here…"

"Easy, baby." I put a hand on Alice's shoulder. "We're just trying to help a friend, and help you too."

Fuck, how many times do I have to remind her? I wondered. *Why can't she just believe me? We wouldn't need to pump her like this if a brother's ass wasn't on the line.*

Em's attitude wasn't making this shit any easier. They locked eyes. Then Alice jerked, throwing my arm off her and shooting me a look that said *back the fuck off.*

No, nothing much had changed since yesterday evening. Despite her cold fucking shoulder, I still wasn't gonna let Em ride right over her. The nurse paced a little more quickly around her now. I expected more harsh words, more vinegar, whatever she needed to say to free her old man.

But I never expected Em to grab my girl's beautiful black ponytail and twist her head back. Alice jerked, whining as Em lifted her face up close.

"Emma, what the fuck?" I had my hands on her shoulders in a second, trying to jerk her off Alice without dislocating her bones.

Fuck, she was holding on tight, begging me to hurt her if I truly wanted her gone. "You guys are too scared to get tough with a girl unless she's being a real bitch. I get it, you don't rough up girls. Thing is, I'm not bound by your club charter. This bitch is hiding something, Sting, and I want to know what."

Bitch or not, Em had no fucking right to talk to her like that – and she sure as fuck didn't have any need to grab her like a stray cat!

"Let go!" I roared. "Stop hurting her!"

I was seriously contemplating throwing the nurse across the room. Only problem was I'd have Tank crush my skull tomorrow if he came home and found out I bruised the girl he was ready to claim.

Fuck!

"Oh, please," Em hissed. "She's had worse. If she'd tell us what, then I wouldn't have to keep doing this."

"Dammit, Em! I'm fucking warning you…"

Alice squealed as Emma's pull tightened. Harsh words, I'd allow, but I couldn't let this fucking torture continue. I shifted my hands to Emma's waist, ready to send her flying across the room, consequences be damned.

Em saw the bluff in my pissed off eyes and called it. She practically tore that sweet black hair out in fistfuls, pulling so hard Alice came off her chair and hit the floor.

My brain snapped. Something primal and vicious underneath my skin broke out. I saw red as I hauled Emma off her feet, running to the nearest wall and crashing her up against it.

"Everybody's losing their fucking mind around here!" I snarled, trying to talk to calm the bloodlust surging through me. "Look, nurse, I know you're upset as all hell about Tank's situation. That's still no excuse for you to treat this poor girl like a piece of fucking –"

Emma was about to open her mouth when Alice spoke behind us. "Okay! I'll…I'll talk…"

All the rage deflated. I dropped Em, too fucking shocked, turning around to face her as the nurse wiped herself off and crossed the room.

Alice said she'd talk, said she'd tell us everything, as long as we let her go. Shit, I told her for the thousandth time that was all in the cards, even though every part of me was howling for the opposite.

She told us about riding with a big man in a truck stuffed with cargo. Had to be Mickey, and if my time in the club taught me anything, she'd been taking a cruise with him in a full blown weapon's shipment.

"Did you guys see a truck when you visited their clubhouse?" Em asked.

I shook my head, still digesting Alice's confession. My heart was hammering against my ribs. She'd finally given us something useful, and I hoped like hell it was true.

"Fuck no. That shit had to have gone somewhere if it was really the kinda shipment she's talking about. Fuck, I have to tell Blaze. If we can find this damned thing or make the Rams cough up what they did with it…"

I took off before I could finish the sentence. The Prez had to know, and he had to know *right now*. The Rams were probably covering that shit up right that second, if they hadn't gotten to it after our little visit.

Harsh words followed me, more insult and anger flying back and forth as Em and Alice came to terms. The clubhouse was so damned quiet the shit followed me all the way to the garages, where I expected to find Blaze. Before I left, Alice dropped one last bomb, and its explosion was still resonating in my fucking skull hours later.

"I can't remember who I am or what I'm supposed to be. All I can do is start a new life, get my shit together, and figure things out. None of that involves you, Stinger, or anything remotely attached to the Prairie Devils MC..."

Alice's words made me stop in mid-step, hand on the door leading outside. The excitement throttling my blood at finally having something to save Tank's ass flamed out. Fuck, she was really serious, dead set on leaving this club and everybody in it behind for good.

And *everybody* included me.

It shouldn't have bothered me so fucking much. Hell, if it wasn't for the promise I made after Beth, it wouldn't have. I'd let myself get too close to this weird girl, let her turn my whole fucking world topsy-turvy. All because I couldn't let the past be the past and I wanted to play hero!

The urge to beat my own ass was overwhelming. *Fucking idiot.*

My damned eyes were on her as she angrily stormed outta Blaze's office, stomping right past me, heading back to my room. The door slammed a second later.

My turn. I threw the door open and smashed it in the frame so hard the chrome on every bike outside rattled like thunder.

Outside, Blaze jerked up from the bench, eyes wide, and then narrowing when they landed on me. I was walking over to him, feeling fucking stupid, ready to deliver my report all business like. Too bad I'd blown that chance the minute my piss and vinegar followed me.

The Prez looked tired, exasperated. Didn't blame him. Tank and Emma's endless dance had caused enough fucking drama around the clubhouse for the last few seasons.

Now, it was my turn, and it wasn't about to get better when happiness wasn't in the cards with Alice. Shit, happy with her wasn't even in the same deck.

What-fucking-ever. The beauty with the glass tongue in my room wasn't getting shit from me anymore. *I* was in control.

I didn't fucking need her. And I sure as hell didn't need an old lady when I couldn't even get my lips on this girl without feeling her flak bursting my eardrums.

I kept the report to the Prez short and sweet, giving him Alice's words verbatim, grinding my damned teeth the whole time. On the way back, Em passed by me, slapping a slip of paper in my hands.

"What's this?"

"Test results. You're clean, VP. Near as I can tell, you took a hard turn and twisted your testicles just enough to cause discomfort. You should be more careful riding on these mountain roads." Emma frowned. "I hope you'll be wise about where you stick your —"

I took off before she could finish. Didn't need a goddamned lecture. The ache in my balls was gone, and the lab shit confirmed what I already knew.

I also didn't need to be reminded the only place my cock longed to be was totally off limits. The stone cold bitch in my room might as well have had her legs clamped shut with barbed wire across her pussy.

Fuck me if it didn't make me want her any less, and that meant I was seriously screwed.

The next day was Tank's homecoming.

I was parked on the curb outside the prison, watching Goliath walk through the gates. Emma beat everybody else rushing to him, leaping into his arms and giving him a kiss so hot and long it would've made any man forget their dank, cold cell.

Fuck. Several brothers had their old ladies with.

Blaze and Saffron. Moose and Connie. Roller and Reb sat next to the whores, a quick reach away from throwing their arms around those chicks and pulling them close, warming them up for later.

Marianne and Sangria migrated to sucking and fucking their cocks since I stopped giving 'em so much attention. Couldn't blame them. That scorched earth shit Alice left in my head was really pissing me off.

I couldn't even put out the fire enough to get my dick wet in some chick who'd appreciate it.

Well, fuck her anyway. Fuck her for wrapping my brain in a tornado of lust and rage every single second. Fuck her for twisting me inside out, turning eighteen damned years of calm on its head. Fuck her for making me think about the past I tried my damnedest to bury – almost as much as I thought about throwing her to the wall and ripping her jeans off, pushing my angry cock between her legs, and working out all the crazy shit between us the best way I knew how.

Fuck her for making me think about fucking her when she was nothing but fucking outta reach. Fuck!

I was hellbent on having a decent day anyway. Tomorrow, we'd all be scrambling, trying to find something to get our brother off the hook permanently. But tonight, Blaze and Saffron had a big bash organized, one that promised to be a sendoff or a welcome home for Tank, depending on what happened next.

Forgetting about Alice's shit wasn't so hard when the big guy strode out to us, arms still wrapped tight around Emma. He stopped as Blaze slapped him on the shoulders, giving him a big, brotherly greeting.

I was about to do the same when the Prez stopped everybody and told us to listen up.

Everybody was surprised by how eloquently he spoke. The boy wasted no punches claiming Em as his old lady right there, point blank, promising her she was his and only his, no matter what was coming next.

Hell or high water, he'd made up his mind, and so had his girl.

"As of today, Emma Galena is off fucking limits," he growled. "She's mine, all mine, and only mine. You'll all be reminded soon enough, every goddamned day when she's wearing my brand…"

Everybody went nuts when he was done. Fuck, even I was smiling, so wide I felt my own dimples drilling into my cheeks. Tank returned the grin and nodded at me as he walked past, heading for the bike we'd towed with us to pick him up.

I climbed on mine and rode behind them, ready to get back to the clubhouse and let loose. Em was crazy about his gigantic tattooed ass, and that made him a lucky man. I just hoped his luck would hold and we'd find some way to keep the love and laughter going.

I fought like hell to keep Alice outta my head on the ride home. It was a beautiful day rounding the mountain curves toward Missoula, feeling autumn's crisp bite needling my face. The chill I got on my Harley would make the Jack I downed later feel that much better.

At the clubhouse, Em and Tank said they'd join the bash later and quickly disappeared to Tank's room. Brothers were laughing, quickly breaking into beers and whiskey. Over near the bar, Blaze pulled Saffron close, grabbing her ass as he kissed her, breaking away after he whispered something nasty in her ear.

I stared down the hall at my room, where Alice was no doubt curled up sleeping. Angry lips twitching, I turned away and headed straight for the bar. The sooner we got this fucking party started, the sooner I could forget.

Saffron was already handing out drinks. I took my spot and flashed her a smile big enough to hide all the chaotic bullshit rumbling through my skull.

"Hey, Sting," she purred, clasping her hands. "What'll it be? The usual?"

"Yeah. Full bottle. Might as well stock up before the other brothers do. Wouldn't be the first time we've run out of shit too soon."

Saffron wagged a finger at me as she pulled a full bottle out of a box. "I know how to run my bar, Sting. Nobody's walking away dry tonight. Drink up."

She slammed it down in front of me. I grabbed a fistful of cash outta my wall and threw it on the counter. Money was flowing in real easy from the club proceeds now that all our shipments were flowing West without any problems with the Grizzlies MC.

I didn't even bother using the shot glass she laid out for me. Just popped the cap and tipped the damned thing to my lips, closing my eyes. That first hit was the second best thing to emptying my balls deep inside some beautiful bitch.

Pure bliss written in fire.

Too bad the beautiful bitch I imagined had silky black hair, dark eyes set like secrets, cream colored skin begging to jerk and twist underneath my cock...

"Fuck, that's good," I growled, pausing for a breath.

Saffron laughed. "Well, there's plenty more where that came from. Beer too. We've got whiskey coming out our ears since the prospects brought in this gift box from mother charter today."

My eyebrows went up. That was weird. Throttle occasionally sent presents over from North Dakota, yeah, but rarely booze like this.

Whatever. He'd had Tank in his charter before the big boy came West, so maybe he was paying his respects.

Doctor Jack's magic cure hit my brain with nothing between him and my guts except a light breakfast.

Saffron served some snacks to Moose before she circled back to me a minute later. "Is little miss forgetful coming out to join us?"

I wrinkled my nose. "Fuck if I know. I'm not gonna force that chick to do anything she doesn't want to. I'm done playing those games, Saffron."

She cocked her head, a wry little smile on her lips. The woman looked downright cute when she wore that kinda smile. I'd never dream of going after her now, but I'd tried to have a go before Blaze claimed her, and I didn't regret a fucking thing.

"You sure about that?" she whispered in my ear. "Lot of guys around here say they're not doing the chase lately, but it sure catches up to them."

She winked. I looked past her, feeling my dick stir when I saw the girls coming in. On a night like this, the two club whores weren't enough for all the brothers. The usual gaggle of local girls who wanted to play slut-for-a-night with big badass bikers had arrived.

"I'm not Blaze, and I'm definitely not Tank," I said, knocking back another fiery swig. I stood up and started to push past her.

"Go easy, Sting. Don't do anything you'll regret tomorrow." She gave me a hard stare when she saw me moving toward the ladies.

"You're not my sister, baby. You're the Prez's old lady and you've been here long enough to know your place. Let me have my fucking fun because I'm sure as shit not getting it with Alice."

Her mouth dropped a little, stunned into silence. Maybe I'd been a little harsh. But hell, spending all evening at the bar with Saffron needling me about chasing an ice princess who wasn't gonna thaw out anytime soon wasn't my idea of fun.

The three girls were quickly divided up. Smokey and Stone waited for me to make my choice. They were lowest on the totem pole since they weren't full patch brothers yet.

I pulled aside the two brunettes and left them the blonde. My dick strained like pure stone with some Jack in my system. I hoped like hell these chicks were clean because if I had to use a condom tonight, I'd bust right through it.

"What's your names, girls?" I growled, pulling them both to my neck.

"Sugar," the one with the green eyes said.

"Spice!" yelled the other, licking up my neck and reaching for my crotch.

Fuck! Pure fire ripped right through me. I passed Spice the bottle and she chugged it 'til the fire in her throat was too much.

A couple weeks without getting laid was too damned long. I sure as shit wasn't waiting another hour, and these two girls were gonna help me out, even if I had to fuck 'em in the garage behind the bikes.

They pressed their tits against me, taking turns with the Jack. My arms slid around them and jerked them close. Their hair wasn't as rich and dark as Alice's, no, but I liked brunettes and they'd do fine.

"Easy, girls. There's plenty of this dick to go around." They both moaned as I caught their hair and pulled. "You came here to get fucked senseless, yeah? Then you've come to the right place. You're not walking out of here tomorrow unless your knees are bent and you're dripping my come."

Their grip on me tightened. I grinned, yanking on their ponytails harder. For some fucked up reason, that brought back memories of Em tugging Alice's hair. A sickly sweet vision of me doing the same damned thing to my wonderland girl flashed in my head.

How awesome would it be to finally lay into her and melt that frost clouding her little heart? Shit, how loud would Alice whine if I threw her down beneath me and mounted her from behind, hammering out my frustration against her sweet ass, jerking her jet black hair in my fist like reins?

My cock was at full salute and those thoughts were only making me crazier. I needed Sugar and Spice laid out beneath me *now*. Didn't matter if I'd be thinking about her the whole time I was fucking 'em.

"Come on," I said, grabbing them both by the hand. "I know a quiet spot we can wreck with our screams."

They both laughed as I led them toward the door leading outside. Took a little while to push through the crowd, brothers and girls everywhere, plus some local dudes from town who were looking to become future hangarounds.

I passed by Moose and his family at the table. He gave me a friendly nod and raised his glass, shit eating grin peeking out behind his giant beard.

Right on, brother, it said. I flashed him a quick salute, wondering if he ever missed this shit. He'd been with Connie and had a grown daughter so long he probably forgot what having a girl lick your nuts while you were buried inside another chick felt like.

His loss…

I pushed the girls ahead of me and was about to reach for the door when there was a gigantic crash. Spinning around, I saw Moose go down, the friendly smile he'd given me disappearing in a flash as he fit the floor, grabbing his chest.

His family screamed. Fuck.

I was there first, leaning over and kicking the table outta the way as the older brother thrashed on the ground, kicking his thick legs.

"What the fuck's going on, boss?"

I turned to see Tank, sweaty and half-dressed and holding a glass of water. "Don't know. He just dropped down and started dying in front of me. Get Em!"

When I looked at Connie and Becky, Moose's daughter, I instantly regretted my words. I leaned down, shaking my head. No, no fucking way was he dying here. If it was a heart attack or something, we'd get him whatever he needed to keep his ticker going.

"Come on, brother! Stay awake…"

Easier said than done. *Shit, shit shit…*

Moose groaned and his eyes closed, slipping away a little more by the second. Connie clawed her way past me, grabbing his hand. Becky fanned his face, beaming her terrified eyes at me.

Em and Tank showed up again a second later. I helped Tank lift our brother up on the table, then backed away, listening intently as they worked on him. Over in the corner, Sugar and Spice stared at the scene with huge marble eyes, looking like the devil himself walked right off our cuts and spat in their faces.

I walked past them, heading for the bar. I had to find the Prez and let him know what was up.

"What're you two looking at?" I growled, waving my arm at the two sluts I'd been so fucking close to taking. "Get the fuck outta here. Party's over."

Hurt like hell to say it. Even worse, I rounded the whole clubhouse, and Blaze was nowhere in sight. Finally, he and Saffron came through the side door, laughing as they entered. I was back by Moose, watching as Em checked him over. The grim look on Tank's face said it all.

Then it hit me. My guts lurched hard, like some fucking demon crawled in my stomach and started tying shit together. I reached for the edge of the table and missed it, falling on my ass.

Fire. Nothing but pure fucking fire ripping through me, a blinding white roar smoking my tissue from the inside out.

More brothers groaned. I heard Blaze swear and hit the floor, and then Em and Tank rushing past, their faces filled with horror as the entire damned clubhouse started dropping like flies.

"Poison. Motherfuckers!" I swore, remembering the mysterious box of whiskey Saffron broke into. That shit hadn't come from mother charter at all.

I wanted to force my feet to work, get back up, and go slit the Rams' fucking throats one-by-one. I spread my hands on the floor and pushed with all my might, trying to lift my ass up.

But then my guts tightened fiercer than ever, locked with the inferno rushing through them. The pain swelled, harsher and deeper, so fucking bad I couldn't think about anything at all.

IV: Freedom Is a Lonely Business (Alice)

I tried so hard to ignore their stupid party. Burying the pillows around my ears couldn't blot out all the noise, and the linens smelled just like *him*.

Every time I breathed his wickedly sexy scent, I almost felt bad about telling him where to stuff it and rushing off after the bitch nurse questioned me the day before. Almost.

Then I remembered he was one of them, just one more loud mouthed idiot chuckling outside my door. I didn't doubt for a second that Stinger was probably drinking and sucking face with some skank after the way I'd treated him.

It shouldn't have pissed me off. But it did. God damn it, it did.

I hadn't gotten a wink of sleep all evening. Slipping out for a hot shower while the clubhouse was empty, picking up their friend from prison, was my only comfort. Since they'd returned, I tried to ignore it, tried to think long and hard about how I was going to leave this place and where I was going to go as soon as they let me.

Mostly, I tried to forget him, ignoring the tears that stung my eyes whenever I thought about Stinger.

All my efforts came crashing down with the insanity erupting outside my door. The first few crashes, I jerked up, throwing the blankets and pillows off me and straightening my clothes. I knew men like these made enemies all the time, and I hoped like hell this place wasn't getting attacked.

Creeping up to the door, I pressed my ear to the wood. People were screaming, some of them yelling like they were hurt really bad.

Screw it. I had to stop being so fucking scared and see what was going on. Taking a deep breath, I reached for the handle and ripped it open.

I'd been ready for a lot of things: men with guns, fistfights, bottles breaking apart on heads. But I wasn't ready to see half the brothers and their women strewn out on the floor, retching in pain.

I took my steps one-by-one. Seeing Blaze laid out with his girl really freaked me out. Emma kneeled over him, phone in hand. I heard her calling for support.

"Hey! We could use some help here!" The nurse spotted me in the corner and pointed, her finger like a dagger.

Jesus, her attitude burned me up. Still, this wasn't the time or place for petty personal conflict.

I followed her over to the spot where she was with the whore named Sangria, tending to several other girls passed out on the ground.

"Just make sure everybody keeps breathing. If they stop, you yell for me or another nurse. My friends'll be here soon…"

If it weren't her, I would've protested. If I'd taken a First Aid class in my life, I couldn't remember it, and now I was having wet cloths shoved into my hands, plus buckets for chilling drinks to catch vomit.

I worked on Roller while Emma's backup from the hospital filed in with their gear. The youngest brother stared at me, his eyes strained and narrow like he'd swallowed glass.

"Need the bucket, babe. Sorry, but I…shit!" I had one second to get it underneath him.

My own stomach rumbled as he emptied his, and I turned away in disgust. Of course, I picked the worst place in the world to look. My eyes fell on the exact spot where Stinger was suffering alone, coiled up on his side, his big body trembling each time he rocked in agony.

I had to make my way over to him…one of the pros took over for me with Roller, the first of two young men who'd come to help Emma, along with that older lady from the hospital. Whatever the hell the club's nurse had done to me in the past, I was grateful for her connections. Half these people could've been dead by now if her friends hadn't shown up.

Other sick people on the ground stopped me along the way, begging me to turn them over or wipe their faces. I did what I could, welcoming the distraction. Guilt twisted me in knots, and soon as I was feeling sick too, wondering if having me close would only make Sting feel worse.

Rumors about poison were floating around. Tank and the prospects seemed to be the only guys who weren't hit, and they disappeared entirely after a little while. One of the slutty girls who hadn't gotten sick was tending to Stinger when I tried to slip by.

I was about to pass when a hand shot out and grabbed my collar. I spun, anger flaring when I saw it was Emma clawing at me.

"This man needs you, and there's only so many of us. Help me out!" She pointed to Stinger, shooing the slut aside so I could move in.

I relaxed a little when I saw he was halfway out of it. I kneeled by his head, gingerly blotting the sweat off his face, checking the IV in his arm like Em told me to make sure it wasn't pulled out.

"There's something else I need to know," she growled, shooting me the look that said she wasn't going to take no for an answer.

She asked me about the Rams' clubhouse, more than ten minutes of back and forth, once again forcing my memory into dark places it refused to go. I tried to describe the filthy place as best I could, focusing on Stinger's handsome face to soothe the pain.

Finally, she darted off, satisfied. I must've given her something useful without knowing it, but the woman was nuts if she intended to go there alone.

Sting opened his eyes for the second time and looked at me.

"Alice? What're you doing, baby? Alice..." This time, he fought to keep them open, whispering my name over and over like a healing mantra.

"Don't fight me...you're gonna be okay. Just rest," I told him, dipping my cloth in cool water and running it across his brow again.

It was a long hard night. Stinger's chills and dry heaves faded after a few hours. I stayed with him the entire time, cooling off the artificial fever induced by the poison, watching his breathing and making sure the IV stayed in his arm like the nurse told me.

The paramedics and Em's friend, Linda, worked all around us. I kept thinking about where Em had taken off too. I had a bad feeling she was going to catch up with Tank and the other guys. The bitch nurse was tough, but I wasn't sure she was ready to fight *those* demons.

It was near dawn when the prospects rolled in. Stone got wheeled in bleeding and went straight to the infirmary. Looked like he'd been shot.

Tank and Emma showed up about an hour or two after that, right around sunrise. I watched her drag him in, both of them heading for the little table where Blaze was stretched out with Saffron. The giant's face was twisted and his arms hung limp. They were both scratched up, bruised, and a few blood splotches were visible on their clothes.

Whatever, at least they'd come back alive. That gave me hope the Rams had lost the latest fight. My ears perked up and I listened closely for confirmation. Tank was speaking quietly to Blaze, sitting next to the Prez with Em's support.

"Yeah, boss. Yeah. All fucking dead. We made sure. My arm's kinda fucked from busting out when they tied me up. I'll be fine. We just gotta saddle up and go back to their rathole to take out the bodies and comb the place over…"

My hands started shaking. My tormenters were dead. Finally.

My memory was still scrambled six ways from Sunday, but at least I didn't have anything left to fear. And if the club had finished up with their rivals, there was no reason to stay here a second longer.

I looked at Stinger again. He'd fallen into an uneasy sleep, twisting and grunting every so often, his body working quietly to re-charge after sheer hell rampaged through his veins.

No, it wasn't just Tank and Emma and the rest who'd freed me. There were times when I hated the handsome man beneath me, but he'd been looking out for me. He'd tried.

That had to count for something, right? I couldn't just run off without saying goodbye…

Without much thought, my hands slipped into his, still trembling with shock. Sting opened his eyes when he felt them. His fingers tightened, stronger than I expected for his weakened state.

"What's wrong?" he asked, struggling to raise his head. "Everything all right, Alice?"

"Yeah." God help me, I smiled. "Never been better. I just wanted to apologize for being such a bitch this past week. I know things have been rough – really fucking rough because of the situation with Tank and the Rams. I get why you did what you did now. You needed to help your guy…"

His grip tightened. He shifted his hand, covering all of mine. Guess it would take a lot more than some stupid poison to lay out this man and sap his strength permanently.

"It's not too late, Alice. We can put all this shit behind us. Forget about the past. All you got to look forward to is your future, and I can help give you that."

I couldn't break the intensity in his gaze. The light in his eyes said he was offering me something equally amazing and scary. It was my turn to feel my stomach twisting, anxiety circling every muscle I had.

"Maybe you don't want that," he said. "I get it. You need to be your own woman, go off for awhile and figure shit out. Whatever happens – don't run. And you damned well better not forget me. Because you need anything, baby, anytime and anyplace, just call. I'll be there in a heartbeat. Don't give a shit if I gotta go all the way to Timbuktu to find you."

"Stinger…"

I closed my eyes. *Crap.* Leaving was going to be a real bitch with the trip he was laying on me, thicker than sin.

He raised his free hand to his lips and hissed. *Shhh.*

"You don't have to decide shit today. And you don't have to spend your time looking after my sick ass. I'm feeling better…pretty sure I can take it from here."

I wasn't a hundred percent sure about that. He was well enough to move without puking his guts out, yeah, but his color was so pale. Half the guys laying around the clubhouse looked like ghosts. The crap in their whiskey had really taken a lot of out them.

"Fuck that! I'm staying until I'm totally sure you're better, Sting. That's what Emma told me, and I'm going to listen."

"Really? You two are on speaking terms now?" He flashed me a huge smile. I watched his lips quirk up and melt into dimples, feeling my heart spin when he did.

God, he was adorable. Well, about as *adorable* as a big, mean, heavily tattooed biker could be. I ran my fingers up over his arms, absentmindedly thinking to myself, wondering if I should really leave.

To be honest, I wasn't ready to be out in the big crazy world by myself again – especially when I hadn't figured out who the hell I was or where I'd come from. But I wasn't ready to stay here either. I definitely wasn't ready to be with this man.

I saw the way life was around here. I'd come from a rough patch, I figured that much, but I wasn't cut out to be anybody's old lady. And if I let Stinger in, even a little bit, wouldn't it be jerking him down that path?

I nodded slowly. "Yeah. I can put my grudges aside, Sting. Especially the petty ones."

He reached up, circling his arm over mine, grabbing me near the wrist. He sat up higher, reaching for the water bottle at his side. I watched him drain it as he held onto me, fully up now, swinging his thick legs over the side of the table.

"You can do a lot more than that, girl. You've got a good heart, and you're motivated when you're not letting that wall of fucking ice cloud up everything." He was still smiling, more softly now, beaming at me like his belief alone was enough to patch my whole screwed up world.

"You really believe that?" I whispered. "How the hell do you know?"

"Because I never want anything unless it's worth it." His self-assured growl told me his energy was returning quick. "And I want you, Alice. Need to see you get over whatever the fuck happened to you before. I gotta see you thrive, baby. You deserve to be happy doing whatever the hell you want, and no asshole's gonna hold you back when I'm here."

Are you? I wanted to say, but stopped just short of it coming out of my mouth. *I never invited this and I'm not sure I invited you either –*

He flicked his wrist. Stinger jerked me toward him easily, like I was light as a feather. I sprawled to the edge of his lap, reaching one arm around his neck when I stumbled.

Exactly what he was waiting for. Lightning flashed in my head with one second to spare before his lips touched mine.

It was like dynamite going off. I quaked, I purred, I shuddered in total, absolute shock as he pulled me tighter, closer, burying his lips against mine. Thank God he'd cleaned his mouth because there was no stopping this.

I want you, Alice. I remembered that part, a thousand times more important than what came after it, stronger and sincere as the lightning in his lips.

Stinger groaned into mine, tasting them, smothering my mouth with his. Then the groan began to melt into a long, low, drawn out growl. I realized I was smooching with a beast that had been kept on a very short leash for far too long, and no poison was going to stop him when he finally had his chance to frolic.

He kissed me hard, deep, thrashing his tongue against mine. I melted in his arms, amazed at the uncontrollable purr coming out of me. Power and fury picked me up and carried me away, all while the same conflicted questions burbled to the top, the only things preventing this from being a moment of pure perfection.

I didn't know if this was our first kiss of many or our only parting kiss. Hell, what did it matter?

Right here, right now, living in the present instead of the foggy past, I gave myself to him. When he sensed me folding, edging up onto his lap, his kiss came hotter and faster.

He only gave me a couple seconds of air before diving in again, pushing his tongue deeper into my mouth, exploring me, opening me, loving everything he tasted. His hands went places...up around my back, tracing down my spine, accenting the tingle sizzling through every nerve. Then they dove low and cupped my ass, giving it a fierce squeeze as he thrust his tongue against mine, back and forth, rhythmic and wanting, a wordless play that told me how bad he wanted to –

"Fuck. Fucking shit, baby. You taste so goddamned hot." He broke the last kiss, struggling for air.

I did the same. He'd sucked the life out of me, all my vital heat, leaving me empty and needy, but still craving more each time I let my eyes wander up over his broad shoulders and study his gorgeous face.

My hands were locked around him, shaking like leaves. Jesus, the sickness hadn't blunted that spicy masculine sent I'd inhaled before.

Comforting. Consoling. Mostly just *strong*.

I breathed deep. Every part of me was on fire, bending in a blaze that swept to my toes and then rushed back between my legs. It burned straight through my skin, leaving nothing in its wake except the sopping wetness melting in my panties. I wondered what it would feel like to have my hands around his neck while he was between my legs, fused to me, pushing his trademark growl into my ears as he took what we both needed so bad.

I moved in for another kiss. Most of the other brothers and their girls were asleep around us, or else so focused on each other it was like we had the place to ourselves. Still, we couldn't go all the way here.

Stinger stopped just short of pressing his lips to mine again. "Come on."

Without another word, he grabbed my hand and led me up. We were halfway down the hall to his room when he lurched and fell against the wall.

"Shit!" His curse bounced on the floor and hit the ceiling. "Sneaky motherfuckers and their poison…hope Tank and the boys hurt 'em bad before they bit it. What kinda assholes lay a grown man down with something he can't even see? I can handle bullets, knives, bombs, but this shit…"

He couldn't see it, but he could obviously feel it. Stinger was on his knees now. I rushed in to hold him up, sighing as the flame coiling up my brain went out. Getting him back to a hundred percent wellness was all that mattered now.

We were both idiots to let lust runaway with him in this state. Let alone how I'd feel after going into that room, running on pure instinct with this dangerously sexy man…

Fucking him was absolutely crazy. I had to get him down, safe and secure and comfortable, for more reasons than one.

Inch by inch, we struggled forward. I pushed the door open and helped drag him through. When I helped him onto the bed, I held my hand to his head, and then two fingers to his neck. His pulse, breathing, and temperature weren't worrisome enough to summon any of the medics.

He'd tried to do too much, too soon. We shouldn't have kissed.

Not that I regretted it for a single second. If this was goodbye – and I had an ugly feeling it had to be, for everybody's good – then he'd left me something wonderful to remember.

"There." I pulled the blanket I'd been using for days up over his shoulders.

He was fading out as he lay there, the savage energy I'd felt before dying in sheer exhaustion. He grunted, turning over. I slid into the little nook next to him.

He'd held me like this the very first night I was here. Now, it was my turn. I wrapped my hands around him, marveling at how hard he felt against my palms, warm muscles mingling with smooth cold leather. His chest was just like the rest of him – rock slabs packed together tight, hard as the Bitterroot Mountains, dark and menacing and beautiful if they were as inked as his arms.

Had to be, if the shirtless brothers I'd seen around the clubhouse were any indication.

"Baby..." he whispered, trying to fight passing out. "I'm fucking sorry. I regret not getting my hands on those bastards myself. I should've fucking killed them, slaughtered their asses after what they did to you..."

"It's okay," I said, resting my cheek against his. Rough, short stubble made a delicious contrast against my skin. "Just rest up. It's all over now. I won't leave until you're better."

"You'd better not," he growled, pinching my hand against his chest with his one last time. "Cause after that sweet taste of your lips, I'm gonna need a whole lot more when I wake up. I *want* you, Alice, need you under me so fucking bad..."

Holy shit. Even when he closed his eyes and started snoring next to me, I couldn't stop thinking about what he'd said.

It left me frustrated, hot, achingly wet. I closed my eyes and tried to sleep for several hours. When I couldn't, I watched through the blinds, waiting until the sun was just about all the way overhead.

I kept my promise to stay with him until he was well. Hadn't slept a wink myself by early afternoon, just listening to the sound of his sleep, less troubled than before as the hours went by. Downright peaceful, actually. He sounded like a big bear hibernating.

Seeing him, feeling him, smelling him made it so hard to break away. But I knew if I stayed a second longer, it would only be worse when I finally did.

I had to get out of here. I had to leave this clubhouse, and then find a ride far, far away from Missoula. I needed to get away from Sting before I never wanted to escape ever again.

Grounding myself here meant I'd be permanently grounded when Stinger woke up. He really did want me, and I wanted him. Thinking about what would happen if we gave in chilled me to the core.

How could I give myself to this man – to any man – if I didn't even know who I was? Sure, I could offer him sex, indulging in the carnal delights I'd always wanted.

But it wouldn't be honest. My whole life was still half-suffocated underneath a shroud. I couldn't offer this man anything when I didn't know what I had to give.

Waking up in a dark closet with a corpse next to me and clawing my way to sanity left me an emotional wreck. I'd treated these people who gave me shelter and safety like shit. Shit, I'd treated myself the same way too.

I had to go, and I had to move now, when Stinger was safe and blissfully asleep. With him out, there'd be no painful goodbye, no fighting him when he wrapped me in his wild grip and told me to stay.

Tears prickled my eyes, the same thorns tangled around my heart. Slowly, I slid off the bed and stood next to him. I leaned down and planted a kiss on his forehead.

All the determination I had welling up inside me to figure my crap out didn't mean anything to my tears.

They overflowed, spilling down my cheek. I sniffed and wiped them away, careful not to make too much noise. I threw a few shirts and toiletries in an old backpack he'd given me and quietly shut the door, taking the long hallway to the bar area in hurried steps.

I'm the one who's sorry, Sting. So fucking sorry. I just can't do this.

It's better this way, better for us both...

I'm not the right girl for you. I'm not even sure what kinda girl I am. All I can focus on is finding out.

The clubhouse was a lot quieter now. Some of the guys were in their rooms and the rest were home, recuperating from the party gone bad. Blaze was sitting up, hunched over at the bar with a huge carafe of water. He looked like hell, and jerked a little when I gently tapped him on the shoulder.

"Hey."

Anger shot through his eyes. Probably pissed that I'd rattled him a little without meaning to. "What the fuck do you want?"

"Sorry," I mumbled, clearing my throat. "I heard about what happened to the Rams. They're dead and gone, aren't they?"

"That's club business. Not yours," he snapped. Then after a long second, he grunted and rolled his eyes.

Blaze gave me a slow nod, leaning closer to me. "Keep that shit to yourself. Not everybody knows. I haven't even had time to debrief the club after everybody's been puking their guts out all night. Thank fuck Tank and the boys got their asses *good.*"

The way he growled it left no doubt the Rams suffered. Filled me with a sick sorta satisfaction, and that only stiffened my resolve to get on with my life now that this awful chapter was done.

Shit, I needed to get away, before I became like these men and their old ladies, hard-nosed killers.

"I want my freedom," I said sternly. "You all promised me I wouldn't be kept here once the Rams were gone. This clubhouse…it's been great…"

Yeah, real great. Yeah, right.

I was starting to trip on my words and I definitely didn't want Blaze to see me tearing up. Had to talk fast.

"Look, I appreciate everything you've done for me, but now I've got to go. I have to figure out my past and future. I think this where our paths are supposed to end."

Blaze cocked his head and looked at me, a strange smirk on his lips. "You ready for that, woman?"

"Yes."

No, no, no, my mind screamed. I stood my ground, unmoving, ignoring the needles poking at my eyes, wanting to bring the tears back whenever I pictured Stinger sleeping peacefully where I'd left him.

"Then here." Blaze moved fast. I watched him pull out his wallet and rummage through it, plucking a handful of crisp bills and shoving them toward me.

My jaw dropped as he pressed over a thousand dollars into my hands. "No! No way. I can't take this."

He snorted. "Pay it back when you get on your feet if it really gets under your skin. You know the fucking address here, Alice. Just take the money and go. Your info helped us. This club looks out for the boys and girls who keep it safe."

I didn't know what to say. The next hour was a blur as I mouthed a thanks and stumbled away from the bar. Saffron was right behind, talking to Blaze, wondering what I wanted.

I'd heard those two were due to get married soon. Made me wonder if Blaze had always been a big bad bastard with a good heart, or if having Saffron as his old lady had softened him. Whatever the case, he'd given me my ticket out of there.

I vaguely remembered how to drive, but without a license, rentals and cheap clunkers were out of the question. I called a taxi instead and spent the next few days holed up in a hotel just outside town.

Winter was about to settle in over Missoula and the Bitterroot valley. I was getting out just in time, heading West. Putting some mountains and a few hundred miles between the Prairie Devils MC and myself seemed smart.

By some miracle, my emotions stayed in check all week. It didn't hit me until I actually climbed on the bus parked at the station and it took off for Coeur d'Alene.

I couldn't resist looking back at the long highway leading into town from the window, remembering how warm and strong and loving Stinger felt beneath me. Remembering his smell, his kiss, his taste…God!

Why couldn't I forget the things that hurt worse than anything the dead Rams did to me?

The bearded guy in camo several seats over stared at me like I was nuts as I broke down and covered my face. I let it all come out for several dozen miles, gasps and tears and hurt, one last bitter avalanche before I left Montana forever, trying to forget the man who would've given me everything.

V: Cold Blooded (Stinger)

Months Later

The club's Christmas Party was a real fucking drag. I'd been looking forward to it for a couple weeks, hoping it would take my mind off the deep freeze clouding my head ever since she left, but it just did the opposite.

The brothers and supporters with their families had come and gone. Now, it was mostly just the single brothers, and the raunchy business was in full swing. I was at the bar, pouring extra Jim into my beer, ignoring the face sucking and excited gasps going on in the corner behind me.

I lost my taste for Jack the same night my appetite for fresh new pussy went out the window.

Had to switch brands of whiskey and started drinking a lot more beer since the night the Rams fucked us. Puking your guts out'll do that.

Or maybe the shit reminded me of Alice too damned much. The scent of Jack was heavy in the clubhouse the last time I saw her, before she kissed my unconscious head one last time and blew town.

I should've been in my old room railing Sugar and Spice right about now. Of course, I missed my chance about an hour ago, when they took off with our newest patched in brothers. Smokey and Stone were probably railing their little asses and high fiving each other right that second. All while I sat by myself trying to get blasted, wishing my dick could get hard to some girl who wasn't cold, scared, and completely fucking outta reach.

Fuck. I picked up my tall pilsner glass and dropped more whiskey in my dregs of beer before swaggering off the bar stool, wandering the clubhouse by myself. The place was a wreck like it always was after a big bash. This one started out low key and gentle as any family event hosted by the club, and then devolved into crazy shit later on after the kids were gone.

I dragged my ass to the window facing the main drag by the gate. Snow was falling, crisp and neat, making for a white Christmas just a few days before the big day hit.

Also meant I was really trapped. Christmas put a cold stop to all but the most essential club biz. Brothers disappeared and spent more time with their old ladies and their families. After this bash, the bars wouldn't be as well stocked for a little while. Worst of all, hopping on my bike and going for a ride was out of the fucking question with powder and ice like this shitting up the roads.

There was nothing to do but shuffle around like a ghost. Blaze and Saffron took off hours ago for their place.

Now, it was just me and the brothers who still got their dicks wet with any hot pussy or mouth they could find.

Wicked reminders everywhere that I wasn't doing the same damned thing, and I wasn't even tied down with an old lady. It was all because she'd gotten underneath my skin and wouldn't get the hell back out.

Didn't fucking matter she'd been effectively outta my life since Jack Frost came to roost. Fuck, I was thinking about her right now, remembering the way she'd ruined my lips forever with her addictive little lips.

If I hadn't been sick as hell that night, I would've tasted a whole lot more.

The poison hit me pretty bad, but it didn't stop my cock from straining like it was gonna rip through my pants, hard and horny and ready to get between her legs. I would've tried it too if that shit hadn't knocked me out.

When I woke up, she was gone, and there was no way short of defying a direct order from the Prez to change that. Blaze wouldn't even let me call her or send the shit we'd found in the Rams' old clubhouse. I had her license and her sketchbook, vicious mementos I couldn't help but pluck out and look at on cold, brutal nights like this. Roller found the ID and gave it to me after they picked over that shithole and dug up the buried weapons shipment that satisfied the Feds to keep Tank free.

I sucked down my brew and left the glass on the windowsill. Halfway down the hall, I heard a woman scream, unmistakably close to climax.

"God! Roller!" Marianne, the buxom blonde, was getting reamed good in the whores' room.

"Fuck!" I watched my younger, leaner brother tense up through the little slit in the door.

His lip ring bounced and thrashed as he ground his hips into her. He snarled and emptied his nuts, pulling her legs tight around him, thrusting as deep as he could go.

My cock wanted a piece of that, and wanted it bad. If only I could make my asshole heart shut the fuck up and let it go.

I walked on. What I found in my old room was a real surprise.

Soon as I was through the door, I heard a woman squeal, the kinda scream I'd know anywhere. Emma looked up with her blonde locks bobbing, chin hooked to Tank's bare shoulder.

The big guy clearly hadn't slowed down one bit since claiming her a few months ago. It took him a few seconds to turn around and see me.

"Fuck! Sorry, boss. Didn't know you were still hanging out in this place."

Em's cheeks flushed beet red. He gently settled her down on the old bed, the same one where I'd been so fucking close to Alice. I sighed and looked at the floor, taking my eyes off them for the nurse's sake. Tank zipped up quick and I heard her clothes shuffling behind me.

"Didn't meant to interrupt anything, brother. Just needed a place to crash. I'm too fucked up to go home tonight. Looks like the party's running on fumes…"

Tank rolled his huge shoulders, settling his cut. He looked at me and grinned. "Not for Em and me. It's okay, boss. We were just getting started. We're gonna head out and keep the party going somewhere we can have some fucking –"

"*Privacy,*" Emma finished, elbowing him in the guts, straightening her pants.

They both looked at me sheepishly. A second later, Tank threw a possessive arm around her, making her squirm playfully against him. Shit, her collar was still way too low, giving me an easy view of the bright red suck marks he'd left on her skin.

"Drive safe," I grunted, nodding politely to Em as she wrestled out of his grasp and walked past me. "The club's finally getting a rest for Christmas time. Well fucking deserved too."

"Sure is," Tank agreed, tugging his leather straight one more time before walking out.

He was almost gone when he stopped with one foot out the door, turning back to me. "You take care too, Veep. Don't get into the same bullshit funk I did. I can smell the shit rolling off you. You're a free man, boss. Don't let some pussy who doesn't want you keep your balls in a vise."

I wanted to laugh in his face. But I was too damned tired for arguing with brothers, especially in this state. Nodding, I watched Tank and Em slip out to the garages for their car. Me stumbling in on them was just a temporary delay.

Didn't take a genius to figure out they'd be going back to the sweet house he'd bought for them and railing her little ass all night. One thing was for sure: she'd been good for the big bastard, and the last man I ever expected to take advice from had actually given me some shit worth thinking about.

I leaned down and sniffed my cut. Fucking *Christ*.

Tank wasn't kidding. I smelled like I'd gotten piss drunk and rolled around in it. What a damned disgrace.

I shouldn't have been moping around the fucking clubhouse – especially not after a big bash like tonight. I should've slowed down on my drinks and gotten home. The little apartment I rented from a local dude who had a son with ties to the club wasn't much, but it was warm and peaceful. It didn't make my skull rattle with bitter memories like every second I spent in this room.

Yeah, there was a lotta shit I *should've* done, but damned if I was gonna. Every fucking second that girl lingered in my head, staring at me with her icy eyes and taunting me with her sweet fucking lips, meant another second I was gone.

Completely fucking lost.

She'd taken me on a bad trip and I wasn't coming back 'til I could bleach her outta my head, or else finally see her again. Best I could do tonight was rip open the old dresser drawer where I kept the only pieces of her I still had.

First, I picked up her old ID, fingering the edges. Same damned card Blaze had stopped me from bringing to her personally before she blew town. If I would've had a forwarding address, I sure as shit would've sent it onto her, but she could've gone all the way to fucking India for all I knew.

I didn't have a clue where she'd taken off to, and nobody was telling me neither.

Blaze was a bastard for keeping her from me, but I had to admit, he'd made the right call as Prez. Last thing this club needed was for the media to hear about a full patch officer riding across state lines and kidnapping a chick.

And yeah, there were days when I thought about that too, just taking off and going the fuck after her, even if it meant my bike skidding off an icy mountain pass or coming home to face a beating from my brothers. If I had any idea whether to head east or west, I'd have done it, consequences be fucked.

As it was, I had nothing. *Nothing*. Not even a single bone left behind to chase my damned tail.

My lips twitched sourly as I picked up her sketchbook. I tore through the pages, staring at the shit I'd seen and marveled over several times before. The girl was good. If she couldn't remember drawing like this, I hoped like hell it would come back some day.

The first page had a castle rising high to the moon in a desolate wasteland. The big, grinning beast behind it had a weird resemblance to the Devils' patch, the big smiling face with its sharp teeth and horns that always leered out our colors.

On page two, there was a cowboy with a revolver in hand. He was one surly looking badass motherfucker, and a couple unhappy girls lingered at his feet, crying on the ground like slaves. Would've been disturbing if it wasn't for the pointy ears she put on everybody.

Then there was one last drawing before the book ran into boring, half-finished everyday things. A shirtless dude with a sword held it up to the sky in triumph, something dark like blood dripping down his six pack, his teeth peeled back in an animal grin. The girl from the last sketch was at his feet, only this time she was looking up and smiling, arms wrapped around his thick leg like she was about to suck his dick straight to heaven.

I smiled like a fucking moron at this. Wasn't sure why. Guess it said my baby had hero fantasies, or maybe she just had a soft spot for real men.

Except she wasn't *my* baby. My smile melted. Alice might as well have been a million miles away on the dark side of the fucking moon. And I wasn't her hero by any stretch.

I'd let her walk, let Blaze whip my ass into line for the good of the club, let her roll into a world that sure as shit wasn't gonna do her any favors. It wasn't gonna cut her any breaks for her suffering either. If I'd learned anything since earning my patch, it was that a person had to earn *everything* in this fucking world from square one.

Lady Luck's hugs and kisses were rare, and they only went so far. They were usually much too fucking late too. Beth taught me that.

Fuck, how many years had it been? Coming up on two goddamned decades?

The shit still got to me like it happened yesterday. I threw the sketchbook back in the drawer and pushed it shut with a snarl.

No use wasting another second in here this cold night.

I walked out and slammed the door behind me. Several dudes on the ground rolled, rudely jostled in their sleep by the sound. I picked up my glass off the windowsill and headed to the bar to finish what I started.

More Jim. More beer. More venom.

No fucking way was I heading home tonight. No point when there was nothing to go home to.

I must've downed two more tall glasses of my gnarly cocktail before the furry heat in my brain started to go black. Shuffling off the bench, I hit the floor and rolled several inches, sprawling out on the empty floor.

Last thing in my head before I blacked out was *her,* and then I swore. Damned good reason to.

Even with enough liquor in my system to choke Tank, I couldn't stop thinking about Alice, and it was scary as shit. I was well and truly cursed, fucked beyond recognition unless I got my arms around her again.

If that day ever came, I wasn't letting go. Not for Blaze, not for common sense, not for anybody. The girl was a goddamned Siren, and the only way to get my dick wet without losing my mind was to find her, take her, and finish what we'd started.

Sometime during the night, my dick jerked. I sat up, and instantly felt something between my legs.

The soupy, pleasant buzz in my head was in that stage where it was turning into hangover torture. Needles throbbed in my eyes when I moved, twice as hard when I saw dark haired Sugar with her face dangerously close to my crotch. The bitch leaned in, rubbing her cheek against my length. My dick didn't give a single shit about the hammering in my head.

"What the fuck?!" I grabbed her hair, fisting it in one hand.

She giggled, obviously drunk herself. Guess Smokey or Stone hadn't exhausted her either because when she leaned up, I saw she was shirtless, her small pink nipples brimming like rosebuds.

"*Shhhh,*" she whispered, holding one finger to her lips. "We both know this has been coming for months. How do you want it? Mouth? Ass? Pussy?"

My eyes wanted to crawl right outta my head. My cock jerked again. It had been a long time, so fucking long. This slut was offering me anything and everything, a buffet of lust and hot white skin spread out for me to devour.

When I didn't answer, she moved for me, going for my fly. The zipper jerked down and her little hand reached in, grasping my whole fucking length.

"Oh! Jesus, Sting…hard as a fucking rock and big too. Can't say I'm surprised." She licked her lips. "I knew you were huge. Let's see if I can wake you up and help shake that hangover…"

My cock writhed in her hand as she drew it toward her lips. At the very last second, my hand jerked, violently throwing her head against my knee by the hair.

"Ow!" She jumped up and scrambled away from me, rubbing her temple. "What the hell's the matter with you? Fucking drunk!"

Yeah, I shook the hangover all right. Hadn't even tucked my cock in when my body bolted up and jumped on top of her, savage instinct boiling in my blood, mad dog killer shit I hadn't felt since tangling with the Rams and Grizzlies.

My hand went for her throat and I pushed her to the ground. Now, she looked genuinely scared. My cock wasn't sure if it liked what was happening or if it was about to deflate in horror.

"Jesus, Sting! I –" I cut her off with another vicious yank of the hair.

"Get the fuck out and go suck another brother, or lick the cold ass ground for all I care. You're a slut, Sugar, you and that other bitch, good for these parties and nothing else. If you *ever* sneak up on an officer of this club again and shit on him in any way, I'll have your ass thrown the fuck out and banned from this clubhouse. Got it?"

Shock and disgust shone bright in her eyes. Had to give the bitch's hair another rough tug to make her listen. Fuck me, her nipples were still hard enough to pound nails. My cock was gonna hate me forever for turning this down.

"I understand."

Done. I released her. She jerked away, scrambled to her feet, one arm thrown across her bare tits. I watched her ass bob as she high-tailed it back to the room she was sharing with her sister-in-sluttiness and the two new brothers.

With her outta the way, my headache stirred with a vengeance. I crawled to the nearest corner and collapsed, turning my face to the side so I didn't choke on anything that came outta my guts. It was a long bitter night sleeping off the worst feeling I'd had since the Rams' shit was in my blood.

I couldn't decide if I was an idiot for poisoning my own stupid ass this time, or if I should blame Alice instead. The girl left her mark, her venom so deep I couldn't find an antidote. And it was pretty fucking strong when it made me turn down free pussy.

"Sting? Stinger?"

Someone was shaking me, and it sounded an awful lot like Sugar. Jesus Christ, what did I have to do to get this bitch to leave me alone?

I popped up before I bothered opening my eyes. The woman shaking me screamed as she was knocked off her knees. Eyes open, head pounding something fierce, my jaw dropped as I saw Saffron sprawled out on the floor.

Fuck! I was about to apologize, but I never got the chance.

A brick smashed me in the mouth and I went down, grabbing for my teeth, tasting pure blood. When I tried to get up, but a boot slammed me right in the middle of my back, knowing where to twist into my spine to cause the most pain. The brutal weight shifted as its owner leaned down to my ear.

"You fucking asshole!" Blaze growled. "You ever push my old lady like that again, and I'll do a lot worse than shake your jaw. What the fuck's gotten into you?"

The boot pressed a little harder, and then came off. Soon as I rolled, slowly, knowing I was in a world of shit, Blaze grabbed me by both sides of my cut and hauled me up, throwing me against the wall.

"Sorry, Prez. I didn't fucking know it was her. I thought it was –"

"Alice?" He snorted and laughed. "Listen, bro, you gotta get over this. She's *gone*, and that's the way it's gonna stay. You're fucking off worse than Tank when Em had his dick all tied in knots."

"Sugar, actually," I said. "The bitch wouldn't leave me alone last night."

Blaze released me, taking a step backward and rubbing his eyes. Saffron was on her feet again, glaring at me and rubbing his shoulder with one hand.

"You okay, baby?" He turned to his old lady, flashing me the evil eye.

"Yeah, I'm fine. We've both had a lot worse than that. I'll be more careful next time about startling a brother laid out on the –"

"Don't bother," Blaze snapped, cutting her off. He pointed at me. "This man getting his shit together is nobody's problem but his own. Thing is, he's *gonna* get his head screwed on again real fast before his bullshit becomes a problem for the club. Isn't that right, VP?"

Bastard was really testing me now. I nodded, straightening my cut. Christ, I needed about a gallon of water to feel human with the hangover tearing through my system.

"What're you two doing here anyway? Thought club business was suspended all week for the holiday?"

"Business for the MC, yeah," Saffron said, resting her face on Blaze's shoulder. "We dropped by to pick up some extra drinks for the house."

"That's not the only reason," Blaze growled. "Also decided to check in to make sure nobody burned the damned place to the ground or fucked a hole in the wall. I gotta watch the clubhouse because you're sure as shit not doing it."

He turned his head, looking at Reb passed out on the ground with his long hair thrown over some skinny blonde's face. A cigarette was still in his hand, a pile of ash beneath it, and several scorch marks to boot. The older brother had taken to smoking a lot more since the cold weather rolled in instead of chewing his snuff.

Thank fuck. The gods of fortune got me off the hook by redirecting Blaze's shitstorm. I watched the Prez swagger over and give Reb a rude awakening of his own.

"Got to make sure everything's set for the deep freeze too," a voice said. "Just because the bikes and guns are sleeping for winter doesn't mean they don't deserve a tuneup."

I turned around and saw Moose standing in the open door leading to the garages. He flashed me a smile, frost clinging to his huge brown beard.

"Let me grab some coffee and I'll be out there to help," I told him.

Tuning up the bikes or cleaning guns sounded pretty damned good right now. It would give me something to do while the hangover faded. Plus I'd be outta Blaze's sight. I wanted to get the hell away before he was done giving Reb hell about burning the clubhouse down.

I turned to the bar. Saffron already had the coffee maker going, and she pushed a huge mug of water into my hand.

"You're a total babe," I said, reaching for the glass and guzzling the coolness down.

"Whatever. You're lucky I'm in a good mood today. Life's too short to be pissy about sleepwalking."

I watched her over my glass. Yeah, the girl definitely had a special kinda glow about her. Christmas was right around the corner, and then it was only a little while longer 'til the big day in Reno.

Getting married to a mean SOB like the Prez was the second best thing a girl could hope for after getting claimed in this club. I just hoped I'd have my shit settled before we all had to take off to Nevada.

Saffron poured my coffee into a thermos. I picked it up from the counter before heading out.

"Don't freeze your ass off too long out there, Sting. You know how Moose can be once he gets into taking things apart…"

Yeah, I knew. The only thing our senior brother knew better than tearing bikes apart was numbers. He'd made club Treasurer by default when the charter formed because accounting shit made everybody else's head spin.

"I'll be fine." I shrugged. "Fucking cold'll probably be good for clearing my head one way or another. Can't think about much at all when your balls are half-frozen to the ground."

Saffron laughed and then leaned across the bar, wanting to tell me something more quietly. Not that she needed to be discreet – Blaze was still laying into Reb like a fucking volcano erupting across the room.

"What's up?" I said, leaning in.

"I don't know how or why, but you're going to see her again. You just have to give it time. When you do, if you can shake this crap, you've got a chance. Give her a man, Sting. Not a jumpy dude who drinks by himself."

Fucking shit. Everybody was handing out wisdom I never asked for. I shrugged and started to walk, heading out behind Moose as fast as I could.

"Whatever. Thanks for the coffee." That was as close as I was gonna get to letting her know I'd heard her shit and taken it to heart.

Missoula's winters had nothing on Dickinson. Moose and I both spent plenty of time in the North Dakota charter before Throttle sent us west, suffering through some real Antarctic shit before we headed for big sky country. Still, the cold crept up on a man when he spent time in it.

My fingers were totally numb after a couple hours. I gave a couple bikes oil changes while Moose ripped more apart, inspecting the nitty-gritty. We made small talk while I cleaned the guns. I hoped he'd be satisfied with my half-assed answers.

No such luck. Moose had a good twenty years on me, pushing his early fifties, and he was arguably the oldest and wisest brother in the club. He'd been there since the MC started back in North Dakota, one of the original crew with Throttle's father, Voodoo.

"Let me ask you something, brother." He wasn't really asking. "We both know Santa Claus is on his way and you're looking at another long cold night in the dark, drunk off your ass."

My eyebrows furrowed. Fuck, was that what he thought? Had I really lost that much respect?

Knowing he was completely right made it pretty damned hard to sass back.

"That's my business," I growled, wiping grease off my hands after snapping a rifle together. "Somebody's gotta hold down this fort during the holidays. I'm volunteering for the job. Don't worry. I can't keep this place tight if I'm not sober."

Well, mostly. Truth was, I planned to repeat the night before on Christmas Eve, running the bottle dry into the big day.

Moose dropped his wrench. It clattered loudly on the ground, echo reverberating through the cold garage.

"Don't bullshit me, VP. I see what's going on here. I've seen it a hundred times before with Blaze and Tank and a ton of other brothers in different charters and different times." He paused, a grin spreading beneath his beard. "You're in love."

I almost choked. I sprang up, locking the rifle in place inside the huge gun vault.

"And you're full of shit. Look, brother, you know I respect you, but we both know where I stand. I fucking let her go. It's done – and there was never anything started in the first place. Blaze told me to lay the fuck off, and I'm gonna listen to the Prez this time. I'm leaving her alone, wherever the hell she went, to rebuild her life. I'll survive and get my dick wet someplace else."

"Yeah?" He took a step closer to me, smoothing his cut down his portly belly. "Leaving the whores alone for months isn't exactly what I call getting over it. Funny how a prickly little thing like her buried cupid's arrow so deep in your ass, bro. Never thought you were the type to fall so hard."

I snorted at the silly imagery. "Whatever, dude. What do you want me to do? I don't get where this shit's going."

Moose laid a thick hand on my shoulder, giving it a good squeeze. With his frosted, graying beard and the warm light in his eyes, he'd make a damned fine Santa Claus himself.

"All I'm saying is, while you're getting over this shit, you shouldn't spend the holiday alone. You're welcome at the table with Connie and my girl anytime. Becky'd love to have you around too. She's doing a project on motorcycle clubs for her smarty-pants English class. Says it's an ethno-graph-y or something like that."

I shrugged. Part of me wanted to tell him to fuck off and then hit the bar, assuming Blaze was done stalking the clubhouse and laying into brothers who'd partied their asses off the night before. But Moose did care about me the way a brother should.

I wasn't that far gone. The club had always been around freedom and brotherhood more than anything else. I patted his hand and stepped away, shaking my head.

"I'd love to help your daughter some other time, Moose. Appreciate the invite too, but I want some time to reflect this holiday. I'm not gonna be the third wheel with a stick up his ass around you and your family. Not gonna get between Tank and Blaze or their old ladies neither."

He gave me a slow nod. "Offer's open all the way 'til the holiday, brother, in case you change your mind."

I watched him walk over to the toolbox and grab his thermos. He drank right outta the top instead of pouring himself a cup of that coffee and Bailey's shit he liked to slug down in the winter for warmth, a bad habit Connie would no doubt give him hell about.

"Oh," he wiped his mouth, turning back to me. "Whatever you decide, you shouldn't be alone. If you're not gonna hang out with me, that's fine. I'm a big boy and it won't hurt my feelings. But you ought to consider taking a trip west, then, and spending it with somebody else."

My eyes lit up and then narrowed. I wasn't sure if he was yanking my chain or if he was really gonna feed me something useful. I threw the rag I'd been using to wipe my hands down and walked toward him.

"You telling me you know where Alice is?"

"Yeah, I do." He raised his hands. "I know what Blaze said too. But I don't see how keeping it from you is for the good of this club. If you wanna track her down for a visit, maybe a drink or a cup of coffee –"

I snorted again. We both knew I had a helluva lot more than that on my mind. But shit, for a chance at seeing Alice again, I'd sit down to a tea party if that's what it took.

"She's in Coeur d'Alene." I sucked in a deep breath and exhaled slowly when he said the words.

"I talk to the Dakota boys when they come through here with their shipments before heading west, especially Bolt," Moose continued. "They're not supposed to be making many stops in Grizzlies territory despite the truce, but you know how that goes. Those trips are long and the brothers like to wet their whistles, sometimes catch a show or two…"

He winked. Adrenaline shot through my chest when I realized where he was going.

No. No fucking way. He wasn't seriously implying my poor girl was dancing in one of those shitty Grizzlies owned joints, was he?

"Last shipment a couple weeks ago, Bolt told me the main club in town got a new dancer in. She's all the rage. Grizzlies had to step up security just to keep dudes from climbing the stage and getting frisky. Dark hair, snow white skin, full curves stacked on a softer frame…fits the bill just perfect. The pic he showed me on his phone sealed the deal. It's her, all right."

I shook once as the lightning hit me. Unbe-fucking-lievable.

My brain boiled with hot red fire, bringing back the pain of that fucking hangover again. I wasn't sure whether to be overjoyed that he'd told me where she was, or snarling mad that Alice had to resort to dancing for money, showing her beautiful body off to hundreds of assholes when I hadn't even seen her naked and beautiful…

My cock woke from his slumber, straining in my pants. It was wrong, so wrong, terribly fucking wrong, but it didn't matter one bit. My dick jerked and twitched each time I thought about her up on stage, swinging her sweet ass around a pole, same pretty ass I wanted to haul on my lap and hold onto while I fucked her 'til I couldn't move.

And my heart throbbed too, beat like a pendulum coming apart in my chest. Pure killer bloodlust shot into my veins when I imagined *any* little prick putting his grubby hands on her but me.

The only one seeing her, touching her, kissing her while she was stripped bare ought to be *me, me, and only me*. Alice didn't know it yet, but I'd claimed her without even speaking the words 'old lady' out loud. If I had to tunnel my way straight through the fucking Idaho mountains to make her realize it, then I would.

"Stinger? You okay, VP?" Moose cocked his head.

"Yeah," I said, loosening my tight fucking jaw just enough to answer. "Thank you, brother."

I meant it. I gave Moose a quick, strong manly hug and then headed inside.

Blaze and Saffron were heading out. The Prez eyeballed me when he walked past, as if to say, *you'd better not fuck up again, bro. This is your second chance and you don't get three strikes.*

Little did he know I was about to risk my VP patch. My mind was made up. When the clubhouse was clear and lonely come Christmas Eve, I was saddling up and heading for Coeur d'Alene, and I wasn't gonna stop 'til I had her in my arms.

The whole fucking world paled in comparison to feeling Alice hanging around my neck, having my lips on hers, cupping her little ass and shoving her into me, right where she belonged. Blaze was a fearsome badass, yeah, but he didn't promise half the scary fucking threats my screwed up brain was whispering if I failed to follow through on this.

When most of the brothers were gone, I left the clubhouse, heading for my apartment. Stopped at the liquor store to grab more beer and whiskey. I'd need to sober up for the trip, but the next few days I needed it to keep my head on straight.

The dreams were worse than they'd been for years. Drinking was all I had to suppress that shit, the vicious reminder that chasing Alice was about more than how hard she got my dick.

I couldn't face Beth's memory. Didn't fucking matter if years passed by. The guilt would only slow me down. So I resorted to drink, closing myself off in my apartment and staring at my black TV, waiting for the fire alcohol sent into my guts to rush up and bathe my brain in forgetful bliss.

At home, I was about to start on my second beer and Jim mix when I stopped. Outside on my balcony, the snow was coming down, pale white flakes frosting everything below. It looked just like that night when my life went off the rails for good.

Same damned night when the kid everybody called Luke died and I became a man.

God damn it. I gritted my teeth, pushing the shit in my glass away. Wasn't that good if I was really honest about it, and it wasn't doing its job lately either. Probably because I'd soaked myself stupid so many times my tolerance was spiking.

Fuck sobering up tomorrow. You'd better start now. If taking a fucked up trip down memory lane is the price of going after her, then that's the way it's gotta be.

Yeah. Right.

Too bad facing that shit with a clear head and a broken fucking heart was vastly easier said than done. And it didn't help one damned bit that today was the anniversary, the day I got my heart ripped out and my tail glued between my legs forever.

Eighteen years. Eighteen bitter, awful years since fate picked my ass up and dropped me on my head, dragging me into this life of chasing pussy and killing for my brothers.

Eighteen fucking years since that night when I stopped caring…'til Alice.

VI: White Knuckle Loss (Stinger)

Eighteen Years Ago

It was a snowy night on the North Dakota plains, when the state was still wild and towns were tiny, before the great oil boom was more than a twinkle in some prospector's eye.

Eric wasn't my dad, regardless of what the marriage certificate said. He was a drunken, violent, filthy piece of shit my Ma married when I was ten. They shacked up on nothing more than pure desperation and a couple hookups.

Of course, if I wanted to be brutally honest, the real reason they got together was because the asshole had a steady supply of ice from his buddies, all Ma really cared about.

"Luke? You in there?" She pushed my door open and the sharp squeak in the worn hinges woke me up.

"Beth." I threw my legs onto the floor, gawky as all hell at fourteen. Then I looked up and saw her face in the low light streaming through the window. "Holy fucking shit!"

She was my stepsister, the only good thing to come outta that fucked up marriage, just one year younger than me. And always, *always* taking the punishment that sonofabitch doled out when he was high or just plain pissed.

Tonight was no exception. She started to cry when I touched the big red mark blooming on her cheek.

"When did the fucker do this? Before I got home?" I regretted coming in late from detention.

I'd been screwing around later than I should've there with Prowl, the biggest badass in school. Dude was a Senior, but he easily could've passed for twenty-five. The prospect cut he wore for the Prairie Devils gave him some serious fucking bragging rights too, and he drew younger kids with a chip on their shoulders to him like dizzy moths to flame.

I wanted everything he had. None of the town's good old farm boys ever fucked with him, and pussy came flying into his arms like those patches were fucking magic or something.

Still, I knew I'd fucked up when I saw what I was sacrificing to chase my new friendship. Hanging out too long left Beth alone with the jackoff pretending to be our dad.

I shouldn't have left her alone. Eric hit the crystal harder when winter hit, sucking it up his nostrils every second he wasn't fucking Ma or getting stinking drunk.

"No, it just happened," she said, shaking in my arms. "I plowed out the road, just like he showed me. But I accidentally hit the mailbox...I wasn't thinking. I should've waited for you to come home and do it, Luke, but he wouldn't let me. He wanted it now, so he could go to the liquor store later."

"Fuck! You shouldn't have come clean, sis. Should've buried that fucking mailbox in the snow. He's too blasted outta his mind to notice." Poor girl. No matter how many times we went over how to avoid pissing off her dad's psycho ass, she still came clean with him, too damned honest for her own good.

"You've got to lie to him," I growled. "You break anything, you let me know about it. I'll fix it or hide the shit so *this* doesn't happen. Come on. Let's go get you cleaned up."

I started to lead her to the bathroom. The house was colder than ever, a million drafts coming through the old cracks. It was the one thing Ma inherited from her own parents, and probably the reason that asshole was gung-ho to wed a junkie with a half-grown son. He got to do his shit in our decrepit old house instead of the ratty studio apartment he had when I was a kid.

Beth clung to me as I led her down the hall. One of these fucking days, I was gonna be big and bad enough to fight back when Eric did this shit. But I knew I had to bide my time.

I was too short, waiting for my fucking hormones to kick in full force. Prowl and I shot the shit in the school's weight room. I worked harder there than any classroom, hoping for the kinda muscles my older buddy had in a few more years.

Then I'd be able to do something about this shit once and for all.

My asshole stepdad was a big dude, and childhood pals with the town sheriff too.

If I raised my hand against him and stopped short of murdering his evil ass, he'd have me arrested and tossed into juvie, if he didn't decide to put me in the ground first. And then there'd be no one left to care for Beth. Ma was too fucked outta her mind most days to eat dinner, let alone give a shit what was going on with her kids.

Family by blood or marriage didn't faze her one bit. My Ma died sometime before I hit ten, and she wasn't coming back. The thin, greasy mess of a woman who holed herself up in the bedroom shooting syringes meant nothing to me.

Not anymore. Maybe not ever.

Beth plopped down on the broken down toilet. I dug through the sparse medicine cabinet for something to numb the pain and sterilize the small scratch the fuck had on her cheek.

Bingo. There was some rubbing alcohol left and a few random cotton swabs.

"Hang on, sis. You know this shit stings."

"Not as bad as dad's belt. He never uses his hands anymore." She sighed. "Guess he figured out I'm too old for that. Takes more than a rough slap to make it hurt."

My heart sank, and I tried to hold it up. Anger did the trick. The rage pumping through my veins kept me sane, focused, determined to play the long game and win it, when I could get her outta here forever.

Just a few more years, I told myself, holding her hand. Beth's fingers tightened when I brought the cotton to her face. She winced.

Guess I was so busy tracing that jagged line down her cheek and trying not to lose my cool that I didn't hear the footsteps pounding down the hall. The door exploded open before I could turn around, and a giant hand wrapped around my neck, jerking me away from her.

"What're you fucking brats doin' in here?" Eric growled, breath as vile as always.

I didn't answer. He smashed me against the wall, hand on my neck so fucking tight his knuckles were going white. Beth jumped up and pressed herself to the bathroom wall, just as scared as me, afraid for what was gonna happen next.

Eric grunted when he saw the cotton and the wound on her face. "Asshole!"

He whacked the back of my head, hard enough to rattle my whole skull. At least his hand was off my throat, and I'd bought Beth a few more precious seconds.

"You're the reason this bitch don't learn no respect, how to do anything right." He sucked in a sharp breath, obviously high on his own crap. "You little shit…you think you're a man? Huh?"

He stabbed a fat finger into my chest. I grunted, twisting my head away from him, refusing to meet his fucked up eyes.

"A real man would take some responsibility, Luke. He'd be here at three o'clock, on the fucking dot, and I wouldn't have to send this clumsy fucking cunt out to plow my driveway! Where the fuck were you, anyway? Jerking yourself off with that biker kid again?" He snorted, showing me his busted teeth. "Thank fucking God your mama got her tubes tied. I'd take a shotgun to the mouth if I knocked her pussy up and got another shit-for-brains bitch boy like you!"

"Big fucking loss," I hissed, finally looking into his beady little eyes.

Eric blinked. I had a full second to realize how badly I'd fucked up by insulting him to his face before both his gorilla hands were wrapped around my throat.

"Say that again, you fucking cocksucker! Tell me how bad I fucked up clothing and feeding you and sending you to school – both you ungrateful brats! I did it. I did fucking everything for your greedy asses. And now you shit where you eat like a fucking retard!"

I choked once. My throat couldn't handle the pressure anymore. Funny. I always thought it would be a lot worse when all the oxygen in my lungs was depleted, but the death grip he had around my throat was so fucking tight my body barely understood what was happening.

Then he started to bash my head against the wall. I would've died then and there if it hadn't been for the blur behind him.

Beth sprang up, jabbing her fingers into his neck, biting him as hard as she could. Eric howled and dropped me on the floor. Everything was still spinning when I finally sat up, listening to her scream as he cornered her in the bathroom.

The only thing worse than getting my own ass killed was watching him turn on her. I sprang up, screaming for her to run, dragging myself along the wall to the phone around the corner.

Beth made it out behind me. I heard her pound into the basement, slamming the door behind her, safe for at least another minute as the beast behind her broke the lock and followed.

I wasn't stupid. The bastard was too big, too brutal. We could only hurt him in hit and runs before our luck ran out and he finished us off. My cry for help was a shot in the fucking dark.

I was still gasping for breath while I punched in the keys on the phone. No fucking cells in those days, so I had to type Prowl's number from memory, praying he was home.

"Hello?" The voice on the other end wasn't him, but I was too fucked up to care.

"Help me! Prowl, tell Prowl he's gotta come quick. Eric's beating the shit out of us...he's got my sister cornered! He's going to fucking kill us!"

There was a long pause. "You're the Spears' kid – same one who's been hanging around my boy?"

"Yeah," I coughed, shuddering when Beth started to scream downstairs.

"Hold on, son. We'll be down there in ten minutes, soon as I get the crew together."

Beth screamed again and I dropped the phone. Damned thing was hanging off the hook as I ran down the steps, praying it wasn't too fucking late. Took a quick look in the bedroom at Ma, squirming in their ratty bed, laughing to herself and gazing at the ceiling. She was in another world, like always, drugged out of her fucking mind as her sick hubby went nuclear.

Downstairs, I found him choking her. Same damned thing he'd done to me. I looked around for something to hit him with, but the boxes hid all the obvious shit.

Fuck it, I had to do something!

I got in one good punch, hammering the back of that asshole's head, right by the brainstem. Unfortunately, he was a lot faster than I gave him credit for. Maybe it was the meth, or the adrenaline ripping through his veins now that the murderous day of reckoning we'd all been waiting for was here.

The bastard spun. His fist smashed my left temple, so hard everything blurred and sent me down. I fell against the staircase. The blow from the wood was about as bad as his fist. I blacked out instantly.

"Come on, kid. Get the fuck up." A powerful hand reached for me.

At first, I fought it, afraid it was him. No, Eric sure as shit never wore leather. I recognized the huge man I'd only seen once before, Prowl's dad, decked out in his full MC colors.

Prowl was behind him, and he helped steady me, his face all grim. "Don't look, Luke."

He held my shoulders tight, refusing to let me turn around and see what the fuck was going on behind me. Then his dad looked at us both.

"Bullshit, son. He's got dibs on this motherfucker before we blow his fucking brains out." His strong hand reached for my shoulder and guided me away from my friend.

The first thing I saw was Eric, bloodied and whimpering on the floor, his hands tied behind his back with some kinda cord. It would've been the happiest fucking thing in my life if it wasn't for the pale lifeless figure behind him.

She was sprawled out on the ground in a little head, the back of her head split open, cherry red blood pooling all around her. Grief and rage exploded in my throat simultaneously, echoing through our crappy basement.

I tried to run to Beth's cold, dead body, but Prowl's dad wouldn't let me. I jerked against his hands again and again, screaming so loud I expected the floor to cave in on our heads.

"Let it out, boy. You deserve that much. If we'd been a couple minutes earlier, you wouldn't have to. I'm sorry – real fucking sorry we couldn't get here sooner." I could practically taste the sour regret in his voice. "When you're done crying, take this…"

I stopped blubbering just barely long enough to feel the cold, flat thing he handed me. It was Eric's belt, the same goddamned leather he'd used to beat her a hundred times before. Probably the same thing he'd used to choke her to death too, before he did the final blow.

"Pop?" Prowl wasn't looking so badass that day, more scared and unsettled than anything else.

"We got time. The other guys'll have this mess cleaned up in less than an hour…" The man reached down, forcing my fist to close tight around the leather strap. "Go to town. Anything you want, kid. Soon as you're done, I'll finish this asshole and get his carcass outta your hair. We'll figure something out for your sis too, so you can pay her some last respects."

I heard a gun cock in his other hand. Took a good long second to stare at Eric, broken and blooded on the floor, knowing that nothing but hell was ahead.

Beating the piss out of this asshole wouldn't bring my sister back. Just then, I was fucked if I cared. I took the belt and stared bringing it down on his back, hitting him harder than I'd ever moved my fist, tearing his shirt and cutting his skin.

"Grrrr! Frrrk! Irt stiiiings!" Eric screamed the same fucking thing over and over and over.

There wasn't any satisfaction as I laid into him. His screams took over for mine, mirroring my fucking hurt, my urge to slash my own skin and light myself on fire for my fuckup.

I was too late, too weak, too young to save her.

I whacked and whacked that asshole raw 'til the dry sobs shook my whole body. I couldn't feel my arm anymore when Prowl's dad nodded. My friend grabbed me by the shoulder, leading me upstairs.

A second later, a gunshot punctured the cold winter night, sending Eric home to the demon pool that spawned him.

For the next few years, I was in a total funk, living with my buddy and his old man, Slaughter. Some bribes passed hands and Eric's friend, the sheriff, died a mysterious death, whatever it took to keep anyone from asking too many questions.

We cremated Beth and spread her ashes on the open plains. No fucking way was I locking her up in the ground or dumping her off at the condemned farm where we'd both suffered. Ma wound up institutionalized and died a couple years later. I let them toss her worthless ashes in an unmarked grave without even stopping by to see it for myself.

Prowl got the same patch Slaughter and the rest of the brothers wore about a year later, about the same time I got my PRAIRIE DEVILS MC, DICKINSON cut as a prospect. I learned to smile real big and nod at everything the Prez, the VP, and the Sergeant at Arms told me, a big guy named Moose who was a little thinner and less beardy in those days.

I also vowed I'd never, ever let a girl die like Beth if I could stop it. I'd never walk away if anybody I cared about was in the least hint of danger. And I sure as fuck wouldn't be too weak to take out the wolves circling my girl.

After that night, every waking day was about getting stronger, building muscles and brotherhood, learning to kill any asshole who deserved it. And with the club behind me, I was finally unstoppable.

Present Day

I woke up and headed for the bathroom. Vomited in the toilet and wiped my mouth. Re-living that shit in my dreams made me sick to my fucking stomach.

But today, for the first time ever, I was glad I did.

Tomorrow was Christmas Eve, and I'd be down at the clubhouse first thing in the morning. Soon as the other brothers cleared out and Moose stopped giving me last minute shit about spending the holiday with him and his family, I was gone.

I set my sights on the Idaho border, and I wasn't coming back 'til she was with me. True or no truce, the Grizzlies were dangerous motherfuckers, and so was stripping in those demons' lair.

I couldn't let Alice become another Beth. Fuck, even worse, I couldn't let her slip away. I didn't know if she'd give me anything besides pure venom when I showed up, but I was beyond giving a fuck.

If Alice wanted to make a life for herself, then I'd offer her a better one. If she told me to fuck off, then I'd at least make sure nobody was coming after her pretty ass.

Nobody but me. For her, I was on the hunt, one step away from watching my fucking mind rocket into the void if I failed.

Failure? No, that was off the fucking table here. I'd bend the road my way 'til it led where I wanted, no matter how damned long I had to ride through hell and blood or acres of her ice. I wasn't backing down. Not for anything. Alice was gonna be wrapped around me like an old lady should or else I'd tear my own fucking heart out.

I was too far gone, stuck in her crazy sweet gravity, and there was only one way out. Soon as I got her, I was gonna own her the same way she'd got her nails in me. And when I did, I'd make it crystal-fucking-clear that I wasn't gonna hear any nos coming outta her mouth ever again unless she was wearing my brand.

VII: Passions Unsheathed (Alice)

I should've known better. A girl can't just up and leave and sweep her past under the rug so easily.

It only took me a few weeks to realize coming to Idaho had been one big mistake. Securing a room with virtually no credit history took up half the wad Blaze gave me to get out of his face, and running all over town with taxis and buses searching for work took a lot more.

I was down to dregs by the time I finally swallowed my pride and hit the Filthy Crown for work.

I had the body for it and the youth. I thought I was so numb, handling it would be easy, but the first night almost broke me. I stripped on the dirty stage beneath the dim lights, moving like a whirlwind to hide the tears, shaking my tits and ass like a maniac to stop all the leering men from seeing how I was coming apart at the seams.

The type of rough, dangerous looking men who frequented the bar must've liked my pain. Or maybe they could smell a virgin in over her head from ten feet away, showering her in cash like some obscene throwback to ancient, savage times.

The Grizzlies who owned the place took half – all part of the harsh terms I'd agreed to. But even after their cut, I was making plenty, and I started to save like a mad woman for the day I could blow the bar and hope that none of the hard, dirty men who watched me in the darkness would follow.

Stripping for the Grizzlies MC and their biker buddies made me think about Stinger. No, not just him, the whole clubhouse back in Missoula. I realized fast just how different the two clubs were.

Men in Grizzlies colors thought nothing of slamming dirty needles into their veins while they sipped their beer. They rocked in their seats, watching me slide up and down the pole, pumping my hips like the lewdest thing they'd ever seen. Really, it was pure revulsion, horror mixed with a smattering of fear that one day they'd pull me aside like they did to the other girls.

They'd made them offers they couldn't refuse.

Marks was the only man who kept them away from me. Some asshole trying to grab me backstage or hop up onto the stage during my act was a weekly occurrence. But the big man who was always around for security, fighting the ones who went too far off with his presence, and sometimes his fists when he needed to.

I almost thought I'd made a friend until I approached him one icy December night. He was stuffing his half of the club's cash from all the night's performances in the vault, including mine, when I crept up next to him.

"Hey…" He spun to face me, fixing his hard eyes on my robe.

"What the fuck are you doing here? Go home and rest. We'll need you fresh for tomorrow. Lotta dudes coming in looking to blow off steam from the holiday shit at home."

"I just wanted to say thanks for keeping things orderly, night after night. I know it's just work to you, but I'm not sure where I'd be without you…"

He grunted. "You're right. It's just a job, my duty for the club, babe. I keep the civvies and other brothers off your tits and pussy. Don't think it's a favor. I can't have you fucking 'em like those other sluts when you bring in five times as much as the next best girl here. Gotta keep that virgin shit alive – the myth, anyway. Anybody sees you sucking or fucking cock around here, your cover's blown. You do that shit in the privacy of your own home, yeah?"

I swallowed. Didn't like the way he was looking at me. This whole thing was a mistake. I turned to go, but Marks reached out and grabbed me, throwing me against the wall.

"I heard about you, Ginger-Bell," he said, using my stage name. "I know you were close to those Prairie Pussies back in Montana. Listen, that shit's not gonna fly here. Maybe those bitches are happy to let women wrap their fucking balls up in a neat little bow and screw with their club, I dunno. All I know's the truce Fang and the national crew signed with those fucks was a big mistake.

Can't wait 'til the day comes when we're rolling across the state line to pump lead into those cocksuckers again…"

He drew a sharp breath. I twisted in his meaty fist, yelling when he crunched bone. Marks opened his eyes again, the rapture on his face melting away. Disgusted, he let go and gave me another hard shove against the wall.

No wonder he never touched me himself. Sex didn't do it for this kinda man – straight up violence did.

"Just do your fucking job, got it? You're a Grizzlies girl now. Be happy it's this easy. The day may come when the brothers decide you're doing harder shit."

I rubbed my wrist. "Harder? What're you talking –"

"Porn. Straight up suckin' and fuckin' on camera. Personal and paid sex with the rest of the club here in town, and then any old fucks we line up to bang your ass. I know this shy virgin bullshit's a fucking act, and the guys eat it up. That's cool." He paused to light a cigarette, then took a long pull before he finished. "But it's probably gonna fall apart at some point. The day may come when we figure out better ways to make money off you that's a little more involved than flashing your cunt for stacks. Be ready."

Bitter acid churned in my stomach. Then the wildcat inside me rose up, a vicious hatred I hadn't felt since dealing with Em and the guys pumping me for information.

"I signed up for the stage," I said coldly. "Nothing else."

Marks took a good long look at me. Then he laughed, flicking his cigarette on the floor and crunching it out with his boot.

"You're a real cute bitch, you know that? You almost had me. Seriously." Still laughing, he shook his head. "Hope you show me and the brothers one day what the real Ginger-Bell's like. Cause with all these fake fucking masks you wear, I don't got a goddamned clue."

Crazy, suicidal impulses ran through me right then. I wanted nothing better than to stomp up, grab his big dirty beard, and slap him across the face. Of course, he'd end up backhanding me across the head or worse, but at least he'd understand I wasn't kidding.

My stomach lurched again and I had to get out. Marks never said goodbye. I grabbed my things and left, not looking forward to the ten hours or so of rest I'd get before I had to get up and do it all over again.

Didn't sound like the bastards were going to give us any time off for Christmas either. Not that it mattered. Hell, after what he'd said, I'd be lucky if he wasn't pimping me out at the Filthy Crown's Christmas party, which promised nothing but rowdy testosterone on steroids.

Holiday vacations were the least of my worries. I had to take stock of all my cash, bus routes, everything tonight, before I left for another shift. If there was any hint Marks was going to follow through on the crap he'd talked about with his twisted brothers, I had to go.

I had to start over. I had to *really* get away next time, rather than winding up in the same merciless head spinning circle.

There were only two choices: flee to the southwest, where I knew no one and nothing, away from Grizzlies territories. Or else go east, where I'd inevitably run through Missoula and other Devils charters.

The shame of running into any of the Montana crew – or Jesus, *Stinger* – turned my blood cold. But I was so desperate, so fucking sick to myself, I was ready to consider anything. Before I tried to sleep off the screwed up conversation with Marks, I spent a long time staring at my cheap phone.

I still had his number. Sting was just a call away, and I remembered what he'd told me, the offer to come running if I was ever in trouble.

Anywhere. Anytime. Any way he could.

God help me, it made me smile like the idiot I was. I wasn't crazy or desperate enough to make the call, though. Inviting him back into my life would bring even more complications, but they were starting to look a lot less daunting compared to everything else going wrong.

What the hell was I thinking at the club? I must've been delusional. When I reached out to Marks, I was looking for some little inkling that someone gave a shit. I hadn't found it with that asshole. Stinger, on the other hand, was the real deal.

He really gave a damn. And I'd let him down in return, running off like a scared little girl after tasting his lips for the first time. Christ, I still couldn't shake his heat, his taste, his energy, even after all these months.

What I would've given to feel it bathing me in his stern glow…

But I'd shamed myself so fucking bad I couldn't stand to see him. Not now. Thinking about his bright eyes clouded with disappointment, darkness, twisted me in knots.

The tears came, hot and fierce. I buried my face in my pillow and let exhaustion claim me.

Christmas Eve.

The bar and the stage fixed to it were surprisingly sparse. For the first night in a long time, I wondered if I'd get halfway decent tips. It was just a couple other girls and me, go-go sluts with more worn bodies than mine, girls who were used to a lot more kink too.

Men grabbed at them through the holes in their enclosed cages. Half the girls were hooked on bad shit, and they knew they had a good chance at getting more if they put up with the groping, making taking a few guys up on backstage deals if they offered the right hit.

I was all by myself, dancing for a small audience. The music cranked up, reaching its crescendo. I rolled my hips, transporting my brain far away from this place, getting into that cozy grove. When I danced long and hard, I could flick the strings on my skimpy panties without feeling like a debased whore.

The usual hollers rang out when they came off. I shook, undulated, having a tiny flash of pleasure when I imagined Sting seeing me like this. There were times when he intruded on my act, seizing my head at the most vulnerable point.

He got me wet. The men saw it and thought they stroked my lust, feeding their deranged fantasies. If only they knew the man making my body hum was half a state away, and one of their sworn enemies.

Then the heat turned to shame. Christ, what would he say if he saw me like this?

What would any of the men wearing the Prairie Devils patch who'd put up with my crap say? What about Dad?

I was remembering him more every day, our life together and his sudden death. It hurt like hell. A lot of things were as foggy as the low lying, stinky smoke in this place, but my memory was getting clearer, little by little. And it did me no favors except showing me how fucked up my situation really was, how much I'd lost for good.

Men grunted, roared, and pushed their hands up toward the stage. Marks stalked over and slapped away their grubby palms every time. I was nearing the end when the new crew came in, four large men in cuts, pushing their way to the front.

Marks stopped just short of shoving them away from the stage when they got too close. At first, I thought they were all Grizzlies, local guys from his own MC. But their colors were all wrong in the light, and the man in the middle wasn't leering with lust.

He looked at me like I was a literal piece of meat, something he was ready to scoop up and devour.

Shit. Where had I seen that pock marked face before?

I was trying to focus, finish up the act, ignoring his ice cold stare. The big man was in Marks' face. Something I thought would've set the biker-turned-bouncer right off, but no, it looked like he was wilting in the stranger's presence.

The music died just then as it was changing to another track. I cut my act and took a bow, flashing my biggest, fakest smile ever as crumpled cash came bouncing onto the stage at my feet.

"You know who we are…that bitch there…gotta have a good long talk…" My ears perked up as I listened to the man in the strange cut talking to Marks.

Why did he look so familiar? He definitely sent a chill coursing up my back, and it wasn't just because I was naked and the Filthy Crown had shitty heat.

For a second, we locked eyes. He leaned into Marks, hand on the big biker's shoulder, and whispered something in his ear.

Growling, Marks stepped backward, throwing him off. "I don't give a shit what you fuckers do! Just keep my ass outta it. You drag me or any other brother with my patch in, and I'll make sure it goes all the way to Fang. You Slingers assholes can deal with him then."

I grabbed my underwear and slipped backstage. Whatever was happening, it wasn't good. I'd heard the name Fang floated around several times before, always ominously, the national President of the entire Grizzlies MC. Whoever these strangers were, they'd rattled Marks bad enough to threaten tattling on them to the very top of the chain.

I threw my robe on and dressed. Thank God it was the last act of the night. I was beyond ready to get home before the clock flipped over to Christmas morning. I'd keep myself busy with bad TV, counting my savings and laying plans to get the hell out of this situation.

Anything beat focusing on my lonely, crappy holiday.

Fully dressed, I got my purse and jacket, and slipped out the back exit. No need to go through the bar again and risk running into Marks – let alone those other guys.

It was a five block walk to my rental, one side of an old run down duplex. The winter wind was mercifully quiet, but it wasn't much comfort. The streets were eerily dead, like the entire world had gone into hiding for Christmas, lost behind the festive lights and grinning Santa statues in snowy yards.

I walked fast, trying not to let my mind go crazy with all the shadows in the empty streets. One car passed me by, a little too slowly for my liking.

It was just an old man who slowed down to wave. Probably a drunk, some lost asshole who'd just seen my act at the club. Jesus, I was shaking. If it weren't for the freezing ground, I would've kicked off my stripper heels and ran the rest of the way home, taking my risk of slipping on the ice falling on my ass.

That bastard's eyes at the club were so dark, so familiar. So fucking evil. *How* did I know them?

Dad's last foggy memories kept coming back. I remembered a huge shadow behind him at the Rams' clubhouse, beating him over the head, watching his life slip away as the crap in my drink claimed me.

No, I couldn't think about that. I had to just keep going, one step at a time, straight home, where it was neat and warm and safe.

Finally. When I reached the home stretch leading to the door, I fished my keys out of my pockets and dropped them in the snow by the mailbox like a fucking idiot.

The stuff was deep and dark. I cursed, crouched on the ground, and ran my fingers through the snow, searching and trying not to scream at every little noise.

A truck grumbled, its belt squealing in the distance. I shot up, heart banging like a drum, and then softening as the adrenaline bled back into my veins.

Christ. I'd heard the same sound a dozen times before. It was just the neighbor's crappy old pickup across the street…and where the hell were those damned keys?

My hand was going numb, same as my knees on the cold pavement. Snarling, I ripped it out of the snow and shook it. I was about to dive back in when I was yanked up.

They moved fast. The rough hand clapped on my mouth right as another wrapped around my throat, choking off my scream before I could let it out.

"Long time no see, cunt." The same smooth, icy voice I'd heard at the club rumbled in my ear. "Get on your fucking feet and follow us inside. I got a few questions for you. If you don't scream, you'll live. You start barking and ruining the sweet silent night we got here, I'll choke you right here and bury your whore face in the snow."

I whimpered, feeling his hand tighten on my throat. He shoved my face uncomfortably close to the snow and held it there. I thought it was all going to end in a wink, but then he jerked me back by the hair, kicking open my screen door.

He'd found the keys in the snow. They jiggled in his hand as he tried keys and found the lock, seemingly interested in taking his sweet time. When I looked up, I saw why.

He wasn't alone.

Three big dark shapes were grinning at me from the driveway, blocking my escape even if I somehow broke his grip and took off in those stupid heels. Soon, he pushed me inside, and the other three men were right behind him.

There was no sanctuary. Not here. Not anywhere alone.

Just like that, all the nightmares I'd tried to forget followed me inside, and their name was Nero.

Nero, Nero…holy shit. I remember.

He pushed me to the wall and the knife came out, growling about some stupid handwritten map my father had. Memories hit me in the face again and again. If I wasn't so scared, I might've fainted at the sheer force.

I broke. I cried. I quivered.

When I settled down and listened to his harsh questions, I knew I had to answer, especially when he started threatening me with the psycho he'd brought along, the nut with the razors and cuts all over his body.

I gave up Stinger and his club. I forfeit my own life, and I should've known it right then. But I didn't until I slouched, listening to him tell me I hadn't saved a damned thing, much less my own neck.

Everything was past numb, frozen and dead as the snow outside. I watched Nero and his VP, Shark, head out the door with one last wicked order.

"I'm gonna give you boys an hour with this bitch. Have your fun and then clean up the mess. We'll dump her body off on the way to Montana."

The door shut. The truck outside revved its engine right as I ran, hit the basement, wondering how long I could fight them and avoid this death sentence. My whole crazy life up until that point flashed before my eyes. Wasp and lunatic Hatter caught up to me, tackled me to the ground, tearing at my jeans.

My stripper shoes were long gone. It would've been nice to drive one of those spikes through their evil eyes. I kicked anyway, thrashing against them, slamming my bare heels into everything I could find behind me.

One of the men screamed. My foot bashed something that felt like his brow, digging into his eye.

The other man stumbled, snorting like an angry bull. I ripped myself away, got up, and ran, fast as I could. They were still lumbering around on the floor as I tore through the laundry room.

There was a tiny crawlspace in the corner by washing machine. I knocked the old panel down and flung myself in, tugging the panel back into place behind me. I wasn't sure if they'd seen me, but I hadn't bought more than a few seconds.

They were downstairs now, sniffing around like the animals they were. I listened to them go the opposite direction, trying not to cough on all the fucking dust billowing around me in a swarm.

They rifled through the storage closet, the shelves. One of them ripped it right off its old fixtures and tossed it across the room, where it smashed to pieces.

"Fucking cunt. I'm gonna hold her down while you tear her asshole up, bro. Don't give a fuck about sloppy seconds after she punted me in the fucking eye…"

They were coming closer. The single light bulb had broken when the shelf was thrown, but the darkness wouldn't keep me hidden forever. Soon, one of them would feel the draft, or I'd cough, sneeze, giving myself away.

I closed my eyes. This was it. The rest of my life was measured in seconds, maybe a few minutes at most.

"What the fuck? What's the Prez doing back?" Wasp's hand was on the panel when he froze.

Opening my eyes, I listened along with them. A vehicle was out front, its distinct growl slicing through the thick silence, clouding the rage. My heart picked up faster.

Oh, God. Did that asshole Nero come back to torture me himself?

I wasn't sure if Hatter scared me worse than his fearsome leader. I listened to the men approach the basement stairs. There was noise upstairs, and then footsteps, someone heading down.

"Hey! Is that you, Prez? What the fuck's happening up –"

A gunshot exploded. Someone made a sound like they were gargling syrup, and then there was a long pause, a return of the monstrous silence.

Something heavy leaped off the stairs and hit the floor. For the next minute, I listened with my ear pressed against the panel, wincing each time I heard men hissing, spitting, clawing at each other. They rolled on the floor, banging against the wall like feral animals.

It can't be…

I wouldn't dare let myself consider it. This was supposed to be the end of my story, judgment for failing to keep my cowardly mouth shut. I'd stared death in its vacant eyes and realized what an awful woman I'd been.

I didn't deserve to have Sting here, and I definitely didn't deserve to have him risking his life for me.

The men were snarling louder. Another gunshot went off, and one of them screamed. A familiar voice cursed and footsteps hit the floor, going for the backdoor. It sounded like someone jumped right through the glass. The tremendous crash left my eardrums ringing.

I barely heard the new footsteps crunching over the debris in my little laundry room, closer and closer to my hiding place.

Jesus Christ. It can't be him. No fucking way, no how…

A large silhouette stopped in front of the panel.

I was ready to meet my fate. If the gunman on the other side had a bullet earmarked for me, then I'd take it.

I was ready to die. I wasn't ready for the panel to come flying off a second later, bringing me face-to-face with *him.*

"Stinger?" I squeaked, shaking my dusty head in disbelief. "Jesus, it's really you!"

"Fuck, baby. What the hell did they do to you?" He ripped me out, pulling me tight to his chest.

Meltdown came. I bawled, my strength fading against the rock hard chest I never expected to feel again. I took a deep breath, inhaling his scent, strength and violence and sweat mixed together. Amazing how it could be so comforting.

"Easy, girl. I gotta get you out of here." He guided me into the hallway, where there was a little more light streaming down from upstairs.

He saw the cut on my neck where Nero's knife had nicked me. Stinger's face twisted. Before, he looked ready to kill, but now he was positively bent on it.

"Fuck! Does it hurt?" He ran a finger close to the cut.

I shook my head. "No, it's not deep. It could've been a whole lot worse. Trust me."

"I'm gonna kill those assholes. Never heard of the Slingers before tonight, but those fucks just dug their graves. Shit! Can't believe that other fucking rat slipped away with a bullet in his ass…I should've gone after him."

"No!" I hissed, pinching my arms around his back. "Stay with me."

I looked over his shoulder while thunder echoed in his throat. Wasp lay dead on the floor, splayed out, a deep chasm right in the middle of his forehead.

Something inside me snapped. I shook my way out of Stinger's grip and marched over. I planted my bare heel right in his dead guts, screaming like a maniac.

"Holy shit, calm down, baby. He's dead. You can't kill his ass a second time." He grabbed me, wrapping his strong hands around my arms. He held me down, probably scared I'd pop a shoulder or something, but still I fought him.

"You don't understand!" I shouted. "I should be on the ground with him. These men fucked up everything – *everything!* I ratted on you, Sting. I hurt your club. I told them about the fucking map you got from my dad…"

He stopped and stared If he was furious, he did an incredible job hiding it. Finally, he got a better hold on me, whirled me around, and pressed me gently to the wall near the stairs.

Stinger's eyes pierced mine, whirling with confusion. "What're you talking about, Alice? What the fuck happened here?"

It all came pouring out. There was no use hiding it.

I told him everything. I owed him the full brutal truth after he'd saved my life. When I got to the part about how they threatened me with that beast, Hatter, how I spilled the news about the Rams, he bared his teeth.

"I'm going to kill each and every one of those fucking assholes," he said, strangely calm. "Already said as much, but I really fucking mean it. It's gonna happen."

"What about me?" I said, tears beading in my eyes.

"I don't give a fuck what they forced you to do. It's nothing the club can't handle. They want a piece of us, they're gonna get it lodged up their asses. Now come on, baby."

He let go. I kept shaking, staying planted against the wall as I watched him stalk over to the dead man. He flipped over Wasp's body and brought out a knife, tracing it down his collar, cutting a neat oval around the SLINGERS MC patch on the backside with the smoking pistol.

"Stinger?" I swallowed hard, waiting for him to face me. He stood up, the leather he'd cut off in hand.

"I'm done here. Let's get you outta this fucking place."

Upstairs we went. He had me halfway through the door to the driveway, where his truck was parked, when he pushed a gun into my hand. It was heavy, strange, familiar.

I recognized it – nine millimeter. This wasn't the first time I'd held a gun in my life. Heck, one of the first memories that came back was Dad teaching me how to shoot when I was seven. But I hadn't fired one for a long time, and never when a situation really needed it.

"Keep that shit close. I'm gonna let you in the driver's seat with the engine running. Stay there. You take off if anybody comes sniffing around. I need to clean this fucking mess down here."

We were outside. I watched as he unlocked the truck, started the engine, and then stepped aside, holding the door open for me. A crescent moon lit up the weirdly tranquil street, and I eyed him up and down. He looked just like a crazed prince taking me into a carriage.

"You're not mad?" I closed my eyes, forcing out the words. That stupid cut on my neck was starting to burn for the first time, or maybe it was just raw guilt inflaming the wound.

"I already told you – the club can handle these fuckers. So can I." He reached out, helping me up into the driver's seat, leaving no time for my doubt to leave me outside and vulnerable. "You think I'd rather have you dead and quiet than alive because you said what you needed to?"

I looked down at him, shaking my head. I wasn't sure what the hell to think anymore. His eyebrows quirked up and he shook his head.

"Christ, baby. Looks like we're gonna have to start all over. You really haven't figured out shit about my priorities, have you?"

He walked off before I could answer, retrieving a tarp and what looked like a heavy box from the back of the truck before heading inside the house. I slumped in the leather seat, feeling the truck's heat blast out on my chest, trying to revive the girl who'd died in the crawlspace.

How the hell was he so calm and collected? I chewed on that question for the next twenty minutes as he worked to disappear the corpse. I took one last look at the quiet neighborhood and the house, knowing damned well I wouldn't be coming back.

Later, he came out, carrying several big lumps wrapped in the tarp. I had a sick vision of him cutting Wasp down to the size. He threw the bundles in the back and spread a bigger tarp over it.

It was sick, yeah, but I couldn't feel bad about it. All four Slingers deserved to be cut to a thousand pieces for making me flip and endanger the club. They deserved worse than that for killing my father.

Now that I remembered who Nero was and what he'd done, I couldn't get it out of my head.

I put the gun in the glove compartment and carefully climbed over the stick in the middle to the passenger seat as soon as I saw Stinger coming. He slid into the driver's seat like nothing happened, eyes and hands focused on backing the truck down the driveway and getting us onto the road.

We drove right past the Filthy Crown on the way out, heading northeast, leaving Coeur d'Alene behind. It was obvious where we were going, but I had to know what else he had in store.

"Well? What's the plan?" I rubbed my neck. Stinger saw me wince when my fingers brushed the cut.

"We're gonna drop the piece of shit in the back off and let his bones thaw for spring. Then I'm bringing you home."

"Home?" I'd never thought about Missoula that way before, not until recently, when I figured out how fucked I really was.

Couldn't say it felt wrong.

"Yeah. Don't give me any fucking lip about it either, baby. It's not ideal – I get it – but I'm gonna do whatever it takes to make sure nobody lays a finger on you again, much less a goddamned knife." He drew a sharp breath and ran his eyes up and down my body. "You're done running, and I am too. I made my mistake two months ago when I let Blaze keep me from tracking you down. I've seen the light, Alice, and it's fucking blinding. Let's get this straight: if you go running again, I *will* come after your ass. I don't care if you want to put a damned bullet through my skull even more than those other fucks.

"From now on, you're my responsibility. *Mine.* And you're gonna find out I don't let what's mine break or hurt or fucking die. I'll lose everything before that happens. Truth is, I can deal with Blaze and the asshole Slingers. They're a fart in the wind. But you...this shit...I can't deal with risking your ass or having you outta my sight for one more second."

I turned away, staring out the window into the frigid night. His hand reached for mine, pulled me back toward him, refusing to let me sink down into the cold abyss.

Shame and guilt and uncertainty had nothing on his rough, possessive warmth.

I stared at him. He gave me a look that stuck with me before he turned back to the road.

"But Stinger…"

This. Is. Insane, I wanted to say, counting off all the reasons.

I had a thousand buts blowing through my head. So many they all ran together and stopped my tongue in its tracks. His hand squeezed mine tighter, sealing my lips for good.

"Welcome home, baby. You're here, long as I've got you in arm's reach." He paused, running his thumb up and down my hand, circling my palm. "If the next fucking words outta your mouth aren't a thank you, then I don't want to hear any other shit. I want you to trust me."

"I do," I said, bowing my head and fighting down the brutal lump forming in my throat. "And *thank you.* For everything."

He nodded, a low rumble in his throat purring satisfaction. We drove on in silence, making good time. Tonight, the roads were almost completely deserted. We couldn't have picked a better night than Christmas to turn off on a desolate road he seemed to know.

I helped him haul the half frozen pieces of Wasp's body to a small ravine. Stinger took them from my arms and shoved them down the mountainside. We watched them slide through the snow to a frozen stream.

"More snow's forecast for noon tomorrow. Should take care of his bits and pieces for a few weeks. Ninety-nine percent chance his ass is chewed to pieces by predators long before anybody comes sniffing around in the spring. We're good." Stinger winked. Pretty reassuring for a man experienced in death and destruction.

But he only killed when he had to, bringing his outlaw kind of justice to the bastards who got in his way and anything he cared about.

It was a long walk back to the truck.

Numbness gnawed at my whole body, and not just because it was cold. He'd killed a man, a devil, killed him *for me.* I never broke down once when we were finally inside the vehicle, following the highway to Missoula.

My eyes wouldn't stay off him for the rest of the ride, only looking away when he caught me staring for too long. We didn't talk much.

The ride was...peaceful. Safe. Warm.

Everything Idaho wasn't.

All that was quintessentially Stinger surrounded me, and I'd never been happier just to bask in his glow. A deeper tingle started beneath my skin, the same heat that caused me to flush whenever I danced on the stage, thinking about him.

Jesus, we'd just hidden a man's hacked up body together. I'd narrowly escaped getting killed and tossed in the boonies myself. Yet, here I was next to the last man I expected to see, pure need simmering in my blood, an ache in my brain begging to get closer to him, offering every inch of my flesh in gratitude.

Had I lost my mind? Was it even psycho gratitude when this attraction felt *so fucking right?*

I huddled in a ball, folding my arms, pressing my legs together. Wet heat lit between my thighs. So wrong but so painfully hard to ignore…

When I looked at him again, I was smiling. I laid my head on his shoulder, and he didn't resist, despite the little grunt of surprise he made when he sensed me there.

Somehow, someway, I was going to salvage the most fucked up Christmas of my life. Crazy? Probably, but definitely not impossible.

Especially because when I rubbed my head on him, I *felt* his words, true and clear in muscle and leather.

Welcome home, baby.

Home.

The way there had been terrible, and it wasn't over yet. But I was going to give it a chance, and if my home was truly in his heart, then I'd figure it out soon.

Kiss by kiss, tear by tear, wrapped around his gorgeous body. Tonight, there was nowhere else I'd rather be.

"Baby? We're here." He nudged me gently.

I jerked up and rubbed my eyes. Crap, how long had I been out? Did the drive back to Missoula take all night?

There was a tiny hint of blue on the horizon. Today, every normal person across town would be waking up to gifts and good cheer. I just wanted to go back to sleep, safe in his arms. Anything to forget my life taking its latest turn toward shit creek.

"You okay?" he asked, staring at me and rubbing my arms. "You slept like the dead for three hours. Took a little longer than usual to get back with shit icing up. Would've been a lot faster on my bike if we'd had a thaw."

I blinked dumbly. "Seriously? It's the dead of winter, Sting!"

He shrugged. "This bullshit's not half as bad as a real blizzard on the Dakota plains. I grew up during some cold, harsh times. This mountain shit's nothing."

His eyes said he was making a huge understatement. Now, he had me curious. Just when I was going to press him, he clicked off his seat belt and then did the same for mine.

"Let's get inside. I'm sure this isn't the kinda holiday you were expecting…but I can think of plenty things better than yammering on in this cold fucking truck."

I laughed. Maybe it was because I was so tired my emotions were confused, twisted. The man we'd killed and hidden seemed like a million surreal miles away. Whatever it was, I reached for his arm with my hands and gave him a good squeeze.

God, he felt good. Strong. Right.

In a heartbeat, we left the truck and I followed him inside. He made sure to keep his jacket sealed up tight around his cut and the shirt underneath. There were still a few obvious droplets of blood that had to be cleaned.

Upstairs, Stinger's place was a lot cozier than I expected. His unit had a little fireplace, and paintings of thick forests and men on motorcycles hung on his walls. He left me on the big leather couch and went into the kitchen, probably brewing up something to warm us up.

I expected coffee, tea, maybe even a cup of cocoa. Somewhere between the bathroom and the kitchen, he lost his coat and stripped off everything except his jeans. I gawked like a fool when he came into the room shirtless, carrying a long tray full of snacks, coffee cups, and a couple tall glass bottles.

Jack and Bailey's. I should've known a man like him would need more fire to heat his belly than plain black morning brew.

Damn, and *what* a belly. Stinger looked at me and smiled when he saw me studying his skin. His flesh was like a canvass, heavily tattooed from his tight packed abs to his muscular back.

I'd seen other guys at the clubhouse walking around on wild nights, sporting the same big grinning devil, the club's logo, just like the one on Sting's chest. But everything around it was unique, long pitchforks and whips going up his arms; sleek, sharp loops with spikes that might've been the ends of maces or scorpion's tails.

He pushed my coffee over to me with a smile, holding up both liquor bottles. I pushed my finger against the Bailey's. Anything that was sweet and good for taking the edge off was fine by me.

Then again, staring at him was taking me somewhere long before I sipped my Irish cream. Shit, my memory wasn't the only thing returning after all these months. Being in the same room with him, this close and blissfully free from danger, meant the temptations I'd tried to bury were back too – back with a *vengeance.*

I tried to ignore them, focusing on the crackers and meat he'd brought out. It wasn't much, but it hit the spot after a long night dancing and dumping a bastard's body off in the woods.

Never thought I'd take something like this so easy. I guess remembering Dad's murder made me numb to it, or maybe it was just a sorta grim satisfaction at taking down one of his killers that helped smooth things over.

"You really like to play up the Stinger thing, huh?" I said. Maybe if I talked about his tattoos, I wouldn't look like such a freak

"That's my road name, baby. Real name's Lucas."

"Lucas." I rolled it on my tongue. It felt good.

"Yeah. Nobody called me Stinger 'til I was a prospect. I beat the shit out of this fuckstain who killed my sis with a belt before a brother put a bullet in his head."

I almost spat out my drink and coughed. *Holy shit.*

He snorted and looked down. "Sorry. Dunno where that came from. I've never told anybody shit about it. Moose is the only guy who knows because he was there."

"Wow." My fingers were shaking as I took another sip, trying to steady myself. "My dad died too. What am I saying?" I looked at him and smirked. "You and the other guys took care of his body. The Slingers were there when it happened. Their President beat Dad to death with a mug – a fucking mug. We couldn't fight back. They drugged us with something different than what they used on the club."

Sting nodded. I closed my eyes, pursing my lips.

"Whatever. I'm just glad there's been a little payback. *Finally.*"

"Right on," Stinger growled, his face tightening.

So much for Christmas. Normally, just thinking about the nightmare that caused my brain to blackout for months would've caused me to tear up. But here, on this couch with him, our eyes were locked together, too deep and intense to slip into sadness.

Why did the crazy look he gave me look so familiar?

Holy shit. I know those eyes. I see them staring back at me in the mirror every day, hard and full of hurt, tucked away so all the world's predators can't cause more pain.

Jesus. I should've figured it out months ago...

Stinger reached for me first while I was debating putting my hand on his knee. He jerked me close, just barely careful enough not to spill my coffee. I set it down and leaned into him, enjoying his warmth. God, his smell was even better with his bare skin on mine, surrounding me, sweat and strength and just a hint of motor oil.

"We've both put some serious shit behind us, baby," he said, his voice a low, comforting rumble. "And there's probably more ahead. There always fucking is. But you know what?"

I looked up, brushing my cheek on his stubble as I turned. His lips were coming painfully close, and they looked far too good to ignore much longer.

"What?"

"It doesn't matter. Not a damned bit. What's important is having you here so I can grab hold of your pretty head and tilt it at the now. I want you to see *me*, baby." He paused, tightening his grip. "You got any fucking clue what a maniac I've become all these weeks you've been away? I haven't been myself. Not by a fucking long shot. I can't use Jack or sluts or dropping fucks who deserve it to get you outta my head. You're still there, sweet and sexy as the day I met you, hooked in my skull deep. So fucking *deep*."

My breath hitched. He picked me up, twisting me around so I was in his lap. His fingers smoothed their way through my long black hair and took hold.

He wasn't asking anymore. He was taking what he burned for, every hard inch of him, and I was too wrapped up in want to resist.

Sting's muscles tensed, shaking a little as he held me, electrified with the same raw ache sifting through my skin.

"Can't fucking think straight when you're not around. No pleasure or pain's gonna change that because it doesn't exist. Fuck, I can't get the thought of you under me outta my skull, Alice. Just you and me. You, stripped naked, sweating, screaming my name, your pussy shaken to kingdom come while I bust nuts inside you, crazy like the animal I am..." His words melted in the red hot blood hissing to his head, overtaking his tongue.

"Stinger..."

Oh, God. His eyes bored right through me, feeding the fire smoldering inside me again and again and again. My pussy tingled and swelled like it was about to convulse without him even touching me, wet cream thickened between my legs – the same legs shaking when his hand reached between them.

He pushed his thumb deep, teasing my clit. So hard and sudden I gagged myself with my bottom lip, but I couldn't stop the moan when he cupped my mound and pulled me up. He lifted me higher onto him, the better for his savage lips to meet mine.

This kiss was deeper, a sticky, seething mess of emotion running to my core. Distance and serious fucking need had done a lot to make it better, or maybe it was so hot because I was finally *ready.*

Ready to let his storm flow through me. Ready to open to his power, his lust, his crazed hips slamming against mine and shooting pleasure I could barely fathom straight into my emptiness.

My lips parted, melting for him with a moan, and then his tongue pierced through them. He caught my bottom lip on his teeth and held me open, pushing his tongue deeper, making tight strokes in and out.

Evil, lewd, and addictive in every lick. Jesus!

My nipples were like stones. He reached up and tweaked one breast. Liquor and adrenaline quickened, making us both sweat, but lust was really steering the entire ship.

Our bodies twitched with the shifting flames, roasting from the inside out as our lips pulsed, waves of hot slick flesh as steady and inevitable as something that was always meant to be.

If we didn't need to come up for air, I was sure we would've kissed forever. I wasn't sure how long we sucked and tongued and kissed. He chewed my lip gently one more time before he broke, turning his head.

"Fuck!" Stinger growled, pulling on my hair to hold me in place. "I missed those hot ass lips just as bad as the rest of you – everything I haven't gotten a chance to taste. My tongue, my dick, my fucking brain are gonna blow if they don't meet you in a real carnal way, real fucking soon. You got me?"

I just stared, trying to focus on my breathing. "I think so."

"No, baby, we've been doing nothing but thinking since we met." His hands moved, wrapped around my waist, and hauled me up as he stood. He moved to my ass, clasped it tight, and pulled me to him.

If it felt good just laying in his lap, then being plush against his bare chest was divine, one step below the way I knew he'd make me feel if we both shed the rest of our clothes. I turned toward the little hallway nook leading to the bedroom before he clenched my ass again, pulling me back to his lightning gaze.

"I'm done with all that. I've wracked my head for months on end trying to figure out how I could forget, move on, or race to your doorstep and do what I should've done fucking months ago. Having your lips on mine and feeling up your sweet ass tells me what direction we're going." He paused, brushing his lips over mine one more time, teasing. "We're fucking today, Alice. You and me. I don't need to think anymore to figure shit out and be happy. I'm done with that shit because thinking doesn't solve shit. Not unless it comes with some real hard fucking…"

He kissed me again. Harder this time, aggressive, like he wanted to mark me.

The backs of my legs touched the couch and I started to tip, lost in the storm raging on my lips. I was so far beyond resisting him it wasn't even funny.

No, God no. Stinger was absolutely right about one thing: the time for thinking was over. This was all about feeling, sorting things out in a more primal ways beyond thoughts and words. I fell back and he held me by the shoulders, pushing his legs between mine.

Opening eagerly, I slid against him. Nothing could've prepared me for his bulge rubbing between my thighs. His ridge was hard – so fucking hard – and I swore our jeans were going to combust if we didn't get them off in the next thirty seconds

Growling, he hoisted me up, pulling me into his arms, completely off the floor. Sting carried me into the bedroom. Time blurred, lost in the nonstop thud of my heart.

Next thing I knew, he tossed me down on a firm mattress, tumbling down with me. His hand fisted another ponytail in my hair and his lips returned, kissing and biting and sucking, fucking me with his tongue.

He resumed his place between my legs, rubbing harder this time, rough friction coming until I bucked back.

So good. So natural. So intense.

I wanted those pants off so fucking bad, with nothing left between us, but I couldn't do it when he just kept going, dry humping me into submission. Each time I tried to reach down, he caught my hand and ripped it up, pinning it to the mattress. Whenever I opened my mouth to beg, he closed it with another kiss, stealing away my breath, my voice, my –

"We'll take this good and slow, baby. My terms. I've wanted you so bad for so fucking long...I want you to feel it too. I want you to come for me. Right here. Right now." He hissed, rocking his cock against me harder, higher, rougher. "Don't think. Turn your pretty head off. Let your pussy gush and burn and get ready for my dick. Go with it, Alice. Just shut the fuck up and come!"

Holy shit. He'd turned into a total wolf with one thing in his head. The fire in his eyes confirmed what I already knew: he was taking control, and this was going to go his way, the nasty way he'd always wanted it.

The part of my brain that always fought got pissed. But my body sure wasn't. I rippled once beneath him, unable to stop my ankles from wrapping around his legs, all the better to feel the friction he brushed against my pussy over and over.

I heard the bed creak before a long, jagged moan left my lips. Then he buried me in another one of those hellaciously good kisses, hammering his hips on mine, throwing me completely over the edge.

I reared up, wrapping my arms around his back, clawing at his bare skin. It only drove him on to dry hump me faster, fucking me straight through our jeans, catching my clit in each fiery stroke.

Coming never felt like this. My orgasm picked me up and slammed me back down again – or maybe that was his thrusts – shaking me from head to toe. I tensed up and spat pure fire, sucking at his tongue, trying to match his masculine growl with mine as he took me higher.

It was like he'd flipped a switch in my brain. Everything shut down except the insane need to keep this climax going. Everything except the savage desire to feel him inside me, splitting me open, reaching me as deep with his flesh as he'd already gotten with his soul.

When my legs finally stopped shaking around his waist, he took his lips off mine and let me have precious oxygen. He looked down at me, a little more softly than before, but the need was still there, angry and insistent as ever.

"Fuck, baby. You come just as good as I thought. Come on, little rocket. Let's get this shit off and really make you soar."

Perfect timing. I was spread out, trying to recover as he lifted my shirt over my head. He was even quicker with my bra, unclasping it and throwing it over his shoulder. I had just enough strength to lift my hips when he tugged on my jeans.

A low growl escaped his throat when he saw how wet I was. No contest. I was past drenched after what he'd done, and my pussy ached, ready to be taken after too many years a virgin.

I waited for him to rise up and rip off his pants, but he surprised me instead. His fingers hooked near my hips, helping off my panties with some assistance from his teeth. They skidded down my legs and I kicked them away, muscles twitching when I realized I was bare, with nothing left between us.

Stinger knew an offering when he saw it. He let out a sharp breath and started kissing his way back up, climbing higher, brushing his stubble across my thighs. Goosebumps erupted all over my skin.

My fingers fastened on his head tight, nails digging near his neck. I wasn't sure about this, but he wasn't stopping. He shot me one more ferocious look before burying his face between my thighs, inhaling my scent like it was sweet cinnamon.

"Fuck!" He growled the word against my pussy just before he started to lick.

My hips rolled with his tongue. I lost a little more of my mind. He lapped my cream and rode straight up, exploring my folds, opening me gradually with steady, rhythmic strokes.

I never imagined having a man's mouth there could feel so good.

No, *amazing* was a better word, the only word that applied to this man. And when he started to tongue my clit, I knew he was the only man I'd ever allow there, the only one who'd ever taste and suck and fuck this pussy.

Hot waves pulsed through my body. Muscles I barely knew I had tightened in my belly, tuned to his licks, trying to keep up as his tongue glided through my wetness faster and faster.

My thighs squirmed. Stinger's strong hands landed on them, pressing them to the mattress, holding me open until I –

"Oh. Fuck!"

It started in my center and spread, a ball of pure lightning swelling around my womb. I came hard, losing myself in the circular rhythm he licked around my clit, perfectly sucked between his teeth. I didn't think I'd come like this so soon, but every touch from Sting told me I had a lot to learn, and my flesh was a willing student.

My whole body erupted. My fingernails clawed at his head and fingered the powerful muscles on his neck, rolling with me, quick and smooth as he licked through my crescendo

Blood rushed to my head, so hot and hard I thought I was going to pass out. Then I felt him shifting between my legs, raising up, slowly running his hands over my body. His tongue on one nipple helped me regain my senses.

"Fucking shit. I could lay down and lick these tits all day, baby. They're perfect."

The flush circling my neck glowed brighter. Being naked and completely bared to him didn't hit me until now, when he touched my body freely and talked about it like he was discussing a sexy new ride.

"Only trouble is," he said, pausing to sweep his tongue across the other bud, melting me all over again. "This greedy fucking dick in my pants won't let me. Not right now. I gotta fuck."

He smiled, watching me squirm as he pulled away, moving his hands to his belt and looking at me intently. "You ready for me, Alice? I'm asking outta courtesy, but we both know I'd better hear a fucking yes."

I looked at him for a good long second. We were about to fuck good and proper, and I knew there was no turning back.

Jesus, *yes*. I was ready two months ago, when I was too screwed up to know any better.

I nodded, moaning when he laid one hand on my breast, and slid my bare legs salaciously around his waist. That was all the encouragement he needed. He worked off his belt and pushed his jeans down, kicking them off behind him, the same as his boxers a second later.

His cock was just like the rest of him. Just as big, just as hard, just as mean, throbbing in his hand. Angry, ready, and delayed for too damned long.

I panted and shivered as I spread my legs. "Come fuck me, Sting. I need you deep inside me. Lucas…"

His eyes widened when I said his real name. I swore his cock twitched in his hand, but I didn't have enough experience with them yet to know a hundred percent.

Not for long, I thought, running my tongue over my lips. *Goodbye, virgin girl.*

Hello, lover…old lady…whatever he wants me to be…

He pumped his cock in his hand one more time and then reached to the nightstand. I watched his chest rise and fall, heavy breaths fuming anticipation. He ripped open a condom packet and rolled it down his length.

"There's only one thing better than finally being here after waiting fucking forever," he said, sliding his full length up and down my entrance, another rough tease that tensed my whole body.

"Yeah?" I hooked my legs around his, loving his muscular contrast.

"Yeah, claiming this pussy as mine. After tonight, baby, nobody else's cock is ever going in you as long as you're alive on this earth. There won't be any time for that shit even if I allowed it – and you know I fucking *won't.*" His word slurred in a growl, sending a shudder up my spine. "Because we're gonna be so damned busy fucking there won't be time for anyone or anything. I'm gonna fuck you 'til your sweet cunt fits me like a glove, so fucking perfect you won't even think about showing it to any other fuck. Nobody but me. I fucking own this now."

He rocked forward, stroking my clit with his erection. I was completely frozen. Hell, was it possible to be frozen in pure fire?

Right then, it was. It absolutely fucking was, and I twitched into mush each time he slid his length over me, making me want it worse than anything.

What did I have to do? Bite him, beg him, rake my nails across his gorgeous tattooed back?

I was about to try it all when his hips shifted. Subtle at first, but then determined, aiming perfectly for the heat he craved.

It happened fast.

His huge erection found my virgin slit and pushed in, firm and steady, somewhere between quick and desperate, but definitely passionate. Stinger grunted and rolled his hips, thrusting deep, opening me completely.

For a second, my walls stretched, struggling to adjust to his girth. A rough itch burned my brain when something soft tore near my entrance, and then vanished just as quickly, buried in the greater desire to feel him fill me full.

"Ah! God dammit." He held his cock in me, rooting deep. "Even fucking tighter than I imagined. You got a virgin's pussy, girl. Not a single doubt about it."

I couldn't muster the words to tell him he was right, and now I was an ex-virgin by five seconds. Not like this. It didn't matter anyway because he started to thrust, banishing my chances to think about anything except how good his cock felt inside me.

He planted his hands next to my head, one on each side. A perfect view for watching his tattooed muscles ripple as he found his rhythm, working in and out, quickening his pace when he saw I could take it.

Sting leaned down and buried me in another kiss. I moaned into his mouth, pure pleasure sputtering out when he hit my clit. Heavy, powerful thrusts rocked my entire body. Instinct tightened my legs around him, fixed to his body, determined to ride all the way to explosive ecstasy.

My hands reached up high and caught his neck. I scratched him the harder he fucked me, only loosening up in a half-conscious moment when I feared I'd draw blood.

"Fuck, baby. Fuck!" he grunted, never stopping his thrusts. "You can claw me as hard as you want. Just fucking come with me when I bust. I wanna see how tight that pink perfection gets when it's wrapped around my dick."

Filthy suggestion. Filthy man. And what did that make me while I sweated and whimpered and thrashed beneath him, steam kissing my ears every time he grunted his pleasure?

No, the forgetful virgin bitch was dead. I was someone different now, too full of this beautiful man to go back to being the same old Alice.

Stinger moved his hips, filling me harder, faster, growling a little more each time he drove deep. Coming wasn't far behind, and I smiled when I realized it was going to work. We were going to come together, our flesh singing, and it was going to be wonderful.

The devil on his hard chest rocked and grinned above me as he fucked harder. Before the very end, he pistoned so fast I thought the bed would break. The wooden mattress creaked and squealed, springs screaming with us.

My arms and legs both burned numb as I held on tight. Muscles twitched, pulling like the bedsprings beneath our weight, and convulsed in one go.

I threw my head back and screamed. Stinger's lips formed a feral grin, and then his voice buried my girlish vocals in hard, masculine thunder.

He erupted. Even through the latex, I swore I could feel the heat. His cock spasmed as I clenched and pulsed around him. Halfway through, I couldn't tell us apart. Our heartbeats twitched and pumped synchronized into one.

Each muscle exploded like dynamite, smoothed, and then burst again. Pleasure wracked my body. Stinger's weight pinned me down, making little movements as his cock jerked inside me, expelling his hot thick come.

When it was over, I slumped, arms and legs spread out. Dead to the world after a ravaging like that. Stinger smiled at me as he pulled out, drawing off the condom and tossing it in a nearby bin. His dimples were really adorable when I could sit back and enjoy them without wanting to fuck him stupid.

"Best fuck in years," he said. "Can't get over how fucking tight you are, baby. It's like you've been saving that pussy just for me."

I smiled, finding my place in his arms. It was a little cold without a blanket, but it made his warmth stand out even more. I rested on his chest, chin tilted up in my hands, staring him in the eyes.

"That's because you're my first." There. I let it out.

Not much use in keeping secrets from a man with serious carnal knowledge. Stinger blinked and did a double take. He sat up, running on hand across my cheek.

"Wait, are you fucking with me?" He watched me shake my head. "Christ! I wouldn't believe it if I didn't feel it on my dick. That shit doesn't lie…"

"You're not upset?"

He laughed. "Okay, now I know you're fucking kidding. You being a virgin's just the cherry on top of this perfect fucking sundae I could eat all day."

His hands moved, tweaking one nipple on their way down, pulling at my thighs. One went between my legs and stopped. He found my clit and rubbed. God, he was insatiable.

At least spilling the big secret meant good things to come – and I knew they'd be coming hard.

"Now, this is really gonna be the only dick you get to have," he growled. "Fuck. Good thing you chose wisely."

"Yeah, and I'm going to enjoy it," I purred.

It was my turn to reach for him. I grabbed his dick, half-hard after fucking, and gave it a good squeeze. It was new and exciting. I'd learn how to handle him in time, but I already loved the way he tensed and pulsed in my hand.

"Easy, baby. We got plenty of time for this. All you gotta worry about for the next forty-eight hours is me between your legs."

"Better than disappointing you with something shitty," I said, rolling down his length. He was already getting hard again in my fingers. "I mean, it's Christmas. I'd have gotten you something if I knew you were coming..."

He sliced a hand through the air. "Forget it. All I need – fuck, all I ever wanted – is right fucking here. Just you and a bottle of Jack for later. You know I haven't been able to drink that shit in months 'til today? I thought it was because of the fucking poison, but now I think it was because something else was missing..."

Sly, sly bastard. But at least he was mine. I grinned and threw my lips into his.

I knew pure hell was coming when our forty-eight hours were up. He'd have to take me to the clubhouse, explain what had happened to Blaze. And I'd have to deal with figuring out how to make a life here. I had to find a job here sooner or later, and I doubted Sting would let me keep stripping for cash, even if I wanted to.

I didn't.

The only man I wanted to see me naked was right here, hands on my ass, pulling my naked belly against his cock. A little obvious, yeah, but I really didn't give a shit.

His kiss, his sex, his body salvaged my Christmas. And soon, I knew he'd be salvaging the insane wreck that was my whole fucking life.

VIII: Storm Clouds (Stinger)

It was the best fucking Christmas of my life. Serious emphasis on the *fucking* part. We must've done some lasting damage to the old bed I bought off Moose after moving into this place. Damned good thing my twisted balls from a couple months ago were fully healed.

That mattress screamed every waking minute when I wasn't nestled up with her, sleeping off the last two shitty months. Fuck, going to sleep with Alice in my arms, nose over her sweet hair, was almost as incredible as fucking her.

But really, nothing compared to having my way between her legs. When she told me she was a virgin, I totally flipped my shit.

It had been years since I'd taken one, and never any I cared about before her. Staking my claim to her body felt twice as intense as I'd expected when I realized I truly had the only dick that was *ever* gonna be inside her. And I was damned set on keeping it that way.

The day passed in the happiest fucking blur of my entire life.

Before I knew it, it was nighttime again, and I had her up on all fours. Her ass bobbed against me as I hammered her, making those soft, sweet little moans each time my cock sank deep. I'd lost three loads in those condoms before, and I still almost lost another sooner than I liked.

Growling, I grabbed her ass, helping steady her in the new position. She fucking needed it too when I took her right hand and twisted it between her legs, close to where my cock was pistoning in and out.

"Play with your clit, baby. Need to get you used to having no shame when you're coming with me. When we're naked, you're gonna be an open fucking book, and I'll be the man to write it."

She resisted at first. That only made me grin and pound into her harder, making long, teasing strokes, just enough to take her pussy to the fiery brink.

"Stinger…please…Lucas…"

The girl was delirious. Shit, so was I when she said that name. Alice became the only woman who'd said it for years. I hadn't even told my regular sluts because they were nothing but a fuck, something to take care of the ache in my balls.

Shit was so different, so strange, and so fucking *good* with Alice I barely knew where to begin. Thank fuck my cock did, though.

I held it in her, tilting my hips gently, rocking near her womb with my swollen tip. My hands were on her ass and I wouldn't let her move it too much, teasing her 'til she gave me what I wanted. I had to make her lose control anyway I could, make her shudder and come like no tomorrow, showing me she was really ready to take her place as my old lady.

My old lady. Holy fucking shit!

My balls tightened again, making it harder than hell not to start pounding 'til I busted my nut. I'd deal with Blaze and the brothers soon. Prez was gonna be pissed about all this shit – and rightfully so – but it'd blow over one way or another. And when it did, I was gonna claim her for myself the same way Blaze and Tank took their girls.

By next Christmas, she was gonna be in a nicer bed, wearing a shiny new leather jacket with my brand while I fucked her. Her skin was a smooth, open canvass too – surprising for an artsy chick. No tattoos except for a couple sleek black doves in flight at the base of her neck.

If they wanted to carry PROPERTY OF STINGER to the high ass heavens, that was fine with me. Just as long as I got to see it when I had her on her hands and knees like this, filled with my cock, shivering with need.

"Just play with your clit, girl. No fooling. You know how." The last words I growled.

She wasn't the only one starting to burn with need from this fucking tease. I waited another ten agonizing seconds, and then I reached up and gave her little ass a good whack.

She gasped. Shook. God damn if her hand didn't start to make circles beneath my dick, splaying through her folds, fingers finding her nub and rubbing it like I told her.

Good girl. I grinned, excited to do the dirty work for her next time as a reward. That little scream she made when I smacked her ass – there was way more there than throaty surprise.

"Is this how you like it, baby?" I asked, reaching up to fist her hair, slowly anchoring my dick into her soft velvet again, rubbing close to her cervix. "Something sharp to make you behave?"

She gasped again, letting out a loud moan, slamming her hips into mine now that I finally let her. I didn't need to hear her say *yes*. It was all in the way she moved.

"You like it when it stings, don't you?"

"Yeah!" She hissed, pursing her lips. "I like *your* Sting."

That's my fucking name, I thought with a grin. *Don't wear it out 'til I've fucked your pussy senseless.*

Fuck. As if this day, this girl, couldn't get any better…

I rode her hard, throttling my pubic bone to her ass, balls swinging so hard they slapped her clit and her fingers each time I drove deep. She started coming after another minute – about how long I expected – but I wasn't fucking stopping.

I was gonna melt her all the way before I gave it up. My palms stung each little ass cheek several more times. Alice *screamed*, her tight body seizing up in breathless, orgasmic nirvana.

For a virgin, she was a fucking incredible lay. Or maybe it was because she was right for me, perfect from head to toe to heart in every way I'd ever imagined.

Somehow, she kept swinging her ass perfectly, swallowing my cock, her pussy gushing all around me.

Fuck! Even I couldn't keep it up forever with her sweet cunt going all geyser around my dick. I threw myself forward, bracing my hands against the bed, pinning her ass to the mattress.

I came fucking hard, holding her down, amazed at how good it felt to pump my come inside her, despite the stupid fucking condom. I'd have her see Em about that shit soon. For now, I lost my load, growling the entire time, throbbing in her pussy as my nuts blasted thick ropes into rubber.

When it was all over and I had her in my arms again, she brushed her cheek against my stubble. Sexy and strangely teasing, even when we weren't fucking. I wouldn't let her go so easily without another kiss, but she flicked her tongue against mine first.

God damn! This girl...she's gonna kill me, lay me out cold with her lust. I wondered if any dude had ever died from fucking too many times in a row.

"Again, baby?" I said, wondering if I'd misread the signals so soon. No fucking way. I never misunderstood a horny woman, especially when she was as hot as Alice, naked and pressed up against me. "What the fuck's gotten into you?"

"What you said earlier about thinking…you're right. I don't want to spend the night crying over my dead father or your sister or how the Slingers are still coming for our throats."

Anger shot through me. "You're fucking wrong about that last part. They're not getting anywhere near your pretty ass. I promise."

I reached for her hand and grabbed it as tight as I could. She smiled, somewhat reassured. Had a feeling there was still some doubt.

Hell, how could I blame her? She'd been around to see how Em nearly got wrecked several times over before her and Tank caught a break. If she knew about Blaze and Saffron, or Maverick and June…fuck.

I couldn't guarantee beyond all doubts and demons that I was gonna be able to keep her safe. If she was with me right now, like this, then she understood what she was getting into and accepted the risk.

After Beth, I was sure as fuck gonna try to keep her whole, keep her mine, even if the odds were zero because the Slingers had something up their sleeves we couldn't imagine. I'd put my life on the line a thousand times over for her, just a few more times than the vow I made to my brothers by wearing the Devils patch.

Tomorrow, when the Christmas cheer turned into the lonely deep freeze and we headed back to the clubhouse, I was gonna lay it all out for Blaze. He'd want to mop this shit up just as badly as I did. These assholes weren't just threatening her, but the club too, Alice's biz intertwined with club business.

I shook my head, mulling it all over. She must've sensed me rattling my brain. Before I knew it, my dick was in her hand, and she was kissing a trail down my stomach.

I was hard again in an instant. Her sweet, soft lips dipped over my head, eager and unsure and really fucking *hot.* It'd take her some serious practice to get up to the mad dick sucking skills I'd enjoyed with different sluts over the years.

Not that I gave a shit. Training her in was the fun part. I grinned, fisting her hair, one hand on her cheek, gently guiding her up and down my shaft. Just having her tongue wrapped around my flesh was enough.

Fuck. Yeah.

I grunted, and then growled a little more when her tongue hit that sweet spot underneath my crown, making my dick jerk in her mouth.

Shit, training or no training, the girl had a damned good idea what to do. I let her go all the way, running on instinct. She quickened her licks, circling me faster and faster, and then sucking me deep as the tension in her hair wound tighter. My hips rocked deep in the mattress, all I could do to keep from slamming my cock down her throat when I came.

Pure lightning shot outta me, sizzling everything in its fucking wake. She swallowed it like a good girl too. Guess she must've figured out there'd be rewards for that later. Smart.

I licked my lips, blinking back the fire still hurtling through my skull. Before the night was through, I was gonna eat her sweet pussy 'til she climbed the wall, however many times it took for us to both collapse in the post-Christmas gloom.

I got up to get some Jack, some water, and a couple quick sandwiches. We ate and talked but mostly just enjoyed each other. I wished like hell I could've spent days like this, just her and I, naked in bed without any interference.

Too bad the shit storm was coming, like a big ass dragon finally coming into view after breathing smoke down our necks for days. Before it coughed its fire, I was gonna enjoy the rest of the night. With Alice here, I wasn't even worried about going to sleep without my system pumped full of whiskey.

Eighteen fucking years. That's how long Beth's ghost tormented me, and now my sister was slipping away, fading into the mist with the rest of that hellish night.

I had my second chance with Alice. Not just to save her, but to finish building my life. I was a mile from sweet freedom and I couldn't slow down now.

Alice ran her little hand over my cheek, and I pushed into it, turning my brain to sex only. The kisses came, fast and hot, an appetizer for the banquet of tits and pussy and more hard fucking to follow. I stopped thinking about anything except how much I was gonna make her come.

We woke up at the ass crack of dawn, surprisingly rested for fucking long into the night. We snagged some breakfast at a diner in town and then headed to the clubhouse. Easily beat every brother there who'd gone home for Christmas.

I thought the place was empty 'til I saw Roller, buck naked in all his lean, tattooed glory. The young brother jumped halfway to the ceiling when he saw me, thinking he was alone, and then got another shock when he saw Alice with me.

"Shit, Veep! Didn't know you were coming back here...Prez and the others aren't due 'til later."

I nodded, taking my eyes off him as he stepped behind the bar, hiding his bare ass. Alice suppressed a laugh. God damn it was good to hear her do that after all this shit.

"Relax, brother. We're just here early to hang and wait. No need to interrupt anything with the whores for us."

"You sure about that?" He jerked his head toward my girl, flicking his tongue against his lip ring. "Sure looks like some serious fucking business for the club to me. You want me to call Blaze now?"

"You'll get all the details later," I said, shaking my head and curling an arm around Alice's waist. "No need to be worried, brother. I got this."

"If you say so, Veep." Roller shrugged and grabbed a bottle of Jack before heading to his room.

A few minutes later, I heard him strumming his guitar. That surprised me. Guess he'd gotten his fill of pussy the night before.

I knew I hadn't, despite how many times we'd fucked. Every time I touched her, my cock started to get hard, a total fucking slave to this girl. I moved in for a kiss when Alice pushed gently on my chest.

"Come on, Sting. There's plenty of time for that later. We'd better get ready to do what we came here for…"

I grunted, stuffing an unhappy growl as my dick wilted. The girl was right. She'd gone through everything again at the diner: the Slingers' sick obsession with finding the map her dad left, the threats, the way Mickey was really killed. I'd seen the damned map months ago, before Blaze stuffed it in his office.

The fucks with the pistols on their jackets were after terror. Control. If they got the routes, the whole damned club and plenty more were gonna find their asses raided during runs. The Slingers were too small to be players in shipping, so they hit and ran like scavengers instead. And it didn't make the bastards any less dangerous.

They'd be able to blackmail tolls as high as they wanted, or make mad money smashing the competition with the dirtiest bids imaginable. Sometimes, information was more lucrative in this biz than black market goods.

We hung around and watched crappy movies on the big TV above the bar. Felt good just to take a load off and get some water into my system. Alice started to get tired. She had her head resting on my shoulder, stirring up my sandman too.

I was halfway dozing off myself at the bar with Roller's distant strumming floating through the clubhouse when the door flew open. Saffron came in laughing, Blaze behind her. Alice jerked up and so did I, stiffening on our bar stools, facing them before they saw us.

Saffron stopped in mid-laugh, locking eyes with me first. "Oh…shit."

"What, baby?" Blaze pushed past her and froze.

When he saw Alice, his eyes lit up like a hound sensing a nearby rabbit, and then he dashed across the room. My girl screamed, barely giving him enough space as he pinned me down, both his fists tight on my cut.

"You fucking asshole!" he roared. "How many fucking times do I have to tell you to leave the girl alone? What the fuck's she doing back here? She's not our club's problem and she sure as shit isn't yours!"

Saffron and Alice both tugged at his arms, trying to get him off me, but he had a tight lock. I didn't fight back. Hurricane Blaze had to burn itself out, and I'd only making it worse by clocking the Prez in his hotheaded jaw, however tempting it was.

"Hold it, Prez! Just fucking hold it. You gotta give me a chance to explain this shit for once –" His hand flew up and caught my throat.

I wasn't a small dude, but Blaze had long fingers, and he got just enough of a hold to choke my ass. Fuck.

"I'm done listening to your excuses! I ought to have your fucking VP patch for this. You defied a direct order, asshole – on Christmas too! Fuck, is there anything you won't do to piss in my face?" Growling, he jabbed a finger at my chest, feeling for my patch.

That fucking did it. No way was he taking shit without a vote and all the facts.

I bolted up like lightning, slamming my chest into his. Saffron and Alice were both screaming, but they kept their distance, afraid to get between us. Roller was back in the corner with some jeans on, his guitar in hand, wide-eyed and stunned as he watched the two senior officers in the club go at it.

"Do it. Strip my fucking patch and demote me to a grunt, Prez. I don't give a shit." I shook my head so hard his hand slipped off my throat, and I stared into his very pissed off eyes, his short spiky hair standing on end. "Before you do that, we need to call church. Alice would've been fucking dead right now or worse if I hadn't taken a ride to Idaho last night and did what I did."

"Idaho? Fuck!" Blaze ripped himself away from me, stretching a hand over his face.

Saffron walked over and laid her hands on his shoulders, trying to calm him down. He broke her grip rudely, stretching his face in one long stroke with his hand.

"Let me see if I get this straight…you not only fucked away what I told you and brought this girl back here – probably the last fucking place in the world she wants to be – but you went into Grizzlies territory without the club's approval?" He shook his head in disbelief, his whole body shaking. "Dumbass! Motherfucker! If anybody wearing their patch spotted your ass, they're gonna think you were spying, and then it's my ass on the line too.

Maybe the whole fucking club's if Fang decides to talk to Throttle!"

He started to walk forward, ready to go back to choking me or maybe using his fists this time. Alice stepped between us before I could grab her.

"That's not true! Nobody saw him. I've been working at a Grizzlies club for months and he only stopped outside before he came to my house. The other girls were off shift when he pulled up and asked them about me – they wouldn't tell the Grizzlies shit. It was a miracle he came when he did." She was on fire, freakishly brave.

I was fucking impressed.

Blaze snorted. Alice didn't look away from his crazy eyes even once.

"Just listen. I came back with him because I *wanted* to. He didn't force me to do anything. And Stinger's telling you the truth, Blaze, whether you want to believe it or not. The men who ambushed me and tried to kill me at home are after you guys. They're after the crap you took from my dad's truck when the Rams still had it. The Rams and Slingers had some kinda falling out...I'm not sure. They were there the night it all went down, when they killed my Dad and took me prisoner. The Rams wouldn't turn it over...and now it's in your hands. You've got to –"

Blaze cut her off, turning away. He wasn't the only one looking pissed. His old lady looked like she was about to lay into his ass, but he walked right past her.

"Fuck this shit. I'll hear the rest later," he growled, striding toward his office.

He was almost to the door when he turned back and pointed at Alice and me. "Church in one hour. You better lay all this shit out then, and you'd better do it nice and neat. Roller, make sure the other brothers get here now. Tell them it's serious."

Blaze disappeared into his office and slammed the door in behind him. Saffron sighed angrily and walked off. Alice turned to me, rubbing my neck, and I slowly eased outta her grip.

"I appreciate you saving my ass and all," I said. "But that was fucking crazy, girl. Don't ever let me catch you getting between Blaze and I again when he's like this. I know how to deal with the Prez."

"Somebody had to do something!" Saffron yelled from the bar. "I'm supposed to marry that man in a month and I still haven't figured out how to stop him when he goes all raging bull."

I couldn't help being bowed up for a while afterward, pissed and worried. But I let it go. Alice really had done me a solid – fucked up as it was – but I swore she was never gonna put herself between me and club shit again.

I didn't care if Blaze wanted my patch or my left nut. Keeping the club whole and my girl safe was all that mattered, and laying things out in the next hour damned well better do that.

We were all gathered around the table, all eight brothers. Blaze kept giving me his patented evil eye.

Whatever. I already owned up to this shit and took full responsibility for it. Even the Prez admitted the club would've been a lot worse off if those assholes killed Alice and we hadn't gotten the head's up.

"All right. We know where we stand, brothers," Blaze said, angrily twirling his gavel. "The Slingers are serious fuckers. Deadly serious."

"That's right," Moose chimed in. "They're the best support club the Grizzlies have got, the imperial guard of their little empire out west. We tangled with them in Dakota in the old days. Mean motherfuckers. Ruthless too. I'm surprised Fang doesn't have them fighting the cartels down south."

"They gotta be here playing rear guard. Or else the bastards have gone rogue without papa bear watching," I growled. "The Grizzlies aren't in the shape they used to be, and that means fewer profits for the Slingers. They've gone pirate like the fucking vultures they are, trying to make up their losses by hitting all the shipping they can, and Mickey held the key."

Blaze nodded, reluctantly agreeing with what I'd said. Then he reached over and picked up the old map book that held everything the Slingers were ready to kill us for.

"This, right here, is a buncha bullshit."

Tank snorted. "Everybody's in agreement about that, boss. Only thing that really matters is how we're gonna deal with –."

"Ten steps ahead of you," Blaze growled. "Listen, this club has seen some hard fucking times, especially this charter. We got our baptism in blood and fire from the very beginning when my bro Maverick was heading shit here. If we've learned anything from all the fucked up threats breathing down our necks the last few months, it's that we can handle 'em. The only times we get hurt, when fellow brothers get *hurt,*" he stopped, staring at Tank, who'd been wounded and patched up several times over in our dust ups with the Grizzlies.

"That happens when we play defense too long. The next few weeks are supposed to be a good time for me, but more importantly, for all the brothers around this table. We can't go down to Reno if we're hovering around, waiting them to hit our winter shipments or raid the clubhouse for this damned map. We can't wait. Not again. Can't sit around with our thumbs up our asses just waiting for them to strike. What I'm saying is, we need to hit them first, and put their asses straight into the ground."

I stared at him intently. Blaze had every right to be pissed that his wedding was about to get derailed, but I seriously wondered if it was fogging his head. Chasing down the Slingers on offense seemed crazy, especially when these bastards had a history of prowling around like panthers, springing out when their enemies least suspected it.

I wasn't alone. The other brothers were looking at him like he'd flipped his lid.

"What?" Blaze looked around the room and then his lips curled in a sarcastic smile. "Figured I'd get some resistance here. Fuck it, I don't give a shit. You all know it's the right thing after what we've seen before – all the brothers and the women who've gotten hurt. Tank. Smokey. Stone. Emma. *Saffron.*"

He clenched his jaw on the last one. Yeah, he was definitely gonna fight like hell for any excuse not to delay the marriage.

"It's not that simple, boss," Tank said. "Our intel isn't great over in Grizzlies country. With the Slingers? It's complete shit. These assholes are phantoms. Best thing we got on our side is numbers, and if we split up going after 'em, we're bound to get taken down piece by piece. They're not the kind to take any prisoners neither. You know what they did to Alice and her pop…"

"That's right," I said coldly, staring Blaze right in his eyes, both glowing like hot coals in his head. "We need to put this to a vote, Prez. Playing defense isn't ideal and it opens us to a lotta shit. I get that. But going after these fuckers and then rushing our asses to Nevada, if we're lucky enough to wipe them in time?"

I stopped just short of saying it was fucking *loco.* Blaze got the message. He looked away, fists so tight on the table they were turning white.

"All right, dammit!" His gavel slapped wood. "We'll start with Sting and Tank because they're leading the fight against common sense here today."

"Nay," I said immediately. Tank was right behind me too, pounding the table with one fist when he said the same thing.

Down the line it went, slow and uncertain. The only other Aye was Roller, who'd gotten his taste of adrenaline running weapons out west just a few months ago. The dude was probably still on a fucking high rather than any genuine need to kiss the Prez's ass.

"Fuck." The gavel hit the table harder. "The nays have it. You guys got any other fucking business before I go drown this sorry ass show in Jack, or what?"

Nobody said a word. Blaze adjourned the meeting and stormed off, leaving the rest of us staring quietly at each other before brothers began to shuffle out. He'd taken it about like I expected.

Typical Blaze. Hell, typical for most MC Presidents I'd served under. Democracy was a cruel bitch to the man at the top, but it made the best decisions – the kind that prevented real rifts between brothers.

I walked off to my old room, where Alice was holed up. When I passed the bar, I heard Blaze whispering to a sobbing Saffron, reassuring her.

"I don't give a shit what the bros decide. Nobody's gonna delay us getting hitched, baby, do you hear me? I'll hunt those fucks down myself and skin 'em with my own bare hands." Blaze said, holding her as they pushed their way into the storage room behind the bar.

Great. Competition among the brothers who wanted to kill the Slingers was heating up.

I wanted first dibs, but I couldn't blame the Prez for being right behind me. No brother in their right mind would. Blaze was a fuck sometimes, no two ways about it, but anyone who'd put their brand on a girl would do the same damned thing.

Speaking of brand...when shit settled down a little, I had to claim Alice right. I'd get my brand on her, loud and proud, screaming to the whole world that she was *my* property. Mine alone. Maybe then I'd finally feel some sanity flow back into my head after that girl shook everything to pieces.

I found her on the crappy old bed where I'd laid with her the first time, right after we brought her home from the Rams. She looked up when I came in.

"What's going on? Are the guys really pissed?"

"Not at you. They understand, and you're welcome to stay under my protection." She nodded, and I watched closely for any signs of reluctance, regret, anything that might darken the fucking heaven we'd enjoyed last night.

Nothing. Just how I wanted it.

"I still can't believe this happened...it hurts that I had to tell them anything to save myself." She looked up. Her lip quivered once before she bit it, hiding the turmoil rushing through her like a whirlwind.

No time for this shit. No time to be sad. The goddamned Slingers had already done plenty of damage, and more was bound to come in the days ahead, but I'd be fucked if I let them screw with her head, her heart.

"I got something for you," I said, rounding past her to the old dresser.

I pulled out the sketchbook and pushed it into her arms. "Something we found in your old man's stuff, along with the shit causing all this fucking trouble."

She looked up, her eyes wide. I smiled. "Go ahead. It's safe. Those fucks will want nothing to do with this. You will."

I sat next to her, throwing a possessive arm over her shoulders, watching as she flipped through the pages. Her stare was dull at first, and I wondered if I'd fucked something up.

But then her fingers caressed the fantasy shit, especially the sketch of the mad-eyed warrior with the girl at his feet, his sword raised up to the sky. Badass.

"Well?" I asked, impatient to see what the hell she had to say.

"I'd forgotten this stuff. Mostly. All the crap that happened before Dad was killed…must've been a year since I'd done any art. I had a mental block for a long time. Couldn't bring pen or charcoal to paper. I just carried these around in my bag, hoping it'd come back."

"It's not too late, baby. You wanna take this shit to the fucking moon, I'll help you. The clubhouse could use some dressing up. If you want me to talk to Blaze, just say the word, and I'll get a space for you to throw something together. If it's half as good as the shit in that pad, we won't be the only ones paying you."

She shook her head and set it aside. "No. The mood's all wrong…I can't just create when I don't feel it first.

That stuff's all in the past, Sting. I'm not an artist. I never really was."

Bullshit. Her denial made me grab her by both arms and pull her onto my lap. She pushed against me and we both fell, slumping on the bed, with her on top.

"Bull-fucking-shit. I don't believe it, baby. That's just all the crap we've had to deal with talking. I've known dudes before with talent. It comes and goes, yeah, but they never leave it behind once they're bitten by the bug." She shook her pretty head, raven black hair waving, still denying it. "You're gonna get your muse back sooner or later, Alice. And when it comes, you fucking talk to me. 'Cause I'll milk that bitch for all she's worth 'til you never have to worry about doing some shit you hate for money ever again."

"Well…if it's any consolation, the stripper days are behind me. I don't think I could do it again, even if I tried."

I growled, moving my hands to her ass, beginning to rock gently. My cock sprang up, ready to go, throbbing like I hadn't gotten pussy for weeks instead of hours.

Fucking shit. This woman, this beautiful dark eyed babe, was gonna suck the life outta me, if I didn't go crazy when I wasn't deep inside her first. I ran my hand to my pocket, feeling for a condom and getting a little shock of relief when I found its bulge.

Thank fuck! I was worried I ran out.

Alice was getting into it now, twisting her hips, little gasps parting her lips each time I rocked against her clit. I started to undo her belt and get her pants off when she fell on top of me, sweet breath close to mine.

"Is this a good place?" she whispered. "Everybody's out in the bar, aren't they?"

"Don't worry about it. All the brothers have heard somebody else fucking. Shit, half the dudes have *seen* it too, wild nights you wouldn't imagine…"

Her dark brown eyes wavered, and then she ran a hand up my chest, sweeping dangerously close to my cock. *Crazy fucking tease!*

And, of course, I loved every second.

"Are you sure I'm going to keep up with you, Sting? You had to have had other women who were better than me…"

Fuck, fuck, fuck. Now, she was really teasing me, somewhere between a sexy joke and serious crazy talk.

My hands cupped her ass tighter and gave it a squeeze, pulling her into me, rocking my hips against hers. I did it hard and fast, ready to make her come in her jeans and panties like last night, even though I was dying to get inside her.

"Bullshit. The wildest, wettest baby girl I know is on top of me right now." Her hips rolled into mine and I grunted, feeling my eyeballs twitch. "Shit, baby. You wanna talk about how the past is in the past? Then I'm gonna tell you it's the same with me. I don't give a shit if I never see another pair of bare tits in this lifetime. You're the only one I want to see, taste, and fuck. You, Alice. Only you.

"You're mine, baby," I growled, jerking her ass up and down into me. "And I'm gonna lock your doubts up and throw away the fucking key when I get my brand on your sweet fucking skin."

That did it. She relaxed. I dove in, kissing her rough, growling as I did. Thunder worked its magic, and I felt her smile a little as I opened her up with my tongue, reaching deeper, owning my woman.

My hands went to work. I jerked off her clothes as we continued to kiss, lifting her legs when I needed, and then pulling away her top. Her bra popped, spilling her perfect tits, ripe and ready for my hands, my mouth, my teeth.

I dug outta my clothes underneath her. Knew she needed it just as bad as me when her hands jerked at my chest, helping me lose my cut, my shirt, and then my jeans. When we were both naked, I flipped her over with another growl, reigning in my rampant cock.

"Don't hold it, girl," I said, kissing my way down to her tits. "You scream as loud as you fucking want, just like when we were in the apartment last night. I'm gonna claim you good and proper soon…but let's drive it home right now. Scream for me, baby. I want my ears to echo with you coming all over me."

My teeth caught her rosy nipple right as my fingers caught the other. She jerked and squealed, grinding against my cock.

Holy fucking shit. I almost sank into her right then without even wrapping my dick up. Damned good reminder to send her off to Em later for some birth control, if I could stop myself from doing something fucking crazy just then.

God damn it was gonna be amazing to pump a baby into her someday. I pulled back at the last second, riding down her stomach. I grabbed her thighs and pulled them apart, loving how she whimpered.

I grinned when I saw it. She was fucking soaked, pussy pulsing and ready, aching with a fiery need I was ready to sate. Except, first, I was gonna see how hot I could make her burn.

My tongue went straight for her clit. Alice's scent, her taste, her sweet fucking skin…Christ, I was never gonna get enough of this woman. Her velvet was softer, ready to open deep since I'd taken her cherry.

I licked deep, tasting the tender flesh, parting her. She did that hot little dance beneath my hands, rolling her hips away from my face sometimes and then grinding into it, like her body wasn't sure if she wanted to throw herself at me or run because it was too much to take.

Fucked if I was gonna let her go anywhere except on my mouth.

"Stinger…" She moaned my name, nails beginning to dig in near my temples.

I rubbed my head against her hands. Didn't give a single fuck if she scratched me to shit. Hell, I welcomed it. Feeling her needle my skin meant I was doing my job, and I was working damned hard between her legs, alternating winding laps through her folds before lashing her clit.

Lips and teeth and tongue kept moving in a flurry. She was back against the headboard and I still wasn't stopping. I'd drive her up the goddamned wall if it made her come harder.

"Stinger!" Her breath hitched. "Oh, God. I'm fucking –"

Coming. And keep on doing it too, baby, I thought. *This pussy melts best on my mouth, and right now your clit's the best thing I've tasted.*

My tongue focused right on her little nub. I sucked and fucked it with my whole mouth; lips, tongue, and teeth, everything I could muster to send her flying off the edge.

It worked.

Fuck, it worked, and my ears hummed happy as she became a whimpering, screaming, spasming mess beneath me. I had to hold her down tighter, jamming her hips into the bed to keep her in place. My girl bucked back, shoving her pussy hard against my mouth, encouraging those rough, relentless licks she craved.

I didn't stop 'til she was breathless and limp. Watching that girl go off like fireworks was the second best thing to owning her heart. Sure, her pussy came first, surest way to claim her. But when I came up a minute later, kicking off my jeans and still tasting her glorious cream on my lips, I saw the total beauty in her deep brown eyes.

That wasn't just lust staring at me. I'd seen that shit a hundred times on every whore from here to Minnesota. No, this was fucking different, and the *love* there filled me with a special kinda fire, straight from my head down to my dick.

I fucking throbbed. I ached. It *hurt* when I wasn't inside her, and I wasn't wasting one more precious second. Tearing the condom with my teeth, I leaned back on my hips and rolled it on, leaking pre-come all over before I got it secured.

Alice shuddered. Her right hand curled between her thighs as she spread wider for me, toying with the clit I'd just sucked, calling me home.

Sweet merciful Jesus. Sweet fucking Satan.

I reared up, throw my hands on the headboard, and drove my hips into hers, finding the mark.

"Fuck me!" she hissed, a brighter shade of red painting up her skin. "I don't care where we are or who we're with…if it's just you and me, Sting, I want it…"

She was struggling, tripping all over her words, chasing shame as she came alive on my cock.

Good fucking girl. My girl.

I started to thrust hard, finding my pleasure, wondering what merciless god kept me away from this perfect pussy for all these years.

Her nails went for my ass. Alice's legs locked around mine. All the encouragement I needed to ride her harder, faster, slamming my dick as deep as it would go. She threw her head back in slow motion, sweat beading on her brow, and drew a deep breath.

Absolute fucking dynamite. The fierce, but feminine growl that hit me in the face rattled my bones. My hips went nuts, jackhammering into her, making sure to drag my trim hair across her clit when I pounded her deep.

She hit me from four directions. Ankles and nails dug into my skin and I snorted like a stallion, losing my fucking mind in the headlong rush to the fire waiting at the finish line.

"Fuck, baby! Don't stop coming, 'cause I'm gonna join you. Come on, firecracker." She oozed more pleasure when I called her that. "Make me blow to smithereens."

Whatever I said was like magic. Her sweet cunt clamped so tight around my cock it felt like the softest silk in the universe sucking me off.

Shit.

I buried myself balls deep and came, cursing and snarling like a motherfucker, pure molten fire shooting out my balls. It was one degree away from perfect – and only one because of the fucking condom – but I gave it up happy. Came so hard my body shook, pulsing like I'd been hit with lightning.

The bolt shot through me, all passion, straight through my girl. I grabbed her little ass halfway through and shook her up and down on my cock, jerking myself off with her sweet body.

Alice could barely open her eyes. She'd turned to stone, locked in the same endless orgasm as me, coming her beautiful brains out.

We both collapsed on the bed a couple minutes later. I ripped the condom off and tossed it in the trash, listening to brothers milling around down the hall outside.

Soon, we'd get dressed and I'd take her home, assuming Blaze wasn't gonna ride our asses about anything else today. Before that, I picked up her sketchpad and laid it on her bare tits, bringing her back to life with another long kiss.

"Sting? What's this?"

"That's me telling you to draw me something. I know, I know…" I held up one tattooed arm. "You haven't got your muse back *yet*. You will. Count on it."

She smiled, shaking her head in disbelief. The light in those dark eyes told me I'd really hit deep. I smiled back. She reached up and ran a light finger over one corner of my smile.

"Whenever you do, baby, I wanna see it. We'll find out real fast you've got life left in those fingers." I reached for her hand and squeezed. "And I'm not just talking about how good they make me feel when they're wrapped around my dick."

Alice laughed. Music to my ears – and they needed it too after nearly being lit on fire while we fucked.

Maybe hell was coming tomorrow if the Slingers caught up to us. Some fuck could put a bullet in my head if I was really unlucky, and I was ready for that. But today, it was just us, and the only fucking world that mattered to me was in this clubhouse with her in my arms, inches from my heart.

It was shaping up to be a long fucking winter. Too bad. I was determined to keep it from icing her up after

I'd thawed her out – especially when the glacier Beth's death left behind was evaporating by the day.

That smile on my face she loved to gawk at and run her fingers through? For the first time in my fucked up life, it was starting to seem real.

IX: Tarnished Hearts (Alice)

Safe in his arms, the darkness in my dreams was deep. Unforgiving.

I saw my Dad's death again and again, those brutal men who'd nearly killed me and defiled me splitting his head on the worn clubhouse floor. Then the gruesome scene blurred into fantasy, all the things I'd drawn in the sketchbook and sworn off.

I was drawing, just like he asked, drawing him.

He filled my empty page, more realistic than anything I could do in real life in that strange timeless way only dreams allow.

When I was done, I looked down and gasped. I tried to make him a hero, a badass knight riding on a white horse, but that wasn't what greeted me on the paper.

Snarling, I tore it the sheet out and started all over, marking up the page at light speed. And each time it turned out the same – darker and scarier than I intended.

Stinger looked like a barbarian rather than a white knight. No matter what I did. The severed head always ended up there, hanging from his fist by the hair, just like the savage smirk on his lips. His eyes were the cruelest part.

They were cold, pleading, merciless – exactly how Dad's looked before he died.

I woke with a start and rolled over. We were back at his apartment after a long night, and he was in the bathroom, shirtless and magnificent as ever, drying his hair in the mirror.

The patterns on Sting's back formed a maze of sharp edges, curled like daggers. They looked like they were ready to fly off his skin and skin the whole world. Wide awake, his rugged exterior made me feel safe, and I knew he truly cared.

But I couldn't explain those stupid dreams.

"Finally." He turned toward the bedroom when he finished with his hair, saw me, and smiled. "I know you need your beauty sleep, baby, but damn. It's almost noon. I was gonna wake you after this. Hungry?"

I shook my head. "I'm good. When do we need to get to the clubhouse?"

"Should've been there an hour ago, but everybody's running late. Moose says Blaze and Saffron haven't even shown up yet. We're okay. It's warmer out there today," he said, smiling as he turned to the window. "We'll take the bike in. Get ready. Put the new shit we picked up to good use and bundle up. Fresh air will do us mighty fucking good before it's all business."

I was actually looking forward to a short ride on his bike now that the weather allowed it. The business part made me cringe. Stinger was off to do God knows what with his brothers.

As for me, I was going to see Em about birth control.

I just hoped Blondie would keep her inner bitch under wraps. Yeah, I'd been bad all those months ago when they pumped me for information. Still, I hadn't forgiven her for flinging me around like a puppet to keep her old man out of prison.

Soon, we were off. The roads were clear and the dense clouds retreated over the mountains, leaving nothing but sun and blue sky. Snow thawed on the rolling hills around us, but there was too much winter left to make it last.

I was grateful for the stop we'd made last night for new winter gear on the way to his apartment – a big improvement over the crappy coat and gloves I had before. Stinger was suited up in nothing but an extra leather jacket and gloves. I had my hands wrapped tight around his rock hard abs as the Harley purred beneath us, a beautiful throwback to the first time we'd ridden.

Out here, with the gorgeous sky and the daylight, he really was my knight, powerful and pure. I shook my head, fighting off the doubts stewing in my dreams.

Yes, this man's violence bled into everything he did. It shaped who he was, and it wasn't going to stop anytime soon. I'd watched him kill for me and helped hide a hacked up body like it was a boring chore.

Accepting him meant taking the whole package, including the brutality that came with his lifestyle in this club. My heart alternated between sinking and fluttering as the cool wind flapped in our faces. Stinger reached for my gloved hand at the stoplight and gave it a good squeeze.

Fuck. Why does love like this have to come with such hard choices?

At the clubhouse, Stinger disappeared into their meeting room, waiting for the other brothers. I was perched on a stool with a tall glass of OJ, something I'd stolen from behind the bar for drink mixes.

The whores walked by and fished out beers, shooting me uneasy looks. I gave my bitchiest stare right back, knowing they'd both been fucking my man not so long ago.

Jesus, my *man.* I slapped my forehead, running tense fingers through my hair. *Was that really what he was? Could I say I'd made up my mind?*

My heart screamed yes, but my messed up head said something else.

"Come on back, Alice," a smooth voice said behind me.

I looked to see Em staring at me. Her lips were quirked and she had on a leather jacket with her PROPERTY OF TANK patch on the back, bright gold hair hung over her shoulders. The girl had definitely fully gotten herself into the life.

I rose and didn't say anything as she led me back. Just like any other doctor's appointment I'd ever been to, only this one was being handled by the last person in the world I wanted laying her hands on me.

During the quick exam, I flinched when she touched me, resisting the urge to throw my nails into her face. Em's eyebrows went up, and then she rose, peeling off her gloves and walking to the waste bin.

"You're good. No sexual activity prior to this?" she asked, keeping it cold and clinic.

I shook my head. "Nothing. I was stripping in Coeur d'Alene. Not whoring myself out."

Emma's eyes narrowed and she looked me up and down. Damn, she had a way of getting underneath a girl's skin with that sassy mom-look. Obviously, Tank must've had a thing for spitfires.

"You don't need to be such a smartass, girl. What happened between you and me's all in the past. Here. Take these pills and pull the stick out of your ass. Just follow the instructions on the box." She tossed a packet of birth control pills at me, one of many sitting in the club's stash, a cabinet stacked high with different kinds of contraception.

"Sorry," I said after a long pause. "It's been very stressful lately. Never thought I'd be back here again…it takes some time to adjust."

Emma cocked her head. "Sounds to me like this is where you're meant to be. Don't tell me you're second guessing what's going on with you and Sting? Tank told me everybody in the clubhouse could hear you two going at it down the hall last night."

I flushed bright red and hid a smile. Lost it completely when Em grinned, a weirdly approving look on her face.

"You'll get used to life here with the guys and us old ladies before you know it. This MC has a good record with picking up misfits and putting them in their place." She rolled her eyes, considering her words. "Well, putting them where they *belong*, I mean."

I nodded, straightened my clothes, and got up, tucking the little pill box into my pocket. "I hope you're right."

"I'd better be. You'll be heading to the wedding in Reno in a few weeks with the rest of us," she said. "If you haven't figured out by then you're old lady material, I'll eat my words with a heaping slice of bullshit on the side."

I smiled, thanked her, and left. Couldn't help but be surprised it went better than expected.

Sitting at the bar, waiting for Sting to finish, I ran through everything again, gently rolling my glass of water back and forth between my hands, watching the circular vibrations.

Everything in the clubhouse seemed super real today. From Saffron sulking around and wiping down counters behind the bar, to the thick tension that filled the room like a furnace. Whatever was going on behind the door, it was dead serious.

Is it really any surprise I've ended up here? All I know is this life, this danger, this violence...

I sipped my water, feeling totally exhausted. It wasn't just the cold. My adrenals were shot, totally spent from the fear of losing my life, the stress of dancing at that shitty Grizzlies club.

Pleasure did it too. I had Stinger's insatiable thrills coming at me each night, churning with the serious doubts bristling in the back of my mind.

"Nice to see I'm not the only one getting beat up by Jack Frost," Saffron said, stepping out from behind the bar with a rag for the counters.

"Today was pretty decent," I said. "We rode in on his bike. First time I've been on it in months."

The ride really did make me happy. Out there, hair tucked tight beneath my helmet, arms wrapped around my man, it was easy to forget there were monsters aiming to derail what we were trying to build.

Monsters, inside and out. The Slingers were a ferocious threat, and I didn't know how to handle them any better than the demons inside me, all the savage ghosts who refused to kneel to my newfound love and lust.

Saffron winked. "There'll be plenty more riding where that came from in another month, girl. We're riding to Reno one way or another. Even if we have to tow the bikes through a blizzard and unload them down in Nevada. Blaze said he'd shoot his way in if the assholes twisting the club's balls cause any trouble."

"So, it's still on, then?" Saffron blinked. I realized I'd said something fucking stupid one second too late. "I mean...I was worried when I saw your frustration with Blaze and Stinger fighting the other day..."

Saffron laughed and shook her head. "Boys will be boys – especially when they're constantly measuring who's dick is bigger and who has the meanest tattoos. Blaze can be a dick, but he never lets me down when it counts. No frigging way will I *ever* take this thing off unless I'm putting on my wedding dress..."

She stood up tall and did a little twirl, showing off her leather, a lot like Em's. PROPERTY OF BLAZE, the mark of her old ladyship, was there on the backside. Even with these stupid doubts screwing with my head, imagining one of those on my shoulders and Stinger's brand on my skin made me jealous.

"I'm really happy for you. For everybody. This club can certainly use some cheering up..."

Saffron snorted and rounded the bar, pulling out a stool to sit next to me. She laid her ruby red fingernails on my shoulder and squeezed.

"It's always something, Alice. You know that? If it's not Tank staring down a prison sentence for beating some guy to death, it's a pack of wolves ready to come in and rip us all to shreds."

Ugh. Was that supposed to make me feel better? I swallowed the rest of my water, hoping to hide the unease building in my face.

"But guess what? I wouldn't trade this leather and the engagement ring on my finger for *anything*. Blaze is worth it. So are the rest of these boys. I used to have the same crap I see clouding up your eyes in mine not so long ago…"

Was she serious? I wanted to blow her off, get the hell out of here. I heard about Saffron suffering her own brand of really bad shit, but I didn't believe for a second it was like mine.

"My brother, Jordan, was mixed up in the Grizzlies MC and all the bullshit they're into – especially the drugs. Still is, I'm sad to say." That made me sit up and take notice. "Before Blaze and the Devils, I thought all MCs were the same. They were all brutal pigs to me. Criminals. Some rogues who went AWOL from the Grizzlies killed my own mother. If there's anybody who should've tucked their tail between their legs and gotten as far away from all this as their little legs would carry them, it was me."

"But you stayed," I said.

Saffron nodded. "For Blaze. He protected me. He took revenge on all the assholes who ruined my family. This club has been through a lot of shit, and I know there's more that'll come. But that's what makes these men stronger and their love deeper. The love I have for my old man, the bond these brothers share…it's not like anything outside these walls. If it means I have to put up with the occasional poisoning or shooting or setup…well, I'm game. It took me a long time to figure that out, Alice. Emma too. I'm not telling you to do anything – your decisions are yours to make like a big girl – all I'm saying is, don't let fear chase you away from a good thing. If I'd listened to my gut, I would've missed out on the love of my life. I wouldn't have found my way home, straight into his heart. I can't imagine being anywhere else."

Saffron let me go. Her eyes were all bright. Genuine proof she meant every single word. No BS here.

I couldn't look at her. Mouthing a thank you, I went back to staring at my glass like a class act drunk, trying not to get a headache as I digested all the food for thought she'd given me. The woman served it up in piles – not that I expected anything less from somebody crazy enough to get with Blaze.

Half an hour later, evening dragged into night, and the door finally swung open. The brothers filed out, anger and worry lining their faces. The three youngest brothers hit the bar, keeping their distance from me. Blaze and Tank scattered, and Sting headed right for me.

I sat up and pushed my way into his arms. God, I'd never get tired of his heat folding over me, a shield of pure muscle and power, bulwark against the fucked up world outside.

If only I could capture it, hold onto it, make it mine when my head swirled with doubt.

"What's wrong, Sting?" His eyes were darker than usual.

"Club business. Can't say more than that, baby. You're safe, and that's the way it's gonna stay. Don't fucking worry about anything else."

I wanted to, though. Before I could ask anything else, he wrapped one hand in mine and pulled me toward the door.

"We're done for the day. Let's get the fuck outta here. We've got a ride through the dark and a cold bed at home that needs warming."

My heart did a flip. Despite all the crap pressing on my mind the past evening, my baser instinct couldn't argue with what was coming. Wrapping my hands around him on the Harley finished off what little resistance I had left.

I leaned on him the whole time, running my hands up Stinger's abs. Jesus, he was so hard, even with all the layers of clothing packed between our skin. I closed my eyes, savoring his scent, breathing deep to keep me warm while the winter air kissed the tiny bits of our faces still exposed.

The constant hum of the bike underneath us didn't help. My panties felt more soaked each time the cool air caught me there. The tension pulling at my womb dashed everything except the raw, primal need to be filled.

It was going to be a long, hard winter. I could worry and drive myself nuts, or I could buckle down and enjoy him, one moment at a time.

Trust. All I had left after we'd both suffered together through so many bitter days. Whatever happened long-term, there was no way this man would let me suffer.

I didn't have much, but I did have faith. And maybe having enough faith in this beautiful, determined man would lead me *home*.

When Saffron said the word, I knew it was paradise.

The days were cold. Short. All the way until New Year's and then beyond.

Sting wasn't around as much as I'd hoped, too busy with club business to show up before I went to bed. I vaguely felt his powerful, warm bulk closing around me, a kiss on the neck. In the morning, he was gone before I woke up, leaving me short texts and notes on the counter about how he'd be back later.

Funny how even a little distance cranked my longing up a few notches. Sure, I was trying to sort out all the crap and uncertainty in my head. And now it was harder than ever without him around.

I hoped to God whatever the club was doing would be finished soon. The Slingers who'd killed my dad couldn't be dead soon enough. I hated the way they were still fucking with me, reaching into every attempt to rebuild my life and shaking all the pieces loose.

A week or two into January, Saffron invited me out. She needed somebody to go with her for feedback on some last minute wedding accessories, and I was the only girl tied to the club who wasn't busy during the day.

She picked me up at the apartment and we were off. I tried to push the grim atmosphere out of my head for the day. I'd never been too deep into fashion, but getting out and trawling bridal shops seemed more appealing than another day cooped up in the apartment, wondering what was eating at my man.

Saffron said Blaze was distant and stressed as all hell too. It didn't make me feel any better.

Whatever was going on with the club, it was bad. All the guys were scarce while they dealt with the monsters at our gates.

The morning passed quickly. Before I knew it, we were on shop number two, more like a crazy looking thrift store than a proper bridal shop. It was the kinda place I would've preferred myself, and Saffron obviously liked it too.

"Well?" She smiled and planted her foot on the leather bench next to me.

"Jesus! You sure you're going to be able to get down the isle without falling in those things?"

She shot me a wicked grin. "Oh, yeah. I've had plenty of practice shaking tail in these getups. Same as you, girl. A woman's got to get creative to surprise her man after fucking him a few hundred times. These heels will knock his socks off."

I smiled. "More like get him off. Those things'll definitely do the job."

"What about something for you?" Saffron winked. "You're welcome to do more than tag along. I'm sure Sting would appreciate some surprises too."

I lowered my face, trying not to flush. All the hard loving with that man hadn't driven away my virgin modesty yet. But I wasn't going to act like a prude around this woman.

I set off, seeking the most outrageous heels I could find. Bypassing the shoes, I hit the lingerie first and found the frilliest violet top and skimpy matching panties. They were a perfect match for the blaring purple bitch heels around the corner.

Stinger flashed in my brain, growling between my legs as I dug my heels into his side. Was I okay with a man fucking me like a braying bull?

The mischievous grin Saffron returned on my way back to her was a *hell yeah.*

"It's going to be an awesome wedding, isn't it?" I teased, still admiring my shoes.

"Fucking better be!" Saffron did a twirl, but then her smile melted. "Yeah, it's going to be great. Just wish I could get my little brother to Reno without any problems."

I swallowed, remembering what I'd heard about his Grizzlies activities. "I've seen how territorial these guys can be. Maybe he'll show up in a suit instead of his colors?"

Sardonic laughter shot out her lips. "Jordan hasn't worn anything except ratty t-shirts and leather since he was ten. Whatever. I kinda hope he doesn't show up at all. It'll just be more drama for me and the guys. My family begins and ends with the club now."

I nodded. Her voice sounded hollow, not totally convincing. How shitty did it feel to have your only flesh and blood in a rival MC – and a very dangerous, brutal one too?

"Let's get out of here and grab some lunch," she said, snapping my heels out of my hands. "It's on me. Least I can do for dragging you out here today."

Smiling, I thanked her. Arguing with free stuff didn't seem wise when I was still living off Stinger's shelter and a little spending cash from my old job at the Filthy Crown.

We paid and headed out. We got halfway to Saffron's SUV when her phone pinged. She dropped the big bag from the store, swore, and began furiously texting back. I dove to pick our stuff up.

"What's going on?"

"We need to go right now," she said, tucking her phone away and looking around. "Blaze wants to send somebody out for escort. Don't worry – I told him 'no.'"

My eyes widened. "Are we in trouble?"

"I...don't know. Something's up. I promised him we'd get back to the clubhouse ASAP. Come on!"

I stuffed our bag in the trunk and clambered inside the truck. Saffron peeled out fast, and soon we were on the main drag, racing to the other side of town and safety.

"Relax," she said. "This kinda stuff happens all the time when the boys are on edge. Probably a false alarm. They're just protecting us."

I felt a little safer in the SUV, but definitely not a hundred percent. She was about to cross a wide intersection when an old truck rolled out and stopped right in the middle of it, blocking our path.

"Shit!" Saffron hit the brakes.

Two blue cars pulled up, blocking traffic. Men jumped out and started banging on the windows. It took a couple seconds to realize they had hammers.

I screamed just as the glass exploded from both sides. Rough hands reached for the locks on the doors and ripped them open.

Saffron was too stunned to floor it. Wouldn't have done any good anyway with the rustbucket blocking our front. Rough hands yanked us out, pulling us in opposite directions at the same time, carrying me through the snow while I struggled like a mad woman. The creep holding me popped the door to the new vehicle and threw me in. I rolled into the mystery vehicle hard and found my face in some guy's jeans, stinking like tobacco.

"We got 'em. Yeah, Prez, both bitches. Let's fucking roll," a man said in the driver's seat.

The whole world was upside down. I struggled to sit up and heard the man next to me laugh. He reached out, helping me at first, even though I tried to swat him away. Then he threw me against the door, clutching at my hair and giving it a rough pull.

"Slow down, darlin'. Wouldn't want to rip any of this pretty black hair out of your head. That's for later, if your Prairie Pussy studs don't come through."

I finally had a good look at him. He was a grimy, nasty man with a long blonde hair, wearing the same SLINGERS MC cut as the man in the front. The man in the driver's seat saw me in the mirror and smiled, flashing jagged silver teeth I recognized.

It was Nero's VP, Shark, the man he'd left with on the night I was almost killed. "Hi, baby doll. Prez is gonna be real fucking happy to see you again. Don't worry. We're too fucking pissed off about losing a brother to your skank ass to kill you up front. We're gonna finish what Hatter and Wasp started."

The man next to me yanked my hair, laughing through his busted teeth. "Fucking cunt. I want her asshole first…"

Blood rushed up to my temples. Savage urges boiled in my blood. I wanted to rake my nails over the demon's face, if it wouldn't get me brutalized.

They'd obviously taken us for some reason. My heart sank as I realized we'd just become the latest bargaining chips in their insane quest for my dad's old routes.

The car jerked into formation behind the other blue vehicle, and the old truck that cut off Saffron's was riding in the front. Behind us, two loud motorcycles roared, operated by more men in blood red Slingers' patches.

I swallowed, promising myself I wouldn't cry. I was too pissed, too determined to live this time. I wasn't giving up. Biting my lip hard drew blood.

The tangy, sharp taste of copper was comforting in a fucked up way. Unlike before, I wasn't scared for my life. Not entirely.

These assholes were too slow for their own good. They'd already made their mistakes. Stinger was coming, him and the rest of the club, and when they did the men in the car with me were all dead.

The crazy fog in my head was melting away. I looked at the brutes and their greedy, violent expressions slowly, finally starting to understand.

This shit-storm's end was in sight before it had truly gotten started.

Hell was going to catch up with them sooner or later. And when it did, I'd finally see just how dark, intense, and beautiful Devils' bloodlust could really be...

"Out." The man in the backseat reached past me, popped the door, and pressed something hard into my spine.

I didn't shake as I slid my feet to the cold ground and crawled out. The wind was blowing snow off the little roof of the old cabin they'd parked next to – a crappy little house that looked like it hadn't been a home since wild pioneers roamed the mountains.

We were somewhere north of the city, right outside the Missoula limits, when the mountains became high and wild. Somewhere in the nearby wilderness, the Devils hid the men who crossed them, monsters who deserved to die.

I hoped like hell they'd add a few more to their deep cold graves after today.

The man with the greasy long hair and his VP marched me out toward the rickety door. Inside, there was nothing but a couple ancient chairs and a worn wood table. Saffron was already there, her hands bundled behind her back in an old chair.

Several feet away, Nero stood with the other guys from the truck. He took a long pull on a cigarette, fixing his cold eyes on me. His gaze was harsh enough to freeze, so cold I wanted to shake instead of laugh at how cliché the nasty scene in front of me seemed.

"Tie this cunt down tight. She likes to struggle and hide. Isn't that right, Hatter?" Nero looked across the table to the corner.

The scrawny, mindless worm near the door laughed, rubbing his bony hands together while he stared at me.

Christ. If Nero's eyes were cold enough to start an ice age, then Hatter's lunatic hyena laugh pulled me beneath the frozen ice, echoing in my poor ears over and over and over.

Several Slingers forced my hands behind me and rolled a cord over them, making quick knots near the wrists, just like Saffron's. Her eyes met mine. They'd gagged her, stuffing what looked like a dirty old rag in her mouth.

Hot anger pulsed through my system. No, maybe they had to keep us safe while they waited for our club, but they'd certainly found more subtle ways to make our lives miserable.

"Got her," greasy hair grunted behind me. "Tighter than what either of these whores got between their legs, I bet."

Nero walked over, flicking his cigarette to the floor and stubbing it with one boot. He raised an arm and pointed at his guy.

"No gag. I want to hear this one's screams. Did anybody figure out which fuckwad is her old man?"

"The VP, I think," Shark said. "Some turd named Stinger. Typical Prairie Pussy name."

"We'll kill him first," Nero growled. "Right in front of this bitch, just as soon as we've secured that fucking map."

He looked at me just as Saffron began to whimper and struggle in her gag. Her body moved like she was frightened, but I could tell her eyes were full of pure hatred.

Nero came closer. He caught my chin, digging his fingers into my jaw bone, too tight for me to jerk away. Bastard.

I thought about biting him, but soon he was down at eye level, so close I could see all the scars sheared across his cheek. Adding one more scratch to his damaged face wouldn't do much more for us.

"Your daddy's the reason we lost one of our boys, and we're probably gonna lose a few more before this night's through. Only fair that you should suffer, bitch. I don't normally play with my prey before I kill it, but you've made yourself an exception. I'm gonna watch you lose your fucking mind before I slit your throat."

Nero spat. He literally fucking spat in my face, and I was left staring at him while his gross, sticky spittle dripped off my forehead.

His words cut deep. I listened to Saffron struggling next to me and thought about Stinger.

His threats were monstrous, but they had a cold efficiency behind them too. They were so vicious, so pissed off, I worried about buying time. I couldn't just let them take us down the same slow, sneaky way they'd done to Dad.

Had to do something. I had to –

My brain flipped off and I kicked. Hard. Nero swerved, but not fast enough. My foot landed right between his balls and caught them in a sickening crunch.

He staggered backward and fell on his ass, slapping the floor with his fists, snarling and cursing. Slingers swarmed me in less than a second. Shark ripped my head back and pressed a cold knife to my throat.

I laughed, despite the uncomfortable lump in my neck pressing on sharp steel. I couldn't help it. The way things had come full circle was way too fucking crazy to process.

"Prez? You okay?" Boots clambered on the floor like someone was helping Nero up.

Then they stomped toward me, quick and deliberate. His breath was heavier now, struggling to contain the pain vibrating his bones. Shark looked like he was a hair trigger away from bleeding me out, especially when I grinned at him.

Fuck you, I thought. *Do it now if you want to live, asshole. Do it before the club shows up and finishes what I started with your Prez.*

"Just say the word," Shark said coldly. "We can tell those fucks it had to be done. She fought us. There's no fucking prisoners of war here."

"No!" Nero said, raising a hand, still slightly doubled over. "That'll fuck up everything. We need her alive. Just a couple more hours. We'll settle with this bitch later. Just get her fucking legs bound. Both these cunts. The Prairie Pussies are gonna show up any time now."

We locked eyes while his henchman tied my feet to the rickety old chair. I refused to look away, even when he came close a second time, one hand on the dagger strapped to his waist.

"Enjoy your fucked up triumph now, cunt. Because when we get through with your guys, you're gonna wish you'd kicked my nuts a whole lot harder." He drew his knife, anger flashing in his eyes while mine stayed fearless. "What I really want is to skin your ass myself, just as soon as Hatter's done with you."

"Do it," I grunted, hissing the words through clenched teeth.

He stared at me for a second, stroking his chin. "I got it now. Looks like I've been using the wrong fucking approach…"

He broke the iron gaze first. Thank God. My relief instantly melted when he walked away, circling Saffron instead. He jerked her head back by her brunette hair, running the flat edge of the knife up her neck instead.

Shit! I started to struggle, rocking in the chair without even realizing how stupid and hopeless it was. Crap quality or not, the old wood and the cords did their job, holding me in place.

"I know you don't give a fuck about your own life, babe. So I'm gonna tear hers up first. Right after we get done with your guys and that pissant named Stinger." He turned the knife inward, baring his teeth as he raked it across her skin.

Saffron shrieked against her rag as hot blood danced along the blade. It slid down her throat, pooling near her breasts. Scary, but not enough to be life threatening.

Asshole was playing with us. Screwing with us both.

"Bastard!" I screamed, kicking as hard as I could against the new cords around my legs.

If I could've picked the chair up and thrown myself at him, I'd have done it in a heartbeat. The demon was right: watching Saffron's torture was far worse than him doing it to me.

Worse? It'd gone to pure crap across the board.

This was worse than being captured by the Rams, worse than the constant worry about what I'd gotten myself into. I wanted Stinger here so bad it hurt. I wanted him to put this sick brute down without a shred of mercy.

Nero stopped after he'd left a straight savage line across her cleavage, dangerously close to her throat. My whole face felt like it was going to explode, blood so hot I couldn't stand it. I rocked my hands until I hurt, fighting the rope, not caring how it scraped my wrists.

I had to stay alive. Focused. I couldn't let my mind shut down again, wiping everything out. I wouldn't let the amnesia return – even if I had to watch Saffron and others die in front of me.

I remembered Sting's face. I tried to remember my Dad, holding tight to all the memories, everything I had.

Just breathe. Breathe deep. No matter how bad it gets, you can't let your mind black out.

My thoughts weren't very reassuring. Nero growled as Shark walked over, getting a strong grip on his wrist.

"Prez? What the fuck? I thought we weren't gonna hurt these bitches 'til –"

"Fuck." Nero reared up, staring at what he'd done. "Blot this shit up and rinse her off. It's not like she'll bleed out. Those fucks won't know shit and she won't tell them a fucking thing either."

"What are you?" I whispered, forcing myself to look him in the eyes.

My brain didn't want to compute the psycho death I was seeing, the walking murder this man represented.

Nero's expression was so cold it was hard to even see the evil. It was like looking into a predator's face, a thing running on pure instinct, beyond right and wrong. The freaks and ghouls I used to draw had more humanity than he did.

"I'm the President of this fucking club," he said matter-of-factly. "Helluva lot better than being a weak little whore."

He paced closer, pushing his face against mine. His breath stank and I twisted away, especially when he donned another twisted, emotionless smile.

"You think you're more than that, don't you?" He turned his head to Saffron. "Both you cunts. Listen to me: you sluts are fucking tools to me, and nothing more. Better get off your high horse, princess, before I whip its ass and you fall off and break your neck. None of this shit would be your problem if your daddy hadn't been so successful fucking people over."

"You don't know shit." My turn to spit in his face.

Nero stood tall, still wearing his crooked smile, slowly wiping his face. I closed my eyes, ready for him to whack me across the face. Getting knocked cold right now would've saved me from hearing Saffron whimpering next to me.

My soul bled for her.

"Suit yourself, cunt. It's not my job to make you repent for daddy's sins before this shit's done. And it'll be over before you know it." He took several steps backward before turning to me again. "You really ought to take a good look at me. When we're through, I'm the only person in the world who's gonna remember your snotty ass. I'll think about the way you fucked me over, and how I fucked you back harder, every time we hit your daddy's routes. You're not a human being anymore, bitch. You're a means to an end, and a very temporary one too."

I wasn't responding anymore. Even his men seemed to keep their distance. Guess the severe, strangely calm threats were too weird for them too.

I was too exhausted for more insults, half-blind with anger, trying not to go insane each time Saffron made a little noise. Insulting the asshole wouldn't do any good. Neither would rubbing my wrists and ankles raw. Houdini himself couldn't have escaped this crap.

Nero staggered away, toward the backroom where they'd set up whatever terrible surprises they had waiting for the Devils. Outside, the wind had really picked up, blowing the loose mountain snow around the windows.

Opening my eyes, I looked at Saffron and instantly regretted it. She wasn't whimpering or crying or shaking any more. Her head was rolled back and she was deathly still, faint salty lines on her cheeks where hot tears rolled down them.

If the wound he'd given her healed before the wedding, she'd be lucky.

Hell, we'd both be falling to our knees and kissing fortune's feet if we left this place alive.

Watching him savage her right in front of me tore at the confidence. I fixed my eyes to the window, trying to look through the scrawny animal blocking my view. Hatter tittered out the window like the lunatic he was, humming some inane, off tune, and ridiculously creepy ditty to himself.

God help me, I shuddered.

All I could think about was *him,* cursing my old stupidity and my doubts. Nero and his killers were one more brutal example of why Stinger did what he did.

The barbarian I saw in my dreams was the hero after all, and I was too stupid to recognize it until now.

Shit, right now, I didn't care if I had to watch him cut their throats in front of me.

I wanted to see the killer in him fight for me, just like the dark warrior I saw in my dreams, a champion so ruthless he'd leave these assholes begging for their lives before he sent them to hell. It's amazing and scary what want, hatred, and a little fear can do to a girl's brain.

Come on, Sting. Where are you? Is this what I get for doubting you?

I kept chewing on that question the entire time while the sky grew dark. It was all I could do to keep myself from panicking and blocking out everything as we both suffered at the edge of the frozen world.

X: Hellbound (Stinger)

I heard the crash in the office first and went running. Sounded like the whole fucking clubhouse was falling down.

When I got to the door, I half-expected to find Blaze buried underneath a pile of rubble. Instead, I found him standing in the middle of the carnage he'd created, red faced and breathing pure fire. His knuckles were scratched bloody.

"Christ! What the fuck set off the dynamite?" I was still eyeing the scene. Everything from his desk to the filing cabinet was crashed on the floor, or dented and leaning, ready to fall over after being hit by the tornado he'd created.

"Round up all the bros. We need to go, Sting. Right. Fucking. Now." He walked fast, pushing past me and heading for the garage.

I ran after him. "Whoa, whoa, whoa. Is this about wherever you sent Smokey and Stone an hour ago?"

Blaze stopped near the bar, jerking his hand into one pocket. He pulled out his phone, spun, and pressed it into my chest after tapping a few keys.

"Read it and move your ass. Just fucking listen to me for once." He was gone, swinging the door open and heading straight for the big vaults where we kept the guns.

I saw paper clenched in his other hand, the faint outline of the map the Slinger's wanted. Fuck.

Then I looked at the text messages. The replies were furious and badly written.

FOUND UR OLD LADYS TRUCK. GONE. BOTH GIRLS. GLASS BUSTED OUT. COPS SWARMING IT. LOOKING FOR A TOW.

"Fuck!" My scream echoed through the clubhouse like a stray bullet.

My heart sank to my guts and then shot up, blood turning hot, red hot rage lighting up my blood. I knew Saffron invited Alice out that morning from the messages she'd sent me.

It was bad enough having the Prez's woman captured by those motherfuckers. But now they'd gone one step further and made it personal, taking mine, stealing the girl I'd sworn my fucking life to protect.

I stuffed the phone in my pocket, then pressed both hands to my head, compressing my skull.

It was all I could do to avoid wrecking more shit in the clubhouse when I needed my energy. I needed it for the fucks who'd hit me deep.

Fucking up close and savage, sinking their fangs into my soul. I had to lean on the wall as I started to shake, heart pumping pure adrenaline. If it wasn't for Tank coming up, looking all confused, my fists would've started putting holes in the fucking wall.

"What the fuck's going on here, boss? Why're you and the Prez going totally fucking –"

"They've got Alice! They took her, brother!" I jumped up, grabbing at his cut, regaining my balance with the grip. "Alice and Saffron both…taken by those goddamned jackals…I need to find Blaze…"

"Shit!" Tank grabbed me before I could storm off, heading for the bikes and the guns.

I struggled against him like a mad man as he held me tight. My brain was fucking rabid, and I wanted to punch right through him, through anything holding me back a second longer from going after my entire universe.

"Easy, boss! Just take it fucking easy. We'll get this shit done. But we need to keep our cool."

One more jerk and I was free. Tank grunted, but he didn't come after me while I headed for the door. I turned back at the last second.

"Round up all the others! We gotta get the crew together and ship out. Can't waste a fucking second…"

"Got it."

I was out in the cold after a quick stop by the hangers to grab my jacket, throwing it over my cut. The frigid air in the garage didn't do shit to freeze up my veins. Tank was right, one more reminder that he was pretty damned smart for being such a tight lipped giant.

Just now, though, nobody's golden wisdom was gonna settle the firestorm seething in my veins. Every time my brain couldn't believe it, couldn't fully grasp what the fuck was happening, the harsh venom in my blood brought me back to life, straight back to staring at the awful fucking reality.

I fucked up royal. The whole club did, but it was Blaze and I bearing all the consequences.

Those fuckers lulled us into lazy scouting. We'd been chasing them too long, letting our guard down, expecting them to pop up at the clubhouse. We started to think they wouldn't come for awhile, maybe not until spring.

Rubbing my eyes, I fought the headache turning my head into a pressure cooker. My ears were fucking ringing with how absolutely *wrong* we'd all been. Shit, going after them like Blaze wanted would've been better than this.

Fuck. And I'd been too lax with my baby too, swept up in club business, barely coming home in time to get a few hours of shut eye and hold her tight.

When I thought about how I might never hold her again, I wanted to get on my bike and go. Fuck waiting for the rest of the brothers. I raced past Blaze and headed for my locker, where all my shit was stashed for action, a heartbeat away from saddling up and raining down hot death in an instant. We organized our gear for situations exactly like this, when the only thing we were able to think about was neutralizing the threat.

Slower, calmer, my hands freezing, I rifled through my shit. I fished out my Magnum and replaced the nine millimeter on my belt. This little cannon would turn anybody's head into cherry mush when it found its mark.

Perfect for this job.

Because when we caught up with the Slingers, it wasn't just a matter of taking them out, making sure they couldn't do anymore damage. By taking two of our women, they might as well have pulled down their pants and pissed on our colors while stabbing through our ribs.

This blow went straight to the heart. And when this club gets hit, where it really counts, nobody's coming home 'til the fucks who've done it get shredded to nothing.

All the brothers assembled within minutes, Tank urging things along. We stood in a circle in the garage to hear Blaze. A weird heatwave wound through my body. The expression on their faces told me I wasn't the only one out here burning up despite the arctic chill.

"Truck's been towed," Smokey said. "Took some wrangling to get the badges off our asses, but they know where their money's coming from. We'll have it repaired and scrubbed from public record, no questions asked."

Blaze nodded, and then shook his head. "Whatever, bro. Couldn't care less about that shit. I gotta get Saffron home."

"What's the plan, boss? How're we gonna hit 'em?"

"Charge in and knock their fucking teeth out," I growled, thinking about Alice. Fuck, I couldn't stop my fists from shaking at my sides like rattlesnakes when I imagined her suffering with those pricks. "It's the only way. We can be smart but we gotta be direct. We're already losing precious time."

"Sting's right." I looked up, surprised to see Blaze agreeing with me. "The asshole, Nero, sent me a text from Saffron's phone right after I got off the horn and found out about the girls. We know what he wants…"

Blaze jerked his hand up in the air, shaking the map. "I'll give that motherfucker exactly what he wants, face to face."

"No fucking way, Prez. You're seeing too much red to think straight." Tank shifted his weight, scraping an irritated boot on the ground.

"Didn't say this was a negotiation," Blaze said. "And it sure as fuck isn't a surrender either. This goddamned thing has been nothing but trouble since we picked it outta Mickey's shit. Should've burned it a long time ago."

"It sounds like you've got a plan. Wanna tell us how it gets our girls home without giving these dickheads a hundred chances to double-cross us?" Moose looked just as confused and uncertain as all the brothers.

I wasn't sure where Blaze was going with this shit either. I shot him a cold look. We didn't have time for any fucking theatrics.

"Go look behind the toolbox, bro." Blaze turned and pointed to the big steel box in the corner.

Moose turned to me. Now I was getting pissed, wondering what the fuck was going on. I beat the bigger, older brother there and did a double take.

Behind me, Moose laughed when he caught up. He reached down, grabbed it by the tail, and pulled it up, shaking off a few flecks of ice.

"Poor little bastard. Looks like he got the shit end of a Missoula winter before finishing his nest."

Snarling, I snatched the dead rat outta his hand. Fucking thing really was frozen solid. Blaze reached out as I walked over, and I passed it to him.

A few brothers suppressed their laughs. Roller was the loudest, and he looked up when Blaze and I pierced him with warning looks.

"Sorry. This is serious shit. Do I wanna know how you're gonna take take those fuckers down with a mouse?"

"Rat. You've seen plenty to know, asshole," Blaze growled, walking to the steel work table near the bikes and unrolling the map, throwing the rat down next to it. "Next time you see this furry bastard, you're only gonna be a little less surprised than those fuckheads."

"Ambush," Tank said thoughtfully. "Give 'em something unexpected. I like it. Better throw in a flash bang and buy us a couple more seconds. Fuck knows I've been blinded by those damned things enough times...we'll have to haul ass. The Slingers are smarter and faster than your average Grizzlies goon, boss. We'll have...maybe five seconds tops?"

"Plenty of time to shoot anything that moves and isn't looking pretty," I said, liking this idea more and more. "Are we done talking?"

I waited for Blaze to nod, then I clapped my hands. "All right. Let's fucking move it. Wrap this shit up and head out."

The brothers scrambled in all directions, gathering weapons and gear, and then moving for their bikes. Reb, Moose, and Roller went for the van. We always brought out different chariots to a battle like this.

I double-checked to make sure my shit was all together, and then headed for my bike. Blaze's ride was next to me, and I watched him get on, fixing his helmet and pulling on an extra layer of gloves for the wintry ride. Thank fuck blowing snow was all we had to worry about on the roads tonight. They were plenty clear, an open route to the hell we were gonna bring with us.

"You and me got dibs on cutting the throats of anyone who's left alive after the wave," the Prez said, firing up his engine. "You're the only bro tonight who understands this shit exactly like I do."

I gave him a nod, tightening my helmet. "I'll race you to the fucking finish line. First man to stop their hearts with his bare hands wins."

Blaze nodded, and peeled out ahead of me, heading for the open gate. I was right behind him, and I wasn't fucking joking.

After what the Slingers had done, it was only fair I gutted them open and ripped their hearts out, the quickest and most merciful shit they deserved. If I found out that they'd hurt my old lady, before I'd even claimed her...

Shit.

Even ferocious wind slapping me in the face wouldn't drown out their screams. I'd drain their carcasses and crawl through the blood if it brought her back to me, safe and whole.

Riding into the dark mountains with the rest of the boys behind me, I knew there were no guarantees. Not 'til these fucks were buried and I had her in my arms. When Alice was mine again, come hell or high water, I was gonna pick up on loving her harder than before, giving her all the attention she deserved, and then some.

I wanted her as bad as I wanted her tormenters dead and gone, wanted her 'til my bones rattled harder than my Harley's engine on the dark road.

I'd let club business blur into the life I wanted to give her. Everything she deserved when she took my brand.

No more.

This was fucking it, right here. Transition. Closing one bloody chapter out and starting a new one with her sweet skin wrapped around mine every waking second.

After tonight, there weren't gonna be any regrets. I'd be too fixed on loving Alice for any more of that shit, or else I'd be dead.

It took about a half hour to get to the location they gave Blaze. It was a shitty little cabin, half its shingles gone, flapping eerily in the wind.

Blaze slowed down as we wound up the driveway. I stopped right behind him, killed my ride, and got off. The rest of the brothers caught up quickly and took their positions, bringing out the heavy guns.

They wouldn't do much good in this fight unless we knew for sure the girls were outta the way. They were really there for intimidation, and we needed a shit ton of it against the Slingers' crazy asses. Their vehicles were parked off to the side, and taking a quick look said we had a slight advantage in numbers. Not that it meant much when these assholes had experience and deadly skill on their side.

Blaze cupped his hands over his mouth, about to yell at the house, when the door opened. A thick man with a mouthful of silver teeth grinned coldly, waving us forward.

The Prez gave the go ahead, and we inched closer. Me, Blaze, Moose, and Tank, leaving the rest of the brothers to hang back in case they meant to surprise us at the door. Didn't fucking think so – not while we had the map. Everything these assholes wanted was scrawled on a dead man's piece of paper.

There was no time to think about fucked up ironies. I was at the door when Blaze pushed something hard into my hands.

"Do the honors," the Prez said coldly, just out of earshot from the line of evil looking bastards waiting for us next to an old table.

Blaze and I walked together, stopping in front of a tall, hard looking man with scars on his cheek. One look at the PRESIDENT patch on his cut told me we were dealing with Nero, the fucker spearheading this nightmare. He spread his hands on the table and spoke.

"I'm glad we could come to an agreement, Blaze. Maybe you assholes are smarter than you look."

"Whatever," Blaze spat. "Where are the girls? You're gonna bring them out there so I can see they're safe before we're handing over anything."

Nero looked at me and allowed himself a thin, cruel smile. "You must be Stinger? They're both in the back. Alive and well, both of them, Alice and Saffron. Now, you can't expect me to trot my hostages around where they might get in harm's way if you Prairie Pussies have something else in mind, yeah? We all care about the girls, Blaze. I didn't pluck a single hair out of their heads, or anywhere else."

The Prez looked like he was ready to explode. My heartbeat sent shockwaves through every muscle in my body. My hands tightened on the paper bundle clutched to my chest, keeping it outta their view, all I could do not to hurl the fucking thing at Nero's ugly face like a brick.

Nero raised one hand. "Shark, let 'em speak so our guests can hear."

The man with the silver teeth and the VP patch walked back toward the room. He said a few words to someone inside, and a second later, Saffron's voice rang out.

"Blaze?" She paused, exploding louder the second time. "Blaze!"

The Prez's eyes lit up. He knew damned well she didn't sound okay, and then my brain started spinning, wondering what they'd done to Alice.

I could feel Tank's eyes boring into me from behind, warning me off doing anything crazy or stupid. Just a few more seconds. We were so fucking close, but there were a thousand ways this could all go to shit.

"The other bitch too," Nero said, giving me a vicious look that said he knew she was mine.

I suppressed a growl. Had to break eye contact with the motherfucker before I wrecked everything. God damn, my fists were hungry, my bloodlust ripping at my throat like a werewolf trying to come out.

Nearly broke my own jaw clenching it tight when I heard her voice. "Stinger, it's Alice! We're okay. We just want to go home. Get us out of here. Please, we want you to –"

"That's enough!" Nero barked.

Footsteps rumbled in the room, and I strained to see what the hell was going on. Probably some fucking roughneck holding a gun to their heads. I'd been in this world long enough to know how clubs kept their bargaining chips in line.

I looked away, and my eyes caught Blaze's. *Don't fuck it up, brother. Just hold it together, a little while longer. Then you can go nuts. We're not walking outta here tonight unless they're all dead.*

Hearing his shit was all in my imagination, but it did the trick. I stopped seething and looked at Nero, feeling a monstrous peace coming over me like my blood turning to ice. Never knew zen could go hand-in-hand with murder 'til now.

"They're both yours. You can keep your fucking guns on us the whole time when we walk 'em out. Just gotta give us that map, Prez." Nero pushed his hands together on the table, cracking his knuckles. "I want my map first."

"Stinger," Blaze said, his voice low, rough. "Give these assholes what they want."

I looked Nero in his beady little eyes as I slammed the map on the table. Thank fuck it was no more than a degree or two warmer in here than outside. The shit in my hands hadn't melted and started to bleed through.

Nero snorted, eyeing the package cautiously. "What the fuck is this? Damn it, jackass, if this is a fucking bomb I'm gonna shove it right down your throat."

Shark came over at Nero's prompting. Blaze swallowed, and I pushed an identical fat lump down my own throat.

"It's all there, asshole," I said. "Wrapped around a rock, just like we found it. Never had much use for it ourselves. We don't roam around like fucking pirates."

"Shut up. That's enough," Blaze said. "Just look at your pretty fucking paper and give us our girls so we can get outta here. This is business, right?"

The harsh note in his voice was fake, not at all the authentic rage storm I'd felt a thousand times rolling off the Prez. Nero cocked his head and nodded, giving his VP permission to pick it up and start unwrapping.

"Call it whatever you want, Blaze, I don't give a shit. Long as you give us what we agreed on, everything's cool and we can –"

An ear shattering scream erupted from Shark's mouth. Nero's eyes bugged out as his VP squealed like a girl and tossed the dead rat high in the air. More Slingers roared, reaching for their guns.

"Tank, now!" I screamed.

The giant pushed through us as we all hit the floor, hurling the flash grenade. Sparks exploded right on the table. The impact blew the shoddy old wood apart, adding more chaos to the deafening flash. The old cabin's groaning wood matched Shark's scream as the shots began.

I covered my eyes with my arm, just like we'd been taught. The Slingers weren't so lucky, but they were still dangerous, firing wildly in the direction where they'd seen us before.

Bullets soared across my head. Smoke and haze clouded everything after the blast, adding to the maelstrom. I aimed my Magnum at a dark silhouette stumbling around. When I saw the bear roaring on the back of his cut, I pulled the trigger. His head exploded before he could even scream.

Quicker than any of these bastards deserved after torturing our women. Fuck, I hadn't even seen her yet, and I could only imagine the way they'd terrorized her, hurt her, screwed her up.

A couple more Slingers went down. I got up, crouched, and crawled through the smoke, passing over the wooden splinters. Some guys were starting to run low on ammo. The whole fucking cabin's walls were shot to Swiss cheese by now, and I stumbled over several bodies, looking closely at their eyes to make sure they weren't playing dead.

Nope. We got the fuckers. Tank looked up from his position on the floor, shoving another clip into his gun. I went down next to him.

"Come on! We gotta find the girls!" Seething, I stepped forward, and then tumbled back when Tank's huge fist caught my boot.

"Not yet! Stay the fuck down, boss." He shoved me down and fired.

A sneaky sonofabitch popping his head outta the back room took a bullet. He squealed, then fell backward, dead.

I got over being shoved around by Tank real fast. He'd saved my ass. I looked around, counting the bodies, trying to remember how many of those savage assholes we'd seen lined up.

Four guys down. That meant there were at least two or three missing. Fuck.

Just then, I heard the movement near the door, where Blaze was heading. It was my turn to burst up before Tank could stop me. I tackled the Prez and threw him to the ground, right as the asshole appeared in the open doorway. Tank's gun barked.

The figure screamed. Sounded an awful lot like that Nero fucker. He grunted, injured, dragging himself out into the dark wintry night. I was about to go after him when Blaze looked up.

"Hold it, bro. Motherfucker won't get far. We can track his blood. Gotta make sure our girls are okay first."

I nodded, holding out a hand. Blaze grabbed it and stood. We navigated our way past several bodies and plenty of debris. Thankfully, it looked like all the brothers were in one piece. A few boys were a little bloodied and scratched from the melee, especially Roller, who'd finished one fucker off with his knife.

We had our guns drawn, heading for the backroom when the corner exploded with a bloodcurdling scream. Blaze and I looked at each other. I took off, heading for the pillar in the corner.

That wiry piece of shit who couldn't stop laughing got up just in time to look me in the eye. One second too long. I fired. The fucker moved like a blur, taking a bullet somewhere in his leg before he jumped out the window. Broken glass rained down everywhere.

I held my hand up and shielded my eyes. Blaze caught up and ran into me.

"Oh, Christ. Shit!" Brushing glass shards off my arm, I cracked my eyes open. My fucking heart almost stopped when I saw what was on the ground underneath the escaping Slinger.

Fuck! Moose was on the floor, his cut a total mess over his gut, head lolled back at a sick angle. Blood pooled all over his beard and ran into his hair, red death spilling outta his right eye socket, the same place that psycho fucking jackal jammed a knife into his head.

Blaze gagged and I hit the floor, shoving my hands through sticky blood, feeling for his pulse. Before I could get a good read, our brother groaned. It was the kinda weak, sickly tremor I'd heard a hundred times from men dying.

Fuck, fuck fuck...

"Hold on, brother. Just hold the fuck on. Prez's gonna get help." I was babbling like a fucking idiot, knowing the odds of living more than a few minutes with a freak injury like this were pretty damned close to zero.

Blaze was back in the main room, screaming at the rest of the brothers. More guys ran to the spot where I was holding the man who'd helped shape my ass into Stinger, trying not to move him too much. But fuck, there was so much blood, still flowing right outta his poor brain.

"Fucking shit, boss. This is way beyond Em's skills..." Tank said to Blaze, sucking on a sharp breath.

"I don't give a shit! Get on the goddamned horn and call her. Get her to bring in the old bird from the hospital who helped our asses out when we were poisoned." Blaze's fists were trembling at his sides, and then he looked toward us again. "Shit, can't you see he's turning white as a sheet? He's gonna fucking die!"

My heart sunk like granite. The Prez wasn't bullshitting. Moose wasn't groaning anymore, and his skin was going paler by the second, his life draining away with his blood.

The cabin went deadly silent. I forgot all about the shitheads outside we still had to put down and the dying brother in my hands. I just wanted to find Alice and hold her close. When I did, I was never gonna let her sweet ass go, never gonna let her end up like this.

"Come on, VP. We gotta get him to the van. Let us in there…" Smokey put his hand on my shoulder. I looked up to see him, Stone, and Roller standing there, wondering how much time had gone by.

I nodded. "Just be fucking careful. He's not gonna survive the trip home if you jostle him around too much."

Take care, brother, I prayed silently, watching as the boys struggled to lift his heavy body. *You gotta fucking pull through. You just gotta.*

Your family's waiting for you to come home. Connie, Becky, all your brothers…

Stepping aside, I got up, and started to wipe Moose's drying blood on my jeans. Gave up pretty damned fast, seeing as how it was all over my clothes, my skin, grisly reminders that the club had paid a price today for winning a battle. And the war wasn't fucking finished yet.

Blaze clapped me on the shoulder and pulled me aside when I got out. "Come on. Reb's untied my old lady. Yours too."

My eyes went wide. Blaze caught himself and cleared his throat. "Alice, I mean. Come on. Move your ass."

The Prez and I went into the backroom, stepping over the piece of shit Tank shot in the head. Saffron nearly smacked right into me in her mad rush to get to Blaze.

Next thing I knew, I was surrounded by their grabbing, cooing, lip smacking reunion noise.

Then I saw her.

My girl was in the corner, crouched low, looking out the shitty fogged up window. She didn't turn when my footsteps approached. Took me sliding my fingers through her hair to get her attention. It was like the girl was in some kinda trance.

Shit! The bruise on her pale cheek hit me right between the eyes. My jaw clenched so hard I nearly shattered the fucking thing, then ripped her up, pulling her into my arms.

Didn't take much to wake her up. Alice was already throwing herself into my arms. Her little fingers danced across my back, tensing on my muscles harder than ever, really clinging to me.

"Jesus, baby. Who the fuck did this? Huh?" I ran a finger over the tender place, and then followed up with my lips.

She didn't wince. Girl had a different kinda fire in her eyes, hotter and wilder than I'd seen it before, like she'd been cleansed of all the fucked up things clouding up her beautiful irises.

"It doesn't matter. I fought them, Sting. Kicked, bit, and scratched when they drove us in here. I had to after what they did to Saffron." She swallowed. "My only regret is playing pretend when that bastard held a gun to her head...I wouldn't have said shit if it was just me. I wouldn't have put you guys in danger."

Blaze growled, overhearing us. I turned my head, just in time to see him pull Saffron to the wall, asking if that was true. His hand stretched her collar down. When he saw the messy cut around her neck, he started to shake. I ground my teeth to nubs.

Right then, we were more than just brothers wearing the same patch. We were hell bound to take out every last fucking demon who'd done this. There couldn't be any loose ends.

Christ, it was a small miracle they hadn't hurt them as bad as Moose…

It took all my energy not to tremble. Alice looked deep into my eyes. The crazy determination there was almost spooky. She was amazing before, but the woman looking at me now was like something that had hatched outta its cocoon, reborn in pure brimstone.

"Baby…"

"They were gonna set you up," she whispered. "I wanted to stop them so bad. If it wasn't for the gun…God, I hate being helpless!"

"I know. Don't you worry about that shit. It's almost done. Most of the fuckers responsible are dead. Just wish I could kill some of those motherfuckers several times over…"

Alice curled her fingers down my back in long strokes, sending tingles straight up my spine, soothing the neon red need to kill. Damned good timing too, because the beast inside me was screaming for blood. My anger shot higher when I realized it was just a matter of time before I had to step away from her again to finish the two fucks who'd escaped.

"Jesus! You're bleeding!" She finally noticed all the blood on me, stumbling back.

"It's not mine. They got Moose. The boys are hauling him home for treatment as fast as they can. Same little wily shit I shot at the first night in your old apartment did the deed. Fuck, do I regret missing his ass the first time around. Hate it even more he crawled away *again.*"

"You mean, there's still a few out there?" Her eyes narrowed, and then she leaned up, making me feel those crazy fucking tingles all over again as hot whispers passed into my ear. "Stop standing around with me. You have to kill them. Every last one."

I grabbed her by the arms and held her close. Alice looked at me with ice and fire mingling in her expression, everything sharp and harsh and nasty.

In one tug, I jerked her into my embrace one more time, crushing my lips to hers. Christ, I loved this girl, just as much as I hated crawling across these knives to chisel our love just right. But finally – fucking *finally* – she fit perfect, part of my world forever, the last goddamned piece that ever mattered.

I kissed her. Hard.

Kissed her 'til she rocked on her heels and then pushed my chest for support, meeting me with an equal ferocity.

If it wasn't for all the bullshit that had just gone down, my cock would've been unstoppable. Even now, the urge to throw her down on the floor, tear off her clothes, and fuck her right on this battlefield was lighting up my blood.

I broke the kiss with a shudder. She drew herself away slowly, giving my bicep one last squeeze.

"I'll be here when the job's done, Lucas. Do it. Do it for me. They need to pay for my Dad too."

The look she gave me – holy fucking shit. I'd never seen her so cold, so determined, and the same killer bitch gaze told me it was time. I nodded, turning to Reb.

"Make sure the brothers keep her and Saffron safe while we're gone. Don't leave this place 'til you get the word from me or Blaze."

"You got it, Veep," he said, digging in his pocket for a light to spark the fresh cig hanging outta his mouth.

I had to practically drag Blaze away from Saffron. But each time his eyes saw the cut around her throat, I wasn't sure who's eyes were crazier, more obsessed with murder.

We were about to go when I turned around and took one last look at Alice. Fuck, she was beautiful. Even with her hair all tangled and the blemish some bastard left on her perfect skin, she was perfect, the only woman I'd ever want 'til I drew my last fucking breath.

I couldn't move another step. Not without doing something first.

"Hang on, Prez. I need you to see this. You and Saffron both." Blaze eyed me warily as I took his old lady's hand. She seemed to welcome the distraction, anything to push the shit they'd done to her behind them. "I need a couple witnesses."

Reb nodded, chewing his tobacco. He knew what was coming. Had a feeling everybody in the room did except Alice, who just stood there as I pressed her into my arms again, wondering what the hell came over me.

"Baby, I can't go out there without doing what I should've done a months ago. We've had a lotta fucked up shit behind us, and we both know there's more ahead. Doesn't matter to me. Not a single damn. I'm not gonna let any crap get in the way of what I've been meaning to do for a second longer."

She drew a breath. I waited 'til her eyes were bright, totally focused on me, starting to understand.

"You're mine, baby," I growled. "Knew it from the second I saw you. Took me all these months to get my head screwed on straight, but now it's tighter than ever, hard as the way I wanna throw you to the floor and let everybody know who you belong to."

"Sting…it's been so long."

"Too fucking long." I looked up, staring at Blaze. "We got business to do, so I'm gonna make this quick, long as it's heard loud and clear. You're not walking outta here shaken and cold after dealing with those fucking animals. You're leaving this shitty cabin my old lady, Alice, and the whole fucking world's gonna figure it out fast."

Blaze gave a firm nod of approval. Saffron smiled, wiping her eyes, overwhelmed with something happy after we'd all stared down the reaper. I grabbed both Alice's hands and moved my lips across them, then pushed between them as they wound around my neck.

If the kisses I gave her a minute ago were fierce, then these were pure fucking lightning. I swung her low to the ground, grabbing her ass, kissing her like an old man should when he tastes the best thing worth living for.

I kissed away the hurt, the misunderstandings, the untamed demons ahead. I kissed her 'til she gasped and scratched at my neck, right in front of Blaze's ferocious eyes and Reb's chuckle, kissed her 'til my lips were numb as the ice covering the ground outside.

"Jesus, Stinger," she whimpered, tottering backward when I finally let her go. It took her a few tense seconds to regain her balance, and then we locked eyes. "Finish it. Go wrap this shit up so I can treat you like an old lady should."

"You heard the girl," Blaze growled, throwing one hand on my shoulder, giving it friendlier squeeze than I expected. "First thing you'll learn about an old lady is it's hell disappointing her. Let's move the fuck out so that doesn't happen."

We turned and started to walk, dead set on doing exactly what Alice said.

The Prez didn't say another word as he followed me outside into the snow. Tank was already crawling on the ground, tracing the blood they'd left.

"Fuck. Looks like the trail ends about here." We followed him to the point where he stomped his boot in the snow, around the side of the building, not far from several bikes the dead Slingers left parked against the wall.

Both assholes were wounded, but they'd somehow made their escape, taking a dirt path going down the mountain. Dead brush and packed snow said the route they'd chosen was the most fucked up place for two wounded dudes ever.

I started to walk without asking. Blaze cupped his hands around his mouth when I'd gotten several feet and yelled after me. "Hey! Where the fuck do you think you're going?"

"Going on foot's a lot safer than tracking 'em on our bikes. Those bastards couldn't have gotten far…"

For a minute, I wondered if either brother was coming. Honestly, I was past giving a shit. Hurling a bullet through both Slingers' skulls when I found their frozen asses would be even more satisfying alone.

Then I heard the crunch of boots quickly plowing through the snow. Blaze and Tank were right behind me.

My heart was dive bombing in my chest when we finally caught up to our targets. I was starting to wonder if those fucks had actually made it to the highway, but then I saw the smoke, heard a roar, and smelled the unmistakable stink of a straining engine.

Not a Harley after all. The fucks had taken a truck, and plowed right through several small glaciers in the process, snapping ice and rocks and branches, tossing their debris everywhere.

"You wanna take this shit from here?" Tank asked, drawing his gun.

"Fuck no. We hit 'em both earlier. They've gotta be wounded by now, disoriented. It's time to put their sick fucking faces outta commission." My fingers tightened on my Magnum.

I had just enough bullets left for these assholes. And that was if we didn't slam them into the snow first, finishing things up slowly and painfully.

We all saw them at the same time.

Their bastard President growled orders at the junkie psychopath next to him, both trying to free the truck's rear tire from where it had gotten stuck. We stepped up, steady and determined, ready to lay into them long before they saw us.

Not how I wanted it to go down. I wanted these assholes to turn around and see how fucked they were, drop to their bloody knees and beg for their lives, then tell us if cutting their throats would put an end to their entire fucked up MC before we went ahead and did it.

Too bad all this shit was destined to wrap up a lot quicker.

The way Blaze was aiming, he wanted it over now. Couldn't say I blamed him.

Whatever, I thought. *Long as they bleed out in the snow, we'll just get our girls home sooner, and see about Moose…*

I held my gun up, and the bastards turned. Blaze fired first. Tank and I were right behind him, spraying the truck with bullets.

"Shit!" I darted out ahead of the brothers. The fuckers went down and rolled. Looked like only one found its mark in the skinny freak, who hit the ground, letting out a high whiny sound like a big balloon deflating.

Nero ran. I slid on snow down slope, crashed against the truck, and fired, narrowly missing the fucker's head. Blaze and Tank slid right behind me.

Tank kicked at the asshole on the ground, Hatter. The big guy was quick, but the scrawny junkie was faster, rolling like a toy into the brush, not far from the thicket Nero ran into.

"Hold on!" I screamed, finally getting a good fix on the skeletal lunatic with my gun.

Right before I could pull the trigger, the dagger he pulled out went into his own throat. The only thing more fucked up than putting a sick fuck down is watching him do himself in right in front of you. The freak was determined, twisting the blade in his neck, gurgling as he went down.

"Holy fuck," Blaze said, slapping his head, pointing with his gun.

It wasn't just Hatter offing himself that had the Prez so winded. Nero was heading toward us, his hands out, collapsing just a step away from his dying brother.

I looked at my boys, trying not to grin. This was too fucking good. Maybe we'd get a chance to give this fuck a little more of what he truly deserved before making sure Satan's Scythe found its mark.

We all walked toward the fuckstain who'd caused all this misery. The asshole was paler, and a lot more deflated than before, his eyes bleary as he looked up at us.

Blaze leaned down, his stubble twitching, pulling his knife outta the holster near his belt and running the flat end across one thigh. "Fuck me. Didn't think you'd be the kind to pussy out, especially after your man here did the dirty work himself."

Tank grinned. I was fucking seething, ready to draw my own knife and plant it into Nero's eye the second Blaze started carving him up. Every goddamned cut was gonna be payback for everything he'd done to this club, everything he'd done to my old lady, and *especially* the shit he'd done to Moose.

Couldn't think of a better place to start than the bastard's eyes. If our brother lived, he was gonna be half-blind for the rest of his life.

The piece of shit at my feet wouldn't live long enough to find out what that was like, but at least we could make him understand for a few minutes. An eye for an eye, pretty fucking literally.

Nero stayed tight lipped. Pissed me off even more. I brought my boot down on his bad leg, twisting hard near the bullet hole, wanting this asshole to scream.

Fuck. Nothing. He just rolled his eyes in pain, lifted his head up, and looked right at me.

"You Prairie Pussies really think you're something, don't you? Just like your whores…" He looked delirious, like he'd lost way more blood than I'd guessed. "Fucking funny…I used to think the same damned thing."

I looked down. His hand was jammed into the dead man's cut, a noticeable bulge below it.

"You fucks…somebody's gotta wipe the smug fucking grin off your devil. Let's die together."

Tank hit the ground and ripped his arm out right as I dove for Nero's throat.

I had a flash of something bright, round, and metallic before I flattened the asshole to the ground and hoisted my knife to his throat.

"Fucking bomb!" Tank roared.

Blaze and Tank both went apeshit, scrambling to get the grenade as far away from our asses ASAP. I lost it in a different way. My murderous rage hit a hateful pitch. The need to see this fuckface dead overrode everything, even base survival.

I went for the throat, stabbing him there again and again, holding him down as he jerked beneath me. Nero's blood splashed all over me, adding to Moose's, and all of us screamed at once.

No fucking way were we all gonna die in a fireball without this motherfucker getting his finale at my hands. I closed my eyes as I kept on stabbing, seeing Alice the whole time, praying we'd all come home in one fucking piece while this asshole took the bullet train to hell.

"Down!" Blaze yelled, adding his bulk to the crazy pile. Tank fell next, bellowing, throwing the hot death in his hands into the woods with all his might. He had little more than a second to spare.

Nero jerked one more time before he went still. Then the grenade exploded in mid-air, raining fire and metal in all directions.

I'd never felt so fucking numb, right to the bones. It took several breathless seconds waiting for the agony to hit, wondering if I was torn up or bleeding out myself. It never came.

No, fuck no, I was still in one piece. A couple seconds later, I felt my brothers stir on top of me. Blaze and Tank popped up fast, sliding their hands over their bodies, checking themselves.

When Blaze saw everybody was good, he pumped his fists into the air and let out a whoop. "Fuck! Just. Fuck!"

"You said it, boss," Tank growled, extending a hand to help me up.

Staggering to my feet, I turned and looked at the mess we'd created. At last, every asshole here with a Slingers' patch lay ruined, too dead to cause more mischief.

Blaze pushed between us, looked at the scene, and nodded. I wondered if he'd be pissed because I'd hogged the kill to myself, but he just looked at me with a thin smile, the kind a man wears when he's glad to be fucking done.

"Let's clean this shit up and haul it up to the cabin. The sooner we light all these fuckers up, the sooner we go home. Come on, brothers."

It took us another twenty minutes to force the truck out of its muddy spot, throw their carcasses in the back, and ride up to the cabin. Took us a little longer than that to stack all the bodies in a pile. We ripped the patches outta their cuts and then threw them all into a heap in the middle of the cabin, stacking extra wood around it, ready for the gasoline we'd brought along for cleanup.

I was moving fast, wanting the cleanup to wind down so I could hang with Alice and make sure she was all bundled up for the ride home.

"Hey…" I looked behind me, doing a double take when I realized Alice was watching me check dead dudes for burning.

"Shit, baby! Go back outside. You shouldn't be in here for this."

"Really?" She quirked an eyebrow. "When you claimed me, I thought you'd figured out I'm used to this crap. It doesn't bother me. Not anymore."

I blinked like a fool. "Still…it's club business, baby. You shouldn't have to –"

She cut me off, shoving something into my chest. *What the fuck?* I reached down and took the crumpled up paper, wrinkling my nose.

It was Mickey's fucking map, the thing that started this shit. And I hoped like hell I never recognized the stink of frozen rat juice again.

"I found it caught in the door. Don't know what you want to do…" The answer was damned clear in her pretty eyes, and I agreed.

"I do. Just let me run it by the Prez first."

I turned, looking for Blaze. He was several feet away, just finishing up a phone call – probably an update on Moose.

"How's he doing?" I asked, tightening the hellish paper in one fist.

"Em thinks he'll live. Lost a lot of fucking blood, though, and his eye's as good as gone. There was no choice but to bring him into the hospital. Her contact there says they're gonna start checking for brain damage tomorrow."

"Fuck!" My head was absolutely fucking spinning. I inadvertently raised the shitty map over my head, fist shaking, scratching at my ear which was suddenly hot as the goddamned sun.

"What the hell's that?" Blaze pointed.

I brought it to my chest, unrolled it, and shoved it toward his face. "Something we'd be wise to get rid of. This fucking thing almost got our old ladies *killed,* Blaze, and our brother too. Do we really want this demon hanging out in the clubhouse, drawing every evil cocksucker to us like a fucked up magnet?"

I expected him to put up a fight. I was tired, chilled to the bone, aching just to be alone with a drink and my girl next to me. But I was determined to hold my ground. Anything to wipe this hell out once and for all.

In one quick jerk, Blaze snatched it outta my hands. He started to walk. I stood up, bristling, yelling so loud Tank came over, ready to break up the fight.

"Just fucking hear me out!" I growled. "You know we're asking for trouble by keeping that fucking thing. Even if we got it in an air tight vault, it's like these assholes can smell it ten states away. Anybody who finds out the Devils are screwing with all these routes is gonna find out *real fucking fast* we've got an inside leak. Don't do it, Blaze. Mark my fucking words, they'll come for it again."

"Boss, just settle the fuck –"

I shoved Tank's hand off my shoulder, still following Blaze. He stopped, stood like a statue, running one hand over his chin, deep in thought.

"Prez?" I was waiting, but he wouldn't look at me.

What the fuck?

Then he started moving again, this time a shorter distance. My fists were twitching and all the crazy bloodlust I'd had while killing Nero was back. I followed him. It was doused with total confusion when we stopped in front of Alice, next to the door.

"I'm not gonna lie, I was on the fence about keeping this shit. I really was," Blaze said slowly. "Then I remembered why I voted for such a hardass VP when we got this charter going. It's your job to ride my ass so I'm not making any fuckups that'll hurt the club. And today, Sting, you did it. You fucking did it."

"Shit, Blaze. I thought you were gonna get greedy and keep that fucking thing." I relaxed, and so did Tank.

"Don't apologize," he said, his eyes narrowing on Alice. "If I wasn't a greedy bastard, I wouldn't be wearing this patch. But I ain't stupid. Since your old lady's not afraid of a few bodies, I wanted her to do the honors. Here."

Blaze held the map out to Alice, right back where it started. She took it, staring at it sadly. Then she nodded and reached for my hand, walking for the pile.

"Make sure that shit gets soaked in gas! Don't want a fucking speck flying outta here that isn't ash before we hit the road," Blaze yelled after us.

I helped her find the perfect place, right between two planks of wood next to Hatter's corpse. His face was twisted and his eyes had popped open. Growling, I reached for the dead maniac and pushed them shut again, wishing I had some rocks.

"There. I'll get the gas. Don't look at that piece of shit, baby. You just look at me."

We soaked the whole area, covering the corpses and the cabin. Reb was finishing up the other side, dousing some extra fuel in the splintered cracks on the floor. With the dark winter night and the isolation, it'd probably be springtime before anybody found the scorched ruins out here.

Blaze was serious about letting her do the honors. Saffron and I were at Alice's side as I watched her light the match, all our bikes and vehicles ready to depart as soon as the inferno started.

Shit billowed up fast. I pulled Alice back while Blaze did the same with his old lady.

We should've hit the road, but the fire was hypnotic. Like watching every wall thrust up between our hearts crumble in a crackle of cleansing orange. My girl's fingers tightened on mine.

The storm was fucking over. I had my old lady and my life. Only thing left was getting my brand on the baby girl next to me, and reminding her every single day that I was never gonna stop loving her.

What we had was as hot and insatiable as the flames consuming the darkness.

XI: Smoldered (Alice)

He was so different on the ride home. Ever since he stepped into the cabin after finishing off the men who'd hurt me so much, who'd made me doubt that what we had was *right*.

When I pressed my hands around his abs on his bike, riding into the darkness with faint, unsettled sparks behind us, I wondered how I doubted this at all.

This was exactly where I belonged, here up against him, the wind running through my soul, my new family riding front, rear, and side. The pain and violence scared me, but it was what I needed to find my way to justice.

Now, I had no doubts. Vengeance was the way home, and home was Stinger.

I leaned into him, breathing in his scent. God, it was addictive. I wondered what kinda crazy magic made him smell even more masculine than before?

Pure, raw warrior flowed up my nostrils and mixed with something in my blood. I couldn't stop myself from scratching at his belly, rubbing my bruised cheek on his neck, mad with need.

Things weren't perfect by any means. Saffron would probably need a few weeks to recover, pushing her wedding back after those bastards hurt her and nearly murdered Moose. I could barely imagine the terrible night that was just beginning for his old lady and his daughter when they heard the news.

But tonight, all the exhaustion, darkness, and heartache didn't do a damned thing to dash the insane need tearing through me with every mile.

I wanted Stinger right now, worse than anything I'd wanted in my entire life. I kissed at his neck when we were entering Missoula's city limits, loving how his body tensed up each time my lips warmed his flesh, my warmth mingling with the sweet coolness left by the wind.

When we roared into the garages, Em was sitting outside on the stairs. She ran to Tank as soon as he parked. I overheard her spilling grim updates about Moose's condition.

Jesus, and I thought Saffron and I were frazzled after being prisoners most of the day.

Blaze reluctantly walked off with Tank and Emma to hear the latest, leaving us to help Saffron inside. She'd twisted her ankle really bad, trying to fight when those assholes dragged us into the rear room.

We all headed for the bar and took our seats. She uncapped a fresh bottle of whiskey and pulled out a few glasses, shoving them toward us.

"Here. We're gonna need a lot of this to take the edge off tonight. Hurry, before Em comes in and starts nagging us about drinking our water. Dehydration's dangerous, ya know." She stuck her tongue out.

I laughed, relieved to see her spirits were returning after we'd left hell behind. Stinger was quiet, sipping slow shots as we talked about the wedding. When I mentioned those wicked heels she'd picked up right before our world went to crap, she lost it, cracking up and crying on my shoulder.

"It's okay! We'll be in Reno before you know it. All this shit will pass…right, Stinger?" I looked at him hopefully.

His eyes were intense, real. No BS hidden in his dark whorls.

"Damned right, baby. This club's seen enough mayhem for a few more months. Come on, Saffron. Blaze's gonna tell you the same fucking thing I just did, and you're gonna believe him. We don't need this shit to keep the edge off. We need our friends and our lovers."

His eyes shifted back to me. Reaching for my hand, he pulled mine close, his grip reassuring and insistent at the same time.

The door slammed and I jumped. Sting held on, refusing to let go, even as Blaze approached.

"Go get some fucking sleep. They won't let us see Moose 'til morning," he said. "We'll debrief on this shit tomorrow. Roller's keeping guard with the family, just in case the Slingers had any rogues out there in sleeper mode."

"Got it, Prez," Stinger said. "We're gonna crash in the clubhouse tonight. Too tired to drive after all this warming up."

He picked up the bottle of Jack and shook it. None of us had really had much at all, but Blaze got the point. He pushed past us and grabbed Saffron, easing her onto her feet, before reaching for the bottle and downing a good third of it.

"Come on, baby. You shouldn't be drinking this shit in your state, so I'm gonna have enough for both of us."

"Asshole!" Saffron playfully slapped his chest.

Seeing them smiling like kids made me smile too. Next thing I knew, we were all alone, listening to the door to the bathroom slam shut. If anybody needed a long, hot shower after tonight, it was Blaze and his blushing bride.

Not to be outdone, Sting grabbed my other arm and pulled, lifting me totally onto his lap. A sticky, shaky heat spiked through me, pooling between my legs, reigniting the animalistic need I'd had on the back of his bike.

"I hate that anyone had to get hurt, but I learned some lessons tonight," I whispered.

"Yeah? Enlighten me."

I leaned closer to his ear, resisting the temptation to nibble on his lobe. "I learned that I'm not afraid of this anymore...the MC, the things you've got to do, what we've got. It's my life, and I'm not running."

"You got no fucking clue how long I've been waiting to hear that, baby." He moved in for a kiss, but I peeled away, holding him in suspense just a little while longer.

He looked at me, surprised. "You gotta be kidding me. There's more?"

"Yup. Tonight's the first time I can safely say I've wanted to throw you down and fuck your brains out without anything getting in the way. No, more than want. I *need* it, Lucas."

I could practically feel the current running through him when I hissed his real name. This time, there was no wriggling out of his grasp – not like I would've wanted to anyway. He threw me over his shoulder and started down the hall, turning toward the infirmary near the bar.

"Gotta clean up first, baby. Fucking love getting down and dirty, but screwing with other dudes' blood drying all over me is something else."

Wise words. I'd forgotten about the streaks all over him, death paint left by friends and enemies alike. We headed into the infirmary and locked the door behind us. He sat down next to the big sink Em used for medical crap. I ran the faucet for him, trying not to go crazy as he peeled off his clothes, one piece at a time.

The blood hadn't penetrated his skin as badly as I thought. It was mostly his arms, his neck, and little flecks tangled in his dark brown hair. I ran my fingers through it, reaching for a sponge.

Sting groaned as I soaked it in warm water and blotted around his neck. Then I made the mistake of looking down at the huge erection straining in his jeans, unmistakable proof his blood was throttled with the same need coursing through me.

Let's get this over with, I thought, biting my bottom lips. *Not that I wouldn't love to stand here and worship these muscles all day...*

Understatement of the decade.

Jesus, he was hot. I worked the wet sponge in between the tight grooves of his inked up muscles, cleansing the sweat and blood dotting his skin, putting the killer to bed and reawakening a different beast. I wasn't sure whether my strokes were loving or shaking with pure lust.

He loved them either way, gently growling and rolling his head back. When I washed beneath his arms, he couldn't keep his hands off me, snarling as he cupped my ass and pulled me forward.

His mouth went up underneath my shirt, kissing at my belly. I laughed, trying to bat him away without melting into a puddle at his feet. His tongue raced up high, pushing my shirt up, shoving my bra aside and going for my breasts.

Holy shit! This is really it!

You know you've found the man you're meant to be with forever when he makes you feel like this after feeling death breathing down your neck.

Right now, there was something else pouring pure hot breath on my skin. This big, beautiful, unstoppable badass named Stinger. Death was no match, and neither was sorrow. He choked the life out of both those evil spirits with his kiss, his touch, his –

Shit!

His teeth found my nipple and sucked, lashing it with his tongue again and again. I tottered backward toward the stainless steel table, falling back when he rose.

Bath time was over. Thank God.

He fisted my hair and moved up for a kiss, smoothing his tongue on mine, straight up mouth-to-mouth fucking. I barely realized when he broke away, unable to concentrate on anything except the swollen ache between my thighs.

"It's my turn," he growled, giving the sponge in one hand a rough squeeze. "Strip for me, baby. You're gonna have to let me run this shit over every inch of your sweet skin before you get my tongue, my dick…"

He flipped me over, rubbing my ass with his hips, making me feel how hard he was. *Holy, holy shit.*

What little shyness I had left went up in a fury, raw need lighting up every single nerve. I stripped fast, loving how he looked at me, nothing but two predatory eyes devouring me one atom at a time.

My jeans fell, and then my panties, the last thing to go. Not fast enough for him. Sting reached around to the gusset and yanked it, ripping soaked cloth down my legs, growling and brushing my tender neck with his stubble.

Oh. Shit.

I really was his. Owned. And really, truly happy to be possessed.

My nipples hardened and everything beneath my waist turned into a hot, wet morass, aligning to the rhythm he sent into my skin with every touch.

His erection rocked against my ass again. Another growl, and his fingers circled my thigh, moving swiftly between my legs. He found my clit and started to make the fierce, hypnotic strokes that never left me any choice but total surrender.

"You're gonna come for me, baby. Right here. Right now. Real fucking hard." His teeth nicked my ear. "Then I'm gonna shove this dick inside you and find out how goddamned incredible you feel with nothing but your pussy wrapped around me. No condom this time. You've been taking that shit Em gave you, right?"

I nodded, trying not to draw blood out of my lip. He tweaked my nipple with his free hand, quickening the strokes with his fingers.

"Good girl. Keep it up too. Now that you're my old lady, I'm never using a fucking condom again. I wanna feel you deep, Alice, every beautiful inch. We're fucking all the time, skin-to-skin, and we're not stopping 'til your pussy cries for my load every damned day."

God. Damn!

The tense strokes coupled with his rough words were officially too fucking much. My knees buckled and I held the edge of the table tight, hardly realizing what was happening as he sank to his knees, running his deliciously scratchy face across the backs of my thighs.

Sting buried his face in my cunt from behind. Sucking, tonguing, opening me with his fingers, his teeth close behind them. He wouldn't quit until my whole body was shaking, bobbing against the table. He pinned me down, holding my thighs open while his mouth did all the work, covering my clit in the steady wet flap of his tongue.

"Do it, Sting," I moaned. "Make me fucking come. I wanna be your old lady and please you better than any of those stupid sluts ever –"

Oh. Fuck.

Jealousy only amped up the raging climax racing through my system.

Every muscle in my body tightened up and I couldn't gasp another word. He wanted me to come?

Fine. I'd go off hot, bright, and screaming, the best grand finale he'd ever seen.

There was no faking it. It came natural, my body losing itself in sharp bliss. All I could do was scream as he rammed his face deeper, lapping at my folds, slapping my clit with ferocious licks again and again and again.

Orgasm hit, explosive as all hell, volcanic as all the emotions he'd throttled through my body. It started in a red hot flush on my cheeks, and then everything in my belly exploded, resonating outward in a sultry rhythm that echoed my old man's power, his love, his passion.

I came.

Stinger growled with satisfaction, never letting up. His tongue kept working me deep, making me shudder on his face that much harder. My fingers balled white knuckled fists on the sleek cool table and I screamed, all I could do to handle the ecstasy ripping through me.

The terror and love of the past twenty-four hours melted in a blurry, breathless sacrifice to this man I'd chosen, the only one with the presence and power like the strongmen who lived in my head.

His grip on my legs tightened as I started to collapse. He flipped me around, helping me onto the table to rest. I wrinkled my nose, knowing I'd have to spray this place down or at least leave Em a note.

The infirmary definitely wasn't sterile anymore.

Stinger pushed between my legs, pulling me up, stamping more furious kisses on my lips, my throat, my breasts. I tasted faint traces of my own wetness on his mouth, melded with his musk, his taste, everything that was gloriously Stinger and Lucas Spears.

"Fuck this shit," he growled, breaking away. "I'm not sliding into your bare pussy for the first time in a damned sick bay. Come on. Let's go to my old room."

He let go and walked to the door, flinging it open. It was just a short distance down the hall, but I didn't want anyone else passing by and spotting me naked. And he was pretty close to nude himself with that crazy hard-on pulling at his jeans – not that the brothers cared who heard or saw them fucking.

"Hang on," I said. "Just let me grab my –"

Sting rushed over and threw me across his shoulder. He carried me off before I could say another word, swinging me over his hard body. I started laughing, beating at his back, shocked to see the caveman come out. He grinned, slowing his steps, lingering next to the bedroom door way longer than we should've.

"Dick!" I said, giving him another slap. Didn't carry much weight when I was giggling like a stupid sorority girl.

"Nobody's gonna get more than a lucky eye full, baby. You're mine now. You always were. Anybody who wants to come closer's gonna have to kill me first."

He gave the knob a twist and we were back in the spartan little room, the first place I'd suffered with him while he held me close, warming away the icy sorrow I'd absorbed for twenty years.

I stopped play fighting. He spun me around and laid me down on the small bed, undoing his belt as he took his place between my legs. His eyes melted into mine.

All fire. All wild. All loving.

Definitely ready to fuck harder than we'd ever done it before.

My lips trembled once. He was on me with another animal kiss, unable to resist, burying me in tongue dancing goodness while I heard his belt rustling off.

Sting pulled back, showing off his painted chest, leaning to kick away his jeans. His boxers came next, and then he was right up against my wetness, all heat and masculine fury throbbing against my pussy.

"You ready to fuck like my old lady, baby?"

Sweet Jesus. I pursed my lips, wrapping my legs around his hard ass, giving him a little jerk with my ankles.

That did it. He rolled his hips back and then pushed into me. Just when I didn't think sex with this whirlwind could be any better, I realized how wrong I was.

Without the condom, I could feel…everything.

Every twitching inch, every spark in his muscles. Pleasure I barely imagined raced up my spine as he slid up to my womb, thumping his balls on my ass. I gushed, trying to hold back.

Just a few minutes of fucking was all it took before I let go and surrendered to the awesome waves exploding beneath my waist.

"Ah, baby. Fucking shit. You're so damned wet, so hot…" His temperature must've went up five degrees too as he pressed his lips to mine and drove his tongue deep. "Christ. I've never wanted to fill a pussy up so bad in my life."

His hips rocked, slowly at first, then quickly picking up speed. He threw more weight into his thrusts. I was used to his power by now, loving it every time he shook my whole body, but I wasn't used to feeling him so *deep.*

My hands and feet locked on tight, riding the storm between my legs. It wasn't long before my hips gyrated against his, pulling him deeper still, melding his thrusts to my pussy.

Stinger growled, nipping at my neck, sucking so hard I knew I'd have a blemish there tomorrow. And I wanted one too.

It was an honor to be marked, branded. Before I took his tattoo and wore his patch, I needed to be claimed with his teeth, his stubble, the wildfire he kindled inside me.

"Give it!" I whined, pushing my neck to his mouth, throwing my hips into his harder. "Bite me when I come. Make me remember how hard we fucked tonight, Lucas."

I reached up and scratched at his head. His growl vibrated through my breasts. The feel of his teeth pulling at my skin was the last thing I needed to fly off the edge.

Coming hard didn't begin to describe how I melted on his cock. Every muscle below my waist tightened up and convulsed, shaking on his cock, turning me into a whimpering, thrashing, clawing mess beneath him.

He fucked right through my orgasm and kept on going, grinding my clit each time he dove deep with his pubic bone. The poor bed beneath us howled.

I'd gotten more than I bargained for with that love bite. Once he was on me, he wouldn't let go, snarling like a wolf as he fucked his way to release.

Stinger came when I was just gliding down from my high. His cock stabbed deep and the earthquake stopped, one second of quiet before the flood.

And the flood – no, the fucking deluge – came a second after his dick swelled. He jerked, releasing the rough bite, throwing his head back and cursing. Hot seed flooded into me, fiery jets pumping up my pussy over and over and over.

"Fuck, baby girl. I'm gonna bust!"

Throwing myself right back over the cliff didn't take any effort at all. I grabbed on tight and pulled him deep, begging to take everything he gave me, feeling him in the deepest heat a man and woman can have.

He rooted himself deep, and my greedy pussy sucked out every last drop he could give me. When it was over, he held it in me for awhile, making slower strokes, fucking through the mingling of our juices.

"Shit, Alice. Everything you show me just keeps getting better." He leaned in for another long, savage kiss.

I smiled when he pulled away. "I like the slow burn approach. Keeps you interested and here where you belong. Don't want my old man wandering to anybody else."

That made him growl. He pulled out between my legs and rolled, shifting me on top of him, locking his hands on my back.

"I'm done with sluts forever, baby. You understand that?" The look in his eye was the same feral one I'd seen before he went off to kill the Slingers. "All I want forever's right here in my hands right now. Beautiful. Perfect. And all fucking *mine*."

Mine.

That word echoed in my head as his lips smothered mine for the thousandth time that night. It was the deepest kiss yet, the one that went above and beyond all the crap we'd waded through to taste the sweetness.

"This is all I'm gonna need for the rest of my life, baby girl. Burn that into your pretty head and stop fussing. I knew the first time we kissed when I was flat on my back and fucked up with poison that I'd never get tired of this. Taking an old lady's as serious to me as wearing my colors.

How much more fucking and kissing do we need for me to spell it out to you?"

I smiled as he shoved his mouth on mine again, rougher than before. His cock was already starting to feel harder against my thigh.

"Mm. Maybe just a little more. You know how forgetful I am."

He blinked – probably wondering if I'd seriously said that – and then broke into a wide shit eating grin. "Baby, reminding you how much I love every inch of this tight little bod's a pleasure, not a chore. Even if you're coming on my dick for the millionth time. And God willing, someday you will be, and I'll be loving you just the same. I'd rather feel your pulse wrapped around my dick than the growl of my own Harley, and that's something I never thought I'd find with any chick."

His eyes were so wide, so bright, spilling pure love into mine. I lost it. I kissed him first this time, reaching for his dick.

By the time the night was through, I had a feeling I wouldn't be able to even feel the nasty bruise Nero left on my cheek. I'd be too busy with the pleasurable love marks on my lips, neck, and breasts – and that was if I didn't feel the soreness between my legs first.

I didn't expect to wake up so early. Sting was still in a coma after coming four more times, always deep inside me. I reached between my legs and felt the heat he'd left there, one more way he'd marked me as his old lady for good.

The clubhouse was eerily quiet. There were a few times through the night when I swore I'd heard another couple loving their brains out as hard as us – probably Blaze and Saffron.

I smiled, easing myself away from Sting's bulk. He was so warm, snoring peacefully, it was hard to step away. But I had to get up after the buzz in my head.

Throwing on my clothes, I closed the door gently behind me and tip-toed out to the bar, grabbing a pencil and the little notepad Saffron used to organize things at the big parties. I found a clean page and started to sketch.

My fingers moved fast, hurting with the rough little motions, but I ignored it. Sex, safety, and a peaceful side of silence were all I needed to feel my muse purring, guiding my hand, outlining all the badasses on their steel horses beneath a familiar grinning devil.

When the rough blueprint was done, I held it up, nodding to myself. The empty spot on the wall where all the tables sat was the perfect place for a mural.

I was still gawking at my design and imagining it there, heating up the emptiness, when I heard footsteps. I flung the notebook on the countertop and looked up just in time to see Saffron wandering in.

She was in her robe, a few baggy marks under her eyes. She walked past me, straight to the coffee maker, and got the potent smelling brew going.

"How's the cut today?" I said cautiously. God, that coffee smelled good.

"Better." She turned, flashing me a good morning smile. "Blaze was a total sweetheart last night. I'm feeling a lot better about things today. We'll figure out the wedding crap later. Just don't tell Stinger he was right."

I grinned, and then lost it just as fast when my next question came. "Any update on Moose?"

Saffron shook her head. "Not since last night. He's critical. Em's supposed to be heading over there with Tank to meet up with his girls and Roller. She says the best folks at the hospital are working on it. I trust her."

I wasn't sure yet how Moose's tragedy fit into everything. It was glaring, brutal proof that some endings were meant to be bittersweet, the price these men and their old ladies had to pay from time to time for living this crazy life.

My head was still fuzzy with melancholy when the timer for the coffee beeped. Saffron poured two mugs and passed one to me across the counter, noticing the little notebook as she did.

"How'd this get over here?" She snatched it up before I could put my hand down and flipped it over. "Holy shit!"

Instant shame. I started to sweat the same way I did back in school, when everybody else saw my stuff for the first time. The teacher, a real hardass, always took his sweet time mulling things over before awarding me the highest score in the class.

"I got bored. Just a little something I busted out this morning. Couldn't shake it after last night, seeing all the Devils in action..."

"It's...shit, it's beautiful!" Saffron stammered.

I looked up. "You really mean that?"

"Mean it? Girl, I'm going to talk to Blaze when he finally drags himself in here. You need to show him this and get it in the clubhouse." She sat the notepad down, then folded her arms, looking around the empty room. "This place could use some livening up. The brothers are getting older, getting paired up. Hell, getting married."

Saffron winked and I laughed.

"What the fuck's so funny?" I turned just in time to see Sting rip the notepad off the counter. His jaw dropped. "Fuck me...you did this, baby?"

"I was going to wait until later for the big reveal. You wanted me to draw you something, right? Well, I did." Watching Stinger lose himself in my work was the biggest surprise yet.

Without saying anything, he closed the notebook and tucked it underneath his arm, shooting Saffron a protective glare. "I'll get you a new one for the bar. Gotta keep this shit safe 'til things calm down around here."

Saffron stuck her tongue out. "I'm one step ahead of you, Sting. Already told her I'd show this thing to Blaze after Moose's situation stabilizes."

"Yeah," he said, a little more sadness in his voice. "One thing's for sure: soon as he approves it to go up, we'll have something to look forward to again. Besides the wedding, I mean. It's been a rough fucking few months."

All three of us nodded. Then Stinger grabbed my coffee mug and drained the last dregs in it.

"Hey!" I slapped his arm, turning to Saffron to beg for a refill.

Too late. Stinger lifted me up and threw me over his shoulder again, heading for the bedroom. Saffron laughed as she watched him carry me off, kicking and squealing the whole time.

"A morning fuck's the least I can do, baby. And not just because I'm hot for getting between your legs again myself."

"What're you talking about?" I whispered, feeling the familiar heat running through me as I ran my hands across his bare tattooed chest.

"You lit a match in a dark fucking hour with this badass piece of paper. Reason one million I'm going out later today to see about your jacket, and then we're having my brand tattooed on your sweet ass." He grinned, kicking the door shut behind him and setting me down. "Better start thinking about where the hell you want it if it's not gonna be *on* your ass for real."

I threw myself at him, slapping his chest. Big mistake. But it was also the best goddamned one I'd made for the new day when he pulled me in, ripped off my clothes, and slammed me down on the bed.

One Week Later

The tension was unholy.

Em was at my left side next to Tank, and Sting on my right, and they were both so tightly wound I felt like the pressure was going to break my bones. We stood just outside the ICU, waiting to see Moose, who'd finally regained consciousness after a week long battle.

All the other brothers plus Saffron were behind me. Everybody except Roller, who Blaze kept next to the family as a constant guard. Thank God there wasn't any sign yet we needed it.

My old man was tight-lipped as ever about club business. But it *seemed* the Slingers threat was over, and all the men who'd caused so much mayhem for me and the club were nothing but charred ash.

The big metal doors swung open. My heart dumped adrenaline. A nurse whispered something into Em's ear, and then waved us all forward.

I squeezed Stinger's hand tight as we went into the pale white room. Moose's big body was propped up in the blue and white bed, his beefy arms at his sides, a band going around his head to hold in the gauze or whatever the hell they'd given him to encourage healing.

"You all here to gawk at me like I'm a fucking Cyclops, or what?"

"Moose…" His old lady Connie darted up, a disapproving look on her face, one that also feared getting in the way of her old man's suffering.

Sting pulled his hand away from mine and stepped forward with Blaze. Across the room, Moose's daughter Becky nudged her face into Roller's shoulder, trying not to cry. The younger brother looked up, surprised, folding a firm arm around her.

"No, brother," Blaze said. "If I wanted to see a fucking freak, I'd go dig up all the motherfuckers we've put down over the years. And with your help, we dug a few more graves for the trash. I would've called church for this, but seeing how you're cooped up in here, I thought a family affair was more appropriate. Stinger?"

The two men locked eyes. I watched Sting reach into a little black box and pull out a patch made by the same place that did the leather jacket sitting heavy on my shoulders. That PROPERTY OF STINGER patch felt like cool steel on my back, and I had a feeling its weight a lot more as time ticked by.

The whole damned world had gotten heavier around these men.

"This is yours, brother. This club doesn't have a patch to recognize a lifetime of half the shit you've done. But you earned this. You earned it with your life."

He leaned down, giving Moose a manly hug after he laid the patch out next to him on the stand. BLOOD SACRIFICE, it read, something I'd only seen on Tank's cut as the only other guy wounded for the MC.

"I'll have Em's mom take care of it for you, bro. I'm not gonna see you in your cut again 'til that things sewn where it belongs."

As a tailor, Emma's mother did all the patches and modifications for the club. She was hard at work right now on Saffron's wedding stuff, changing up an old dress that belonged to her grandmother. I wondered how it was going to go with those bitch heels she'd picked the day we got captured.

"You all right, brother?" Stinger asked, pulling away and giving Moose a heavy look.

Moose gazed out his one good eye at all of us, running down the line, from Blaze to Sting to everybody else. When he got to me, the sadness hit, an avalanche that made me wonder if one day I'd be looking at my man in a bed like this, torn up in ways I could barely imagine.

No fucking way, I thought. *He's too hard, too lucky. And if somehow his luck deserts him one day, I'll be there, just like Connie.*

I haven't figured everything out about being an old lady yet, but I know half the job is being a rock. I'm going to be the best damned stone Stinger's ever had.

"I'm good," Moose said slowly. "Just quit looking at me."

Awkward. Everybody turned their eyes away, except for Connie and Becky, staring at their husband, their father, in horror.

"Look, this club's suffered far worse shit than me losing a fucking eye," he said finally. "Let's stop dwelling on it and get on with our lives. Another week or two and I'll be outta this place, and then I'm gonna go back to work. Tax prep's coming up for all the club's business, and I'm gonna be there, one eye or none."

Several brothers looked up hopefully. Sting slapped him on the shoulder and smiled. Blaze gave an approving nod.

"Prez promised us brighter days not so long ago, right? Last thing I'm gonna do is let any fucking darkness around me blot out the sun we all deserve. You brothers with your old ladies, your girls..." He paused, reaching for Connie's hand and giving it a squeeze, forcing the tears from her eyes.

"You hold 'em fucking tight, and I'll do the same. You guys who haven't claimed a girl yet – keep on drinking. Keep on fucking. Keep on being free." He stopped, clearing his throat to cover up the way Connie whimpered. "Now, like I said, quit gawking at my half-blind ass. Keep my bike tuned up for me when I get home. We got ourselves a wedding in a few weeks, and I'm gonna be there. Don't give a shit if I show up stumbling around like a drunken pirate."

Blaze grinned. "There's gonna be a lotta that anyway, bro, whether you've got two good eyes or none."

Finally. The tension was cut and everybody laughed. Each of the brothers passed by his bed one more time, patting him on the shoulder and making small talk.

I couldn't help but smile. Yeah, their world was twisted, frightening, ruthless at times. But when I saw Stinger coming toward me, a flood of emotion in his rich dark eyes, I knew I wouldn't trade it for anything.

I'd grown up in the middle of Dad's schemes, as fucked up as anyone. But for the first time ever, I had a family to go with the endless, violent bumps on the road. For the first time, I was really, truly *happy*. My heart soared when Stinger pulled me outside and tipped me down in his strong arms, stamping fresh lightning on my lips.

I love you, baby, and I'm gonna fuck your brains out. I read the message in his kiss loud and clear.

We kissed for a long time while the other brothers filed past. Not to be outdone, I heard Em squeal as Tank grabbed his old lady and flattened her against the wall, whispering rough promises in her ear.

"You know I love you so fucking bad it drains the life outta me, baby girl?" Sting pulled back, running his fingers through my long black hair, tender and seductive simultaneously.

"Not half as much as I love you, Lucas."

I smiled into the next kiss. It was all I had to say to feel his strong pulse pumping with mine. We lingered a little longer at the hospital before we rode home.

With any luck, nobody would ever have to make the sacrifice Moose did again. But if it came, I was ready to pay it a thousand times over, a fair price for loving the badass enveloping me for the rest of my life.

XII: Outlaw Kind of Party (Stinger)

One Month Later

The wedding was the craziest shit I'd ever seen, even by club standards. Honestly, I wouldn't have expected anything less.

It was *Blaze* getting married, after all, and it was time to show the whole Prairie Devils MC how big his dick was as Montana Prez before he gave it to Saffron during their week long honeymoon.

We all departed on a cold day in late February. Had to rent a couple trucks to haul the bikes 'til we crossed the Nevada border, but then we mounted them, just me and my girl surrounded by a whole lotta brothers riding into arid country.

The Nomads rode behind our Montana crew, a buncha mean sons of bitches with a dude named Maverick in the lead, their Prez and Blaze's brother. Also the only guy I'd seen wearing our colors who got away with calling Blaze asshole to his face. His old lady, June, rode with him, another girl who'd taken some seriously fucked up blows before our Montana charter formed last year.

But fuck, wasn't that the test every man and his girl went through?

The sweet thing with her hands around my waist all the way to Reno wouldn't have met me if her life hadn't been a clusterfuck. And if I'd never gone after her, she'd be too dead to love anybody.

Lady Luck slapped the back side of my head every time I pressed my lips to her, reminding me how damned lucky I was. And each time I fucked her, I let her know with every touch, every thrust, every screaming release how much I loved her.

My promise to never, ever fuck this up was written in flesh and blood, and I intended to keep it.

Sure, Blaze had his Saffron and Tank had his Em. Me? I had Alice, and that was all I needed besides my patch and my bike, an entire universe I'd been chasing without even realizing it 'til this sexy dark haired spitfire got her hooks beneath my skin.

Arriving in Reno wasn't all roses. There were always thorns.

The newer brothers kept guard while we settled into our hotel, a fancy ass place connected to a casino and one helluva a resort. It was chilly, but the low fifties without any snow outside the mountains was a big fucking improvement over the frozen wasteland we'd left behind.

The trip started off right. One long night of drinking, fucking, and gambling had all of us feeling refreshed. Even

Moose was smiling again with his old lady and his daughter, chilling at the bar and stuffing himself on the best whisky and shrimp the club could buy.

Alice was at my side the whole time. She appreciated the shit outta the weird clash of ritzy and gaudy travelers find in this city, and it was damned good to see her so excited again. I could tell her sweet head was swirling with fresh ideas.

Throwing the mural up in the clubhouse over the last month only fed her muse. She was talking about picking up work in town as soon as shit thawed. Missoula had a perfect niche market with tons of rich dudes looking for the artsy stuff she could deliver.

And fuck, could she deliver.

She's sketched her tattoo design herself, a raven and thorns wrapped around the only part that really mattered to me: PROPERTY OF STINGER. Poor Tank had to go nice and slow to do it right when he put it on her lower back, right above her ass.

I'd never, ever get tired of seeing my name there while we fucked, whenever she swiveled her hips into me and rode my cock. And it was only getting better the more our bodies worked, two magnets meant to fit together in non-stop lust, tighter and better with plenty of practice.

The girl had a real knack for driving me wild. Did I mention how fucking hard my cock jerked in the getup I was screwing with on the big day?

She came out wearing this red, sleek number all the old ladies picked out. Fucking thing was modest enough for a cocktail party, but it accented her curves perfectly, clinging to her ass and tits so good I started to wonder what they'd look like in lily white. Good thing I had some heavy shit in my pocket, waiting for the right moment, because it helped anchor my cock and dissuade his greedy balls from doing anything stupid before the ceremony.

Couldn't stop myself from running up to her and pinning her to my chest. "Fuck, baby. You look gorgeous. Hot *and* beautiful."

She gave me her lips, and I sucked them hard, running my tongue across them several times to show her how bad I wanted her later. Fuck me if it didn't make things worse down below, but I had to push through it. There'd be plenty of time to suck and tease and fill her soft wet velvet all night after the reception.

Alice had to fight to break the kiss. Laughing, she gave me a little push, narrowing her eyes and looking me up and down.

"You're not bad yourself. Still think all you guys would look better in suits."

I snorted. "This is a biker wedding, girl. Not the flowery prim and proper shit that puts a dude to sleep in the civilian world. Dressing up's for the ladies. All the brothers are here for the party."

"Yeah? Is that why your cut's looking cleaner than I've seen it for months?" She leaned into me and inhaled. "I can't even smell the motor oil! Who the hell are you?"

Growling, I grabbed her ass, pulling her in tight. "You know damned well who the fuck I am, baby. And if you don't, you'll figure it out later when I rip that thing off and fuck your sweet ass."

I gave her a playful swat. "Come on. Everybody's waiting for us down below. Might have to fight a few guys today to keep 'em off you. Christ, you're hot."

My cock strained the whole time while we stood, waiting for the elevator. Tank and Em were in there waiting when the door opened.

Shit. Seeing his big stupid smile deflated the insane wood going nuts against my trousers.

"Going down?" Tank asked.

"You fucking know it. I'd ride a thousand floors to find out if the Prez sheds a tear or two today when he kisses the blushing bride."

Alice swatted my arm. Em and Tank laughed.

At the bottom floor, the door slid open, revealing the spacious casino hallway we had to walk through to get to the chapel. The man right across from us, leaning near the fountain, instantly made me choke.

I had to reach up and rub my eyes, wondering if I was hallucinating. But if I was, Tank wouldn't have flipped his shit and ran for the fucker, tackling him and pining his ass to the ground.

"What's wrong?" Alice's breath caught. "Who is he?"

Em pulled her back as soon as we stepped outta the elevator, making sure she didn't follow me. I hadn't seen that wormy little shit in the Grizzlies cut for months, not since the night we rescued Saffron from the rogues, wearing the same patch who'd gone traitor against their own club.

It was Saffron's brother, an asshole named Brass. The little shit had gone west with the Grizzlies since then, and now he'd wound up here, the last fucking place in the world he belonged.

I barely stopped Tank from knocking his teeth out, pulling him outta the giant's path just before his huge fists crashed into Brass' face.

"Start talking!" I roared. "What the fuck are you doing here?"

"I'm alone!" He roared right back. "Calm the fuck down, you fucking Prairie –"

He stopped just short of saying it. If he breathed out *pussies*, I sure as shit would've let Tank have at it, adding a few of my own kicks to the storm.

"I just wanna see my sis get married. That's all. There's nobody else here wearing this patch. And even if there were –"

Tank growled. I suppressed my own, rolling my eyes instead, relaxing my grip on the asshole on the floor.

"Yeah, yeah. We know. Reno and Vegas are neutral cities. Doesn't mean we won't kick your ass for snooping so close to our club when you're not welcome."

He stood up, dusting off his cut. I eyed Tank. We had to be damned careful here in this place. The ceilings were crawling with security cameras. Scuffling with this asshole wasn't worth getting ourselves pulled aside by some do-right with a badge and missing the most important day of Blaze and Saffron's life.

"You can't go in there wearing that thing," Tank said, folding his arms. "You do, and we won't be the only ones threatening to kick your ass. There's a couple dozen dudes wearing this patch, and one with yours – if you're telling us the truth. What's it gonna be?"

Brass looked from side to side, stuffing his hands in his pockets. "What if it was you? Would you throw your colors off if some asshole from my club asked you to?"

Tank and I stared the fucker down. I was ready to wring his fucking neck, teasing us on our own damned turf like this. Damn, if it wasn't for those fucking cameras…

"Boys!" There was a flap of bright red and Alice was between us, Em at her side. "Why don't you just put him in the back where nobody can see him? Everybody's going to be looking up at the altar anyway. Who'll notice he's even here if he stays sitting and covers up after it's all over?"

Tank's face tightened. Em shot pleading eyes at him, a little less fierce than my girl's.

Why she wanted to fight for this piece of shit was beyond me…

"Baby, I appreciate what you're trying to do, but there's a lot you don't understand about what goes on in our clubs –"

She waved a hand. "I understand I owe Saffron big for helping me get my shit together and make sure this thing goes off without a hitch. She'll be thrilled just to see him here, whether he's wearing his own colors or a bearskin suit. Do you really want me to be the one to break the news that you guys beat the hell out of her little brother when he was trying to be nice?"

"Fuck," Tank growled. "Nice isn't a word I'd use anywhere near that sneaky little mother –"

With a heavy sigh, I turned to my brother and reached up, slapping my hands on his big shoulders. "She's right, brother. I don't like it either, but if I give Blaze a call, I'm sure it'll be fine after he gets over the shock. I think this shit's telling us the truth for once – if the Grizzlies are looking to kick our asses out here, they sure as fuck wouldn't have sent this sloppy bastard to lead us into a trap."

Tank's anger swelled in his face, and then the redness faded a shade. Still growling, he turned away, reaching for his burner phone.

"Fucking fine. I'll make the call myself, boss. It's not like I don't trust the security here. All that's on me for setting shit up. Trouble is, I'm not sure how we're gonna protect this fuck when somebody realizes what patch he's wearing."

"Make sure Blaze gets the message and passes it along to the whole club," I said sternly. "No fucking fights with any clubs. Not unless they're gonna draw on us or fuck this club some other way."

I turned back to Brass. Fucker's eyes were just as beady as ever, but he was looking at me like I'd done him one helluva solid. In truth, I had, but I didn't do it for him.

Reaching for Alice's hand, I grabbed her, pulling her away from the shit in the rival cut. "Let's get going, soon as Tank's off the phone. Brass, you stick close to us and sit your ass down where we tell you to. I'll have somebody find a plain jacket you can throw on for the reception. Then say hello to sis, give 'em your well wishes, and get the fuck on the road. You better be outta here by midnight."

"Never thought I'd make a deal with a Devil." He extended a hand. "But I'm game."

I took his hand and shook it harder than anything meant to be friendly. Least the asshole had been smart enough not to use the phrase 'Prairie Pussy.'

At two o'clock sharp that afternoon, we were all in our pews. Alice and I were up in the front, right next to Tank and Em, all the brothers lined up by seniority, and family on the other side. Brass was way the hell in the back. A shitty view, sure, but so far, nobody had given him a second look.

Alice couldn't stop staring at the high ceilings, the neon torches, the crazy ass 'priest' in the front with a purple robe and big shades. It was a Reno wedding, after all. Crazy and outlandish was the norm with several dozen brothers and their old ladies packing the over-decorated chapel.

When the bells chimed two, the brothers at the big door leading outside opened up, and we could hear the roar dying down outside. Smokey, Stone, and a couple other brothers from Dakota who'd come down for the fun parked their bikes next to Saffron's limo after escorting it a couple blocks.

The bride stepped outta the sleek black car with a hand from the chauffeur and our boys. They carried her long ass veil up the stairs and gently let it glide down, one inch off the ground above the long red carpet.

Shit. Alice suppressed a giggle. Blaze's old lady must've grown at least three inches in those wicked high heels she had attached to the white hose going up her legs. She looked like a total babe decked out in white – but I really lost my mind when I imagined Alice wearing the same damned thing someday.

Fuck, now the little secret in my pocket was dangerously close to starting my dick on fire. I watched Saffron slowly walk down the aisle, some weird rock rendition of *Here Comes the Bride* droning on the speakers. Up front, Blaze couldn't stop smiling.

The Prez's eyes were wide as silver dollars seeing his old lady coming toward him, dolled up to perfection, about to be his in every way imaginable. Claiming her again with a ring, a kiss, and a certificate from the state was only second to putting his brand on her.

Alice's fingers danced in my hand. I squeezed it tight, watching as the music died down and Saffron stopped at the altar, beaming pure love into her old man's eyes.

The priest's jabber was short and sweet. Blaze paid the dude good money to lock down this chapel for us all evening, but he didn't seem to mind him moving smoothly toward the words both those grinning lovers were waiting for.

I heard a whimper next to me and looked over. Em cracked, smiling and blotting at her eyes. Tank flashed me a big crazy grin and pulled her into his chest, holding her like a kitten as they watched the ceremony roll on.

The rings went on bride and groom. Brothers clapped and made the rafters echo with their gruff hoots while the dude officiating waited for shit to quiet down for the climax. Blaze already looked like he was gonna rip that pretty dress off and fuck her right there on the altar.

Couldn't get the greedy bastard in my pants to behave neither. Every time Alice wiggled a little closer, making me feel drunk on that sweet cherry blossom shit she was wearing for perfume, I wanted to take her right there, right in front of my brothers and God, holding onto the leash for my inner beast with all my might.

"By the power vested in me by the state of Nevada, I now pronounce you man and wife," the priest said, smiling as shrill hoots from old ladies rattled the final part. "Kiss the bride like there's no tomorrow, Mister President."

Blaze had his arms around her. They jerked his woman to his chest so fast he was right ahead of the wilder, crazier hollering that broke out. I added my hoarse roars of approval to the mix when he threw back her veil and smashed his lips on hers, kissing her so fucking hard her knees went weak, trembling along with the rest of her while tears slid down her cheeks.

Fuck it. I couldn't wait anymore. Amid all the commotion, I grabbed my Alice, putting my hands on her ass and giving it a good squeeze while I shoved my lips to hers. It surprised her at first, but soon she tucked into it, sweet proof that she wanted it just as bad as I did.

Christ. All the fiery kisses we'd had before were like a ghost of this kiss, all lips and tongue and fire, so warm it flowed right down to my dick and caused it to jolt.

If this was what weddings did to her, then I wanted fucking more of them.

When we finally came up for air, the bride and groom were walking down the aisle, down to the limo waiting, flanked by the same honor guard of brothers as before. Tank was still furiously sucking face with Em next to us, probably overwhelmed with the same crazy ache that was coursing through our blood. Blaze caught my eye and gave me a smile as he passed. I nodded, happy as hell for the man who held this club together through several brutal storms.

If it weren't for him, I wouldn't have the girl wrapped around me right now, safe and tight, all mine. He'd thrown some boomerangs trying to keep us apart, yeah, but overall the Prez didn't stop the love bug once it bit.

We all filed out, my hand wrapped tight around Alice's, heading for the reception. They'd picked a big ass ballroom with a fountain and skylights, one more freakishly awesome contrast between grit and elegance.

The tables were huge and plentiful. Alice and I had one to ourselves, not far from Tank and Em and several other brothers. The back table was even bigger, stacked high with all kinds of appetizers and three separate bars tended by neat dressed staff.

Half the liquor there had been sent down by Throttle with his congratulations from mother charter. Yesterday, the boys and I triple checked every fucking bottle and keg to make sure nothing was outta place. After Dakota heard what happened to us last fall, they put a special Devils' seal on every shipment, clearly identifying where their gifts were coming from so no brother would ever fall down poisoned again.

There was a lotta razzing at dinner, but no clinking glasses. No fucking need. The happy couple couldn't keep their hands and lips off each other. Only thing I couldn't figure out was how Blaze was keeping himself under control instead of dragging her back to their suite early, smacking his girls ass 'til she drove those spiked heels into his his own rear end.

Alice sipped her wine and I had my Jack straight, trying to space out my shots to keep sober for later tonight. Seeing Brass walk up to the bride and groom had me on edge too.

The ass was smart enough to wear the plain jacket Roller scrounged up, covering up his Grizzlies MC patches. Blaze knew exactly who the fuck he was, and he looked none too pleased. But the expression on his old lady's face said it all. She popped up and threw her arms around her brother, smiling the whole time.

Less than an hour later, brothers started to hit the dance floor, mingling with their girls. I pushed one hand underneath the table onto Alice's thigh. She flushed and looked at me with a sly little smile.

Fucking tease. If I couldn't have her yet with my dick between her legs, then I was gonna get my hands all over her on the dance floor.

"You feeling too tipsy to move with me, baby?"

She broke into a wide grin and grabbed my hand with both hers, pulling me up. I laughed. The girl wanted it so damned bad, and who was I to hold back?

We danced close, nice and fluid, to nineties rock. The shit never sounded so strange to me with the high ceiling and crazy acoustics, but damn if it didn't excite her.

"This is a wonderful night," she purred, nipping evilly at my ear. "Just say the word and we can get out of here anytime. I know you're holding back, Sting."

She pushed her hips into mine. My cock went absolutely fucking nuts, twitching in my pants, screaming so loud through my nerves my head rattled.

I grunted, pulling her closer with a growl, letting her feel my hard-on. There was nothing to be shy about here. Half the girls were sluts the Dakota boys picked up and brought down, and they were getting their fingers and tongues a whole lot dirtier than Alice and I on the floor.

One of the Dickinson crew was down on his knees, moving his tongue up some chick's thigh, before pulling her completely off the floor and carrying her to a more private spot.

Sex was in the air, all right, and it would've had me strapped down tight if it wasn't for this last, crazy thing I was gonna do.

"Hang on, baby," I said, grabbing for her hands. She gave me a curious look, slowing the sexy little twist in her hips. "Don't worry. You better believe you're gonna get fucked all night. But before that happens, I got something to say."

"Sting? What's up?"

"Come on." I yanked on her hands and pulled her to the nearest table, right next to Blaze and Saffron, bride and groom about to take off together.

Alice shook her head, wondering what the fuck I was doing as I stood up on the table. Several brothers looked at me with the same confusion in their eyes. Even Moose was following me now, one arm around Connie at his table, his lone good eye locked on us both.

"Listen up, brothers," I said, grabbing a strategically placed shot of Jack on the table. "I gotta make a toast to Blaze and Saffron, my brother and this charter's Prez, the best damned Prez this side of the continental divide..."

A man at the table next to me laughed. I looked over and saw Maverick nodding, genuine agreement and a little sarcasm in his eyes. His old lady, June, elbowed him.

Fuck it, I thought. *Might as well make this quick and dirty. That's the way things have always been with this girl, and I wouldn't have it any other way.*

"But I'm not toasting with this fucking drink." Other brothers holding up their glasses lowered them, adding to the confusion I'd stirred. "No, I'm gonna toast to the bride and groom by following Blaze's example. You see Alice here?"

I grabbed her hand and held it up, giving her arm an exaggerated wave. That got a smile on her face, though she was still looking at me like I'd lost my damned mind. Hell, maybe I had.

"Next wedding you boys are gonna come to is mine, after my old lady gives me a yes." Laughter and surprised shouts rang out.

I looked over. Saffron was grinning and Blaze shook his head, unable to hide his cocky smile. The Prez was probably glad I was making his escape easier for the honeymoon by stealing the spotlight.

My cue to drop to my knees, though I was still kneeling on the table over her, fingers squeezing her wrist tighter than ever before. I reached into my pocket and grabbed the box.

Alice started to shake when she saw it, and it was like the poor girl put her finger in a socket when I popped it open. Hoped like hell her shakes were excitement. Damned good chance with her eyes alive and sparkling, taking in the big ass stone I'd picked out set in the gold ring.

"Will you, baby? Will you marry your old man?"

The three seconds I waited for an answer was the quietest, most agonizing time of my life. Finally, she drew one hand over mine, the trembling in her fingers slowing. Grip tightening, she plucked out the ring and drew it to her lips, lips to die for, giving it a little kiss before she moved it back toward me with her fingers stretched out.

"Of course I will, Sting. You're the love of my life. It just took pure hell and some time to figure that out."

I jumped down and threw my arms around my girl. Her shape was always pure heaven in my hands, but shit, hearing her say that turned her into a total goddess, unreal fucking beauty I couldn't keep my hands and hips and lips away from.

The room exploded. Brothers started pounding their fists on the table. Saffron popped outta her chair and ran over, nearly tripping on her crazy heels. She threw her arms around Alice, purring her congratulations.

Fuck that shit. There'd be plenty of time for girls to celebrate later. I jealously pulled my girl toward me, tipping her back the same way Blaze did at the altar, throwing the most intense kiss I could muster on her lips.

The wedding bells and rock songs blasting earlier today echoed in my brain as we kissed and kissed. When I came up for air, everybody was looking at me, laughing and pointing or just giving approving nods.

Everybody except Tank. I saw the pissed look on his face and did a double take, wondering what the fuck was eating him.

Next thing I knew, he was heading right for me, jerking Em off the dance floor with one hand. He stopped next to Alice and me, blocking out half the brothers at their tables with his huge bulk.

"Congratulations, boss. I really fucking mean it." The giant's arms crushed us both, and then he pulled away, smiling like a fool.

I was relieved, but he sure wasn't moving after his brotherly congratulations. Instead, he took Em, lifting her into the air as she squealed while he jumped onto the same table I'd been on just seconds before.

"I got something to say too, boss. I'm gonna follow *your* example, you and Blaze both, just like you said…"

"Fucking great," I heard Blaze grumble, halfway amused and exasperated with the craziness blowing up the room.

Em realized what was coming a second after the rest of us. When Tank's hand went into his pocket, her hands went over her mouth. Smiling, Alice and Saffron patted her on the back, trying to get her to breathe. The little blonde nurse was the last woman in the world I'd expected to see hyperventilating.

"Babe," Tank said, holding out a box with his own gold ring glowing bright. "I promised I was gonna put a ring on your finger the instant I claimed you. The Prez and the VP showed me the way, and now I'm not gonna wait a single fucking second longer to ask: will you marry me, Em?"

Another long, brutal silence. Then, squealing, Em threw herself into his arms, mouthing a dozen yeses in rapid fire.

Thank fuck.

I threw my hands and lips on Alice all over again as the whole ballroom exploded into commotion. Deafening biker growls shook the room for the next five minutes. Loud as they were, the chaos faded in my ears as our tongues mingled, the entire world slipping into a distant fuzz, disappearing into one hot fucking kiss with the only woman who'd ever matter to me again.

Today, it was just me and my old lady, the girl I was gonna make my wife. And just knowing she'd become PROPERTY OF STINGER in every single way sent lava surging through my veins.

My kisses kept coming, hard and possessive, never letting up 'til she pushed against my chest. We locked eyes with her tilted in my arms, her gaze narrowed.

"Sting, let's go. *Now.*"

No fucking way was I gonna argue with that. Tank and Em were still at it, devouring each other. Blaze was standing next to our little cluster too, one arm coiled around Saffron, the same wild desire in his eyes I knew I had in mine.

We took off to our room, leaving the best damned party the Prairie Devils MC could've asked for. A year ago, I would've stayed for the laughs, the booze, the sluts.

But now, I had something a thousand times better to look forward to. Alice and I weren't coming down 'til morning, when she'd be spent and hoarse from all the screaming, off the walls fucking I had planned.

"Jesus, Sting, take it easy!" Upstairs, Alice whimpered when we got to our bed.

I wasn't listening.

My hand was already on one strap of that pretty dress, pulling it off her shoulder, working the zipper with my other in a race to get her naked. I rolled my hips, pinning her in place.

We had all night to climb into bed and do this slow and sensual. But with time our side, that shit could wait.

What we needed right now was a quick, savage fuck, with her bent over beneath me while I shook her body, balls deep in her tight warmth.

"Don't bullshit me, baby. I know what my fiancee wants when her nips are this hard." I reached up and shoved away one bra cup, tweaking the hard little pebble in my fingers.

Alice gasped, grinding her ass into my crotch. Caught her playing coy red handed, and it was pure fucking heaven.

I let her rise, just enough to help shake off the dress. When she raised her feet, I gently swept it aside, grabbing her sweet thighs and holding them apart.

All the modesty flew out the big glass window overlooking the neon lit city when I sank to my knees, tonguing down the small of her back. Fuck, she tasted good, every bare inch of her skin.

Alice gasped, stretching her arms out on the bed high above her head. Her legs started to shake the second I hit one knee and started rising, moving to her panties, soaked and ready to be ripped away so I could tuck into the sweetness they hid.

Christ, she was wet, and her scent drove me a little more crazy each time I breathed in. I wrapped my arm around her legs tight while my teeth went for the waistband above her ass, tearing it straight to her ankles in a jerk a wild animal would've been proud of.

"Oh, God…"

That's right, baby, I thought. *Better let it out now. Those are the last words you're gonna say before all you can do is scream.*

My dick was leaking pre-come all over my own fabric. I ignored the greedy steel throbbing between my legs a little while longer, diving into her pussy, spreading her open with two tense fingers.

Hot, wet cream bathed my tongue. I licked straight through her folds, loving the way her ass bounced near my head the harder I stroked, feeling her cheeks go taut when I hit her clit.

Bingo.

My mouth drew her nub in, holding it ransom for my tongue, 'til she let go and found her sweet release. When her sweet knees began to shake in my hands, I knew it wasn't far off.

Go on, baby, I thought, mouth too full of the best pussy in the world to speak. *Come for me. Come your fucking brains out.*

I heard the sheets rustling through her moans. She must've been clawing them something fierce, struggling to hold on before her body went nova.

No mercy. No holding back. I ate her like she was the best damned thing I'd never tasted.

Best of all, I didn't have to try, because it was no fucking joke. No lie. Every bit of this was real, from shoving my ring on her finger earlier, to laying her flesh out for the most passionate loving bleeding out my soul.

"Just a little longer," she moaned breathlessly. "Sting – fuck!"

Her hips rolled backward and I held her tight, forcing her to stay open, quickening my tongue lashes. Baby girl rocketed straight into the ether, losing herself in my licks, seizing up as sheer ecstasy lit her nerves on fire.

I couldn't stop smiling as I lapped through her climax, knowing I had a lifetime of this ahead.

It took her a couple minutes to stop shuddering and catch her breath. When she finally did, I kissed my way up, standing and laying one hand on her back.

The insatiable fuck between my legs was finally gonna get what he needed. I popped her bra and squeezed her tits, making her roll her bare ass against me, enjoying the friction for a couple hot seconds as my dick ballooned to full hardness.

"I'm gonna fuck you now, Alice. First fuck wearing my ring. You stay right here, with me, and let it all go, just like we did on the dance floor, baby. You ready for that?"

"What aren't I ready for with you?" She said, giving a little nod.

I smiled. Good girl. My hips rocked against hers one more time, loving how she gasped when my cock teased her cheeks.

My fingers worked fast. These fucking clothes were long overdue to get lost. I dropped everything, kicking outta my jeans and boxers last, then pressed my cock to her ass to savor her warmth.

She bobbed eagerly, grinding her little ass into me.

Fuck, fuck, fuck...

My hand shot up, caught her hair, and fisted it at the same time I sank into her. Started pushing into her with long, ferocious strokes, pounding so deep my balls clapped her sweet flesh. Her ass cheeks rippled each time I drove deep, claiming her pussy, crazed as the first time I ever fucked it.

Hearing her moan, lost in total fire, was all the approval I needed. I fucked her like my wife, my old lady.

Tender. Rough. Intense.

Deep, too – especially goddamned deep.

One fine day I'd pump a live load into her after she went off birth control and get our first kid cooking in her womb. I couldn't wait to have a family. Sure, we'd both had fucked up childhoods, but we'd learned enough tough lessons to know how to do it right.

I didn't doubt that shit for a single second.

We fucked and rocked and sweated, her whimpering and propping herself up on her toes. I breathed in her ear, telling her to come on my dick, leaning back so I could watch my brand bob as she sank down around my cock again and again.

Fuck, I'd never get tired of seeing PROPERTY OF STINGER scrawled there. Just like I wouldn't get sick of seeing the new ring on her finger.

Almost as sweet as hearing her tense up and call my name. Close, yeah, but fuck hearing her gasp and explode had no competition. It always won, and it always fucking would too.

"Sting! Come with me. I want you, Lucas. *Fill me.*"

No ifs, ands, or even fucking buts about that. When I heard her beg for my come, I went ballistic, turning to molten energy, nothing but the fire crackling in my balls.

She started to come a second ahead of me, and I fucking lost it. I bared my teeth, growling, deepening my thrusts so hard they shook the bed through her body. I hammered in tight, held my swelling cock to her womb, and flooded her pussy.

Nothing compared to coming in this woman. Nothing.

Riding into the setting sun on my bike was close, but even that shit didn't give me half the carefree fire I got when I jerked on top of her, staking my claim the deepest, most primal way a man can.

Every romp seemed better than the last, but this one was off the fucking charts. No exaggeration. Her legs pulsed against mine, and she gasped and moaned beneath me, her grunts matching mine as our bodies gushed, truly spending themselves.

It was a beautiful relief just to be done, to be free from that rabid need to empty my balls inside her for a few fucking seconds. Shame it wouldn't last long – maybe five or ten minutes tops.

Hell, shame she was *killing me*, day by day, one hour full of fucking at a time. This old lady was gonna make me draw my last breath someday with her name on my lips, and I was okay with that.

I pulled out, smiling as I wiped my dick and watched her roll, gliding back on the bed to make room for me. Right between her legs was a natural spot for me to take when we started up again, and I held myself there, running my stubble along her neck, kissing a hot path to her lips.

"Sting?"

"Yeah, baby?" I said, loving the sunset in her eyes when she looked up at me.

"Can you believe all the crap we've been through brought us here? Sometimes, when I start to think…I just can't believe it. There were so many times I almost gave up. I almost lost you."

Her voice was strained. We'd been through the wringer emotionally today. Understandable.

Still, I'd be damned if I was gonna let her crack now and dwell on melancholy shit when we had a whole night of fucking ahead.

"Yeah. I can believe it all, girl, because we fucking lived it. All the shit we had to suffer: Beth...the Rams...putting down those Slinger assholes...it led us here because what we've got tonight was meant to be. I'm a big believer in fate, baby, even when it seems like the whole damned universe won't stop spitting in our faces."

She nodded, looking a little unsure.

"You'll come around," I said. "All the years we've got ahead are gonna make all the shit behind us into a distant memory. When you think about it one day with your awesome art trophies and our kids running around, it's gonna make everything we've got that much sweeter. Don't take my word for it, baby. Just keep on loving my crazy ass."

She laughed, giving my chest an energetic slap. "Couldn't quit if I tried. I don't think art galleries and cities hand out *trophies* either."

I laughed, eyeing her tits, feeling my hardness returning. "Baby, you know I love every bit of you – especially that sassy fucking mouth. But I love it even more when it's on mine, doing the next best thing to razzing shit up."

Alice giggled. I was determined to silence that music with another kiss, but she turned away, teasing me with her legs rubbing on mine.

"I love you too, Stinger. Love you and your club. I don't care if we've got to wade through twice the crap – nothing's going to change that. Nothing."

Finally. I kissed her hard, sinking my hips lower between her legs. I didn't need to hear what came outta her sweet lips to believe her. When we fused together, I found all the peace and reassurance I'd ever need for the rest of my life in her pink warm sweetness.

Thanks!

Want more Nicole Snow? Sign up for my newsletter to hear about new releases, subscriber only goodies, and other fun stuff!

JOIN THE NICOLE SNOW NEWSLETTER! - http://eepurl.com/HwFW1

Thank you so much for buying this book. I hope my romances will brighten your mornings and darken your evenings with total pleasure. Sensuality makes everything more vivid, doesn't it?

If you liked this book, please consider leaving a review and checking out my other erotic romance tales.

Got a comment on my work? Email me at nicolesnowerotica@gmail.com. I love hearing from my fans!

Kisses,
Nicole Snow

More Erotic Romance by Nicole Snow

KEPT WOMEN: TWO FERTILE SUBMISSIVE STORIES

SUBMISSIVE'S FOLLY (SEDUCED AND RAVAGED)

SUBMISSIVE'S EDUCATION

SUBMISSIVE'S HARD DISCOVERY

HER STRICT NEIGHBOR

SOLDIER'S STRICT ORDERS

COWBOY'S STRICT COMMANDS

RUSTLING UP A BRIDE: RANCHER'S PREGNANT CURVES

FIGHT FOR HER HEART

BIG BAD DARE: TATTOOS AND SUBMISSION

MERCILESS LOVE: A DARK ROMANCE

LOVE SCARS: BAD BOY'S BRIDE

Outlaw Love/Prairie Devils MC Books

OUTLAW KIND OF LOVE

NOMAD KIND OF LOVE

SAVAGE KIND OF LOVE

WICKED KIND OF LOVE

SEXY SAMPLES: WICKED KIND OF LOVE

I: Fractured (Emma)

Did I have regrets?

Not until I saw him behind the glass and heard the chains rustling on his huge arms. For a man his size, handcuffs weren't enough.

The bastards put two hulking sets of medieval looking irons on his wrists, and it still looked like he'd break right through them if he flexed his arms. His legs were just as anchored, bound as his wrists, but not in any way that would really be able to contain this giant. If he'd wanted, one kick would've snapped the rusty links scraping the floor between his ankles.

But what would've been the point?

Tank was done running. He'd proven that in spades last week when he killed to protect me.

The guilt stung, and I lowered my eyes, focusing on my hands before his eyes could focus on me.

He'd reached the end of the line. Just like me.

Lust made us lovers, and murder made us more, bound together in a pact of blood I thought was only meant for Tank and his brothers.

Wrong? Hell yes. Regrets? No, no, *fuck no*.

Nothing but one. I signed myself to him in blood and sin, and I'd do it all over again just for one more crushing taste of his lips.

The sole thing I regretted was seeing those chains bulging around his rock hard muscle and the ratty orange jumpsuit one size too small for his skin.

We'd reached the end of the line, but at least we were here together. Now, there was nothing left to do but face justice. For him, it was the dingy prison and the solemn faced judges. My justice was all *him,* a heavily tattooed god who'd broken my world and pieced it back together again as he damn well pleased, harder than anything I'd imagined but oh-so-worth-it.

The thick glass between us felt like nothing. It was no match for the raging fire in his eyes. I looked up, trying not to see my own guilt inscribed on his gorgeous ink, the same massive arms he'd used to split a monster's skull open.

I was the reason he killed, the reason he was in here now. And if things were really as fucked up as they seemed, I was the reason he'd be stuck here until he was old and gray, too withered to ride a Harley.

How could I even begin to speak? It would've been better to rip out my heart out and sling it against the glass, savage beating proof that I owed him my life, my love, my soul?

If only it were so easy to pull it out! My heart throbbed so tight in my chest I thought the surging blood flow up my head would cause me to black out in front of him.

My words were obliterated, and they didn't start to return until he was fully seated. I swallowed hard. The bruises and scrapes on his face were still there, only halfway faded, brutal reminders of the damage he'd suffered, a sacrifice that said more than a thousand *I love yous* ever would.

Of course, he'd never flinch at physical pain. Dents and scratches never fazed him, and I wasn't sure mortal wounds did either. Hell, he was so fearless and hard headed he probably didn't care about the real punishment that was only beginning, the imprisonment away from everything he loved.

I wasn't so strong. The crappy orange jumpsuit wrapped around his muscles burned my heart a thousand times worse than my eyes, turned it to ashes when I wondered how much life he'd forfeit in a shoebox cell.

Jesus. Why, Tank? Why?

I shook my head. The answer came a second later, sparking in his eyes.

Because murder doesn't come cheap, and neither does love.

The cop near the door behind him stepped through it and continued to watch us through the little glass pane.

Hell didn't do anything to dampen the way I got lost in his eyes. When he stared at me, I froze, instantly forgetting all the scripted sorrows I'd been practicing to myself in the waiting room.

"Emma," Tank said, breaking the tomb-like silence. "Why did you come?" He turned his wrist, showing off the eagle with the Devil's head in its talons inked on his forearm, two symbols that wrapped up his whole mad world.

Just tell him the truth. Perfect words aren't worth a damn. Honest ones are.

"I had to, Tank. I needed to thank you. He was unstable. He was going to hurt me if you hadn't –"

"They're listening," he warned. "Prisoners got no right to privacy, babe. Especially guys who're part of a club the Feds are trying to brand domestic terrorists."

The damned club! His whole life was folding, and still he stayed loyal, giving his brothers the same grim sacrifice he'd given me.

My whole mouth tasted bitter when I thought about it. If it weren't for the Prairie Devils MC, neither of us would be suffering like this right now. We wouldn't be here with this shitty glass between us instead of in each other's arms.

Then again, there was plenty of blame to go around. I couldn't pin it all on the club, however tempting.

If I hadn't gotten myself into a cash grab I didn't understand patching up their wounds, I wouldn't have met him. If I hadn't met him, he wouldn't be here, and a man's blood wouldn't be on both our hands – and the selfish fucking psycho who deserved everything Tank gave him wouldn't be having the last laugh from beyond the grave by bringing down my man and his brothers.

"That isn't going to happen. No one's going to take down the club." I shook my head, desperate to shake the unpleasant thoughts. "The lawyers are working on it. They'll get your guys off the hook and get you home."

Tank snorted and flashed me a smile. It wasn't a smart ass gesture, though. More like an old man marveling at a child's innocence.

"Blaze's lawyers have got some fancy tricks up their asses. Yeah, the club'll be fine, but nobody's gonna spring me free. Shit doesn't work like that, babe. I'm gonna be cooling my heels in this shithole a good long while. Thank fuck those tours in Afghanistan taught me all about patience."

I took a good long look at his face. Killing hadn't changed a damned thing. Why would it? It wasn't like my kill was his first.

He was beautiful, through and through, a living, breathing contrast to the black heart within. My grandmother used to tell me I had big friends in high places when I was a kid, but her silly little saying never meant anything until I met Tank. And right now, it meant the whole world, my overly logical brain's attempt to justify this mess and prevent myself from breaking down into a weeping pile.

My guardian angel was behind that glass, paying for my mistakes.

"You didn't come to talk business, babe." He leaned forward, close to the glass as he could get. "We both know why you're here. Listen, Emma, whatever may or may not have happened last week – don't ever feel a flap of guilt about it. Not for me, and certainly not for that motherfucker who tried to kill your sweet ass. What's done is done. And I wouldn't have it any other way. I did everything to keep you safe. Nobody but you and my brothers matters worth shit."

Damn! The tear sliding down my cheek burned like lava.

It wasn't supposed to go like this. Maybe if he showed something besides the cool and collected intensity beaming out his eyes, it would've made this easier. I couldn't reconcile him accepting surrender with the fact that it looked like he could get up, break his twig-like chains, bust through the glass, and walk right out of here.

Whatever, just as long as he didn't warn me again. I wouldn't be able to take it. Not after he'd warned me about this life, trying to nudge me away from it, and far away from him.

Couldn't he see there was no going back? I was already tainted, in too deep. At this depth, a girl couldn't have those regrets, or else she'd drown.

I wasn't going to walk away, dammit, no matter how much he aimed those perfect honey eyes in my direction. He was paying the ultimate price for me, but I'd suffered for him too!

Pleasure made walking through pure hell a whole lot easier. I couldn't forget the months I'd spent heating up like a rocket in his presence, let alone the perfect nights when I traced those sexy tattoos with my fingers, my tongue, my everything.

"No, Tank, you listen! It's my turn to talk." I reached up and tapped the glass. So cold against my palm. "We were going to have something new and wonderful before all this crap hit. I still want that, and I don't care one bit how long I have to wait. If it takes you ten years to come home – even twenty! – I'll be waiting. There's nobody else but you, and there never will be. Just thinking about another guy makes me want to throw up. Nobody'll ever fill your giant damned shoes. They can't."

For a second, his eyes went bright, glowing with the same addictive fire I saw when we were alone together. Then it went out, and my heart dropped like a rock. He was determined to turn me away.

"I fucked up, Emma, and I'm not talking about the reason I'm in here. I fucked myself when I decided to go after you. Trapped your heart when I should've set it free. Should've stuck to my guns. Should've kept you away. Should've had the Prez turn you right out of the fucking clubhouse and found a girl half as beautiful and smart to play doctor…"

"Shut up!" I was shaking now, losing more tears in hot, painful streams. "You can't regret this! I have mine, but they're all about the time we've wasted. If we weren't too stupid, too slow, playing games on both sides, we would've had more to remember. But I don't care how much or how little there is. Everything I've had with you, I'm holding onto. I'm not going to let it go just because someone tells me to – even if it's you."

His smile was gone. He moved slow, never taking his eyes off me, never showing the tiniest crack in his rock hard armor. My hand was trembling, splayed out on the glass.

It was hard enough to look at him like this, but I couldn't see a damned thing after he mirrored my little hand, eclipsing it in his huge palm behind the glass. The whole world went blurry, sprouting painful thorns.

"We had our time, babe, but the motherfucking clock's run out. I'm gonna cherish every fucking second we had 'til the day I die." He paused. "This shit cuts both ways, you know. I know it's gonna take some time to get your head and heart fixed. You'll tell me and my advice where to fuck off to, and that's your right. But I'm not gonna let you waste the rest of your life circling the skies for me, wasting your best fuckin' years. Gonna make you listen, and listen good, because it'll make sense someday when days have turned into weeks and weeks have become fucking months."

No, no, no...

Why did my eyes have to fail me like this? Why couldn't it be my ears? Hot, painful tears jerked at my vision.

"Walk away, Em. Pack your shit up and leave Missoula. You can land a nursing gig in Seattle or Portland or Eureka and start all over. Forget the Prairie Devils and my stupid ass too. What went down happened because I couldn't let you get hurt – same damned reason I'm saying this shit now. If you really care about me, you'll do exactly what I say, and do it as soon as you fucking can." He inhaled slowly. "My life's fucked, babe. Yours isn't. Fuck, you were the victim here. Nobody disputes that. I can't drag you straight to Hades like a goddamned boulder strapped to your back. Look at me, Emma..."

He waited. Slowly, I did as he asked, clearing my eyes. If he was really this determined, it might be the last time I'd see him, and I wanted this to count.

"Please. There's got to be another way." My words were faint, weak, defeated because I knew damned well there wasn't.

"There's only one way, and I'm pointing to it." His hand was gone from mine, and he stuck a finger out, pointing toward the exit sign down the hall. "Go. You got strength and beauty, babe. That's gonna make this whole fucking thing easier with time. You wanna talk about regrets? Only one I got is breaking your heart. But if that's what it takes to keep you safe, then I'm game. One day, everything'll make sense, and I'll be nothing but a distant fucking memory. Get the hell out and go live enough for both of us."

I jerked up. I couldn't listen to anymore of this heart wrenching shit. He was right about one thing: the man had a knack for shattering my heart and piecing it back together so many times I'd lost count.

He wanted to confess regrets? Then so did I.

I regretted ever losing my head and falling for this stern, violent, beast of a man. I regretted re-wiring my head to the point where I *knew* I'd never love another man as much as Tank, and I'd keep loving him against all the terrible odds.

I wasn't going to stop. I couldn't. If prison bars or his stupid high ideals stood between us, I didn't care. Not one tiny shred.

He'd keep hammering my heart to pieces – that much was given. But as long as I still had a single beating ember left, I couldn't shut it off. If he blew my love to pieces, the tiny cinders would just keep beating for his dumb ass, and *only* for him.

He owned it all – every fragile piece of me – and he'd keep it if we never laid eyes on each other or spoke again…

Look for Wicked Kind of Love at your favorite retailer!

Printed in Great Britain
by Amazon